DEDICATION

For my husband.
For all the laughs. For all the support. For being my best friend. For always believing in me. But mostly for the nightmare drive to the Minack Theatre.
I love you.

OZ

THE FINDING HOME SERIES

LILY MORTON

Text Copyright© Lily Morton 2018

Book cover design by Natasha Snow Designs

www.natashasnowdesigns.com

Professional beta reading and formatting by Leslie Copeland, editing by Courtney Bassett www.lescourtauthorservices.com

This book is a work of fiction. Names, characters, places and incidents are products of the author's imagination, or are used fictitiously.

References to real people, events, organizations, establishments or locations are intended to provide a sense of authenticity and are used fictitiously. Any resemblance to actual events, locations, organizations, or persons living or dead is entirely coincidental.

All rights reserved. No part of this book may be reproduced, scanned or distributed in any printed or electronic form without permission, except for the use of brief quotations in a book review. Please purchase only authorized editions

The author acknowledges the copyrighted or trademarked status and trademark owners of the following products mentioned in this work of fiction: Vans, Facebook, Grindr, Star Wars, McDonalds, Converse, Land Rover, Volkswagen, Mattel, Hoover, Tannoy

All songs, song titles and lyrics mentioned in the novel are the property of the respective songwriters and copyright holders.

Warning

This book contains material that is intended for a mature, adult audience. It contains graphic language, explicit sexual content and adult situations.

"I do not want people to be very agreeable, as it saves me the trouble of liking them a great deal."
Jane Austen

CHAPTER 1

IT'S NOT YOU, IT'S ME

Oz

"Oh my God, Oz. Shit. Baby, it's not you, it's me."

I stare at my boyfriend of six weeks who is currently dick deep in a strange man's arse on our bed. The sight of the white and grey striped sheets that I'd painstakingly picked out last week makes me incredibly want to laugh.

"I sort of guessed that," I say faintly. "Seeing as my penis is safely at home in my jeans while yours is roaming free." I cast him an acerbic look. "Like a very small wildebeest." I hold up my fingers and narrow the gap between them. "Tiny, really. Minute."

"Wait. Are you saying I've got a small cock?"

I shake my head. "Out of everything to do with our current situation, *that* is what you're focusing on, James."

I turn away from the bed and make my way over to the huge walk-in dressing room. *Time to move on again.* I cast a look around at the room that smells of sandalwood with its light oak shelves and the neat rows of clothes. I think I might miss this more than him.

There's a disturbance on the bed behind me and I wince as I hear the squelching noise as my boyfriend evacuates the arse he's found a home in today. I don't need to hear the muttered complaint from the other man to know that he's dismounted as gracelessly as he usually climbs on. My arse clenches in sympathy. *Been there, done that.*

Footsteps thud behind me and I turn to face my now ex-boyfriend. That's current to ex in forty minutes, which was how long it took me to realise that I'd left my wallet in my jacket and come home unexpectedly. Things move quickly in Oz Land.

"Was he waiting in the cupboard?" I ask. I shake my head as he opens his mouth to interrupt me as normal. "I mean, that was quick work. Me first thing, quick shower, and then where did you find this one?" I look at the small blond man climbing back into his clothes quickly.

"He's my new assistant," James mutters, pushing his hand through his hair.

I laugh. "*Really?*" He glares at me as my laughter continues. I pause and clutch my ribs. "How bloody clichéd and yet how utterly you." I shake my head. "Still, it's a relief. The speed you moved this one into our bed, I'd imagined you clubbing him on the head in the lobby."

He folds his arms over his chest, attempting to look dignified, but it must be difficult with half a cockstand and a wrinkled condom clinging to it. "Well, I didn't have to do that with you, did I? You fell into my bed quickly enough. One look at the Belgravia postcode and you had your legs open quicker than I could get my cock out."

Oh, great. I sense we're moving into the insult Oz stage of the proceedings. I straighten up to my full height which unfortunately is only five feet six, but believe me, I work those feet and inches.

"Well, of course it would have to have been the postcode because really, James, this location does bloody wonders for your personality." I tap my teeth with my nail. "Makes you almost interesting. *Almost*," I throw over my shoulder as I grab my suitcase and battered rucksack from the floor behind one of the cupboards.

I should have seen the writing on the wall when he asked me to move in with him and then proceeded to try and act as if he was living with the invisible man. All my belongings stuffed out of sight. The only place he was okay with me spreading out was in his bed. Even then, everything was his. I'd known it was a mistake, but at the time I thought I liked him. I'd paid attention to the way he held me at night and ignored the way he'd dropped my hand as soon as we stepped out of the flat.

"What are you doing?" he demands as I rifle through the clothes in my bag.

"Just checking I've got everything," I mutter. I click my fingers and move over to the wash basket. Upending the clothes all over the floor and enjoying his wince of discomfort, I sort through the laundry and, grabbing my stuff, I throw it into a carrier bag. *Classy to the end.*

I stride over to the marble bathroom and start to grab my toiletries. He moves towards me and I wave my hand at his now flaccid cock. "James, take that fucking condom off. You look like a complete twat." He stares down at his cock as if forgetting he was wearing it. I shake my head. "So tight with your cash. You were probably hoping to get a second chance at using it. Or maybe it's the one you used with me and you wrung it out and went for it again."

The flare in his eyes tells me I'm not that wrong, and inwardly I want to beat myself round the head. *Why did I move in with him? Why did I even move past the first night hook-up with him?* It had been hot but there'd been nothing else there. I sigh. I think I was bored and he was good at sex at first. That had deteriorated pretty fast though once he'd had me. I'd been flattered when he moved me in after three weeks but I needn't have bothered, because all I'd done was saddle myself with an educated idiot with poor impulse control. And no sense of humour, I remind myself.

I straighten my shoulders. *Not again. I'm not doing this again.* There won't be any more attempts at relationships. I've obviously got the picking ability of Britney Spears. From now on I'm hook-up central and nothing more.

But first I have to finish this. I watch as he removes the condom and flushes it. I think of giving him another lecture on the environment but shake my head. Shallow as it is, my concern for the world doesn't extend to me spending any more time with this man than necessary.

I grab my shaving kit and walk out of the bathroom to stuff it into my bag. When I look up, he's thrown on a dressing gown and has a large judgey frown on his face.

"Oz, this is ridiculous. It's beyond me how you can be flouncing around here like a fucking diva with hurt feelings."

Flouncing, I mouth, and shake my head. "My feelings aren't hurt. My eyes need a good bleaching after the sight I've just witnessed, but my feelings are absolutely fine and hurt-free."

"Really?" he scoffs. "You can say that, but we both know the truth. You thought your arse had got me so love-struck I'd have no need for anyone else."

I shrug, knowing it pisses him off. He thinks it's lazy communication. I say it stops me eviscerating him with my words. I pause to imagine *actually* eviscerating him, but I can't make it mean enough to warrant the clean-up.

He frowns. "I don't know why I expected you to understand, anyway. We're from two different worlds."

"Is mine the one with morals?" I ask lightly, and he huffs crossly.

"*Social* worlds," he stresses as if I have some sort of learning impediment. "You and I are from two very different classes, Oz. You're so very working class. It's written all over you with your accent and your clothes." He shrugs and his expression turns cruel. "You're very pretty, but it was a bit like having a little pet for a while. Just not one I'd keep forever. I thought I'd made that very clear to you. You were only here for a convenient fuck."

He shrugs off his dressing gown and starts to dress as I watch him. When he's finished, he grabs a case that I hadn't noticed and starts to wheel it out. "I forgot to tell you. I've got to go to New Zealand for a month. That should give you the time to clear your pathetic belongings away." He smirks. "And find another job."

Yes, you heard right. Did I forget to mention that James is also my boss? I've been his assistant for six months. I think that might make me an idiot.

He grabs his coat and, tapping his phone, he smiles. "My car's waiting to take me to the airport. I'll leave you to pack. Leave your key on the coffee table, pet. Have a nice life." He looks me up and down. "If you can manage it with such a disadvantaged start."

I watch him until the door clicks shut. Then I smile. "The trouble with keeping pets," I say softly, "is that sometimes they bite."

Checking my mobile for the right number, I grab his landline and punch some digits in. Pausing until I hear the dulcet tones of a woman announcing the time in France, I gently lower the handset to the table. The sound of the woman sending James's phone bill soaring is my soundtrack as I go into the kitchen and remove all the fish from his freezer. There's a lot because he's always banging on about the benefits of a healthy diet. I place these over the worksurfaces until you can hardly see the granite counter and the rest over the radiators in the flat. My final act is to turn the heating up to full. That should guarantee him a lovely aroma when he comes back in a few weeks.

I lay my keys gently on the coffee table and, grabbing my case, I walk to the door. Opening it, I look happily round at my handiwork. "Woof," I say softly, and close the door.

∼

An hour later I drop into a chair opposite my best friend, Shaun. His long hair is pulled back into a ponytail and he's wearing a Red Hot Chili Peppers t-shirt and ripped jeans. He's a roadie and has a never-ending supply of band shirts. He puts his pint down and looks at my bags. A worried look comes into his warm brown eyes. "Shit," he says.

I laugh. "That's one way to put it."

"Is there another way?"

I shrug. "I am now jobless and homeless, so no."

An indignant look crosses his scruffy face. "That fuckwit chucked you out? He only moved you in a few weeks ago." I smile at him, but he carries on obliviously. "I mean you can get on a person's last nerve, Ozzy, but twenty-one days must be a new record."

"Hey," I say crossly but he carries on staunchly. That's the only way to describe Shaun. Staunch. He'd have made a good corporal in one of those old black and white war films. Honest and loyal and completely oblivious to social cues like your best friend grimacing at you like a gargoyle. "He must have done something, Oz. This is the first one you've moved in with. You usually tire of men pretty quickly."

"I do not," I say crossly, and he shakes his head dolefully.

"Used to be if you were still talking after clean-up, it was practically wedding bells."

"Well, there won't be any wedding bells with James," I say snippily. "I just discovered him giving my replacement at work a good dicking in our bed."

"What the hell?" he breathes, his expression turning pink with rage. "What did you do?"

"I like the way you know I did something," I say slowly.

He grimaces. "You'd never let anyone stand on you, let alone some rich plonker boss."

"Well, if he has any second thoughts while he's away, I think they'll be killed stone dead when he gets home. Along with his sense of smell," I mutter.

"Do I want to know?" he asks cautiously, and I pat his hand.

"No. You'd only disapprove." It's true. Shaun is the softest, most gentle person I've ever met. I love him fiercely and sort of think of him as my brother. A six-foot-seven gentle giant sibling who has always been my conscience.

"I only disapprove of the fact that you never loved him and moved in with him because according to you he was good at sex at first."

"Well, there's a reason for that," I say glumly. "He was obviously getting a lot of practice." I shake my head and rub my eyes. "I don't even know what I was thinking of. That wasn't me, letting someone move me in after a few weeks."

"You want to be loved," he says stoutly.

"No, I don't," I scoff but he shakes his head.

"Yes, you do, and Oz, you should be. You're the best. You're funny and clever and really, really kind."

"No, I'm not."

"Yes, you are," he says doggedly. "You just cover the kindness up with that sharp tongue of yours. You should stop that and let someone see you."

I shake his arm gently. "You're the only one to get my soft side," I say affectionately. "Because I love you."

"I love you too," he says happily. "But I didn't like him. Particularly not for you."

"Why?" I sigh.

"Because he saw the outside of you." He flaps a hand up and down by my face. "You're bloody gorgeous. All that black hair and those cheekbones I could use to cut paper and those big eyes. And you're so small and cute." I shake my head in awe at the diarrhoea of the mouth currently going on. "I mean at first you don't notice because of your height, but you're actually really fierce and James should have seen underneath all that." He shakes his head in a very doom-laden way. "He should have seen enough to be bloody wary, because you might be small, Ozzy, but you're like a piranha with fucking sharp teeth."

I laugh, something I didn't think was possible a few minutes ago. "All the better to eat him with."

"I hope not," he says primly. "With that behaviour he doesn't deserve you munching on any areas of his anatomy."

We laugh but then I slump and rub my hands down my face. "What the fuck am I going to do now? I'm out of a job, a home, and a boyfriend. It's like some sort of backwards bingo."

He laughs but sobers quickly. "You can kip on my sofa as long as you want."

"No, I can't," I say patiently. "Because in the end Richard is going to get cross at that."

"We've been friends since we were kids. My boyfriend understands that."

"I don't think he's quite so understanding about the fact that our behaviour is still the same as when we were twelve. Richard's lovely and you should never jeopardise what the two of you have for anyone."

"You're not anyone. You're Oz."

I grab him and kiss the side of his head. "I'm an Oz who needs to sort himself out. Find something I can see through, rather than flitting from one thing to another."

"You'll stop flitting when you find the right thing," he says loyally. "You just need to find *your* right thing."

"Well, it's not going to be around here," I say sourly, looking out on the dirty and dusty London street. "Fuck, I'm so tired of here," I sigh. "Always the same faces, the same conversations, the same jobs. I just want something a bit different to wake me up. Are you okay?" I pause and say curiously as he sits up straight and gestures wildly at me. "Have you sat on a drawing pin again?"

"Shut up," he gasps. "Oh my God. Perfect. Can't believe it. Just read it. Here you are and hmm. Perfect."

"Vowels," I say slowly. "Verbs and connections. They help sentences come together. Like a barn dance for words."

"Look." He reaches into his jacket, pulls out a magazine and points excitedly at a box in what I see quickly are the job vacancy pages in ...

I turn the magazine over. "This is *The Lady*," I say slowly. "Is there something you're not telling me, Shaun?"

"Like what?" He's instantly and easily diverted. However, this time he snaps back quickly. "It was on the table when I sat down, so I read it while I waited for you." He taps the shiny pages. "It's actually got some really interesting articles and recipes."

I grin at him. "It's like I don't even know you anymore. You've changed so much."

He growls at me and taps the page menacingly.

I shake my head. "I can't imagine what ad I'd be any good for in *The Lady*," I say idly, pulling the magazine towards me. "I'm not nanny or new mistress material."

"They actually advertise that?" he gasps, looking like he's thinking of grabbing the magazine back.

"They might as well because that's what normally happens. It would be refreshingly honest." I pause before saying in a very posh voice, "I am advertising for someone to take the position of my wife. Lavinia has been a good breeder, but her hips are too wide now and she no longer has the time to pretend to be interested in my boring conversation about stocks and shares and shooting weekends with men like Albert and Wills. I am therefore looking for a younger filly who hasn't let herself go. Live-in position. Job requirements are the ability to fake orgasms to a high level and look good on my arm. Job tenure is probably short term because second wives don't last long."

Shaun stares at me. "You've actually got cynicism down to degree level."

"Thank you," I say, bowing slightly and making us both laugh. I tap the magazine. "The only job advert in there for me would be one asking for someone who is PhD level stupid enough to move in with their boss." I laugh. "No references given."

We both stop and think before he shakes himself like a big dog. "Just read it."

I obediently look down at the box and read out loud. "A vacancy has arisen for a House and Collections Manager for a manor house in Cornwall. You will need to have excellent management skills and experience of managing a team. A degree level qualification in Fine Art or the History of Art would be desirable but is not essential. Experience in overseeing house renovation is necessary."

I look slowly up at Shaun who grins with happiness. "See? It's perfect."

"What about this job says a perfect fit for me?" I say slowly. "This is obviously some sort of country house full of history and very rich, upper-class people. How is an Irish boy from a tower block in Tottenham going to help? They'll have heritage going back hundreds of years. I can only name my mum and auntie because my dad didn't exactly stick around long enough to give my mum his pedigree."

He shakes his head stubbornly. "You're bossy enough that you can tell people that it's good management skills. You have a degree in Fine Art and History of Art."

"Which has qualified me for nothing," I argue.

He lets it go, but when I stand up to leave he tucks the magazine under my arm. "Just think about it," he says softly. "It's perfect. It's a six-month contract so you won't be there long. It's away from London and all the old, well-worn paths. Maybe this is what you need." I look up at him and he smiles. "An adventure, Oz. You need that because you're bored enough to make stupid decisions at the moment."

∼

An hour later I look at the lift in the block of flats I grew up in and sigh. A big sign saying 'Out of Order' sways gently in the breeze from the door. "Fucking lifts."

A chuckle sounds behind me and I turn to see my mum's friend, Mr Pearson, behind me, his arms full of carrier bags. "Took the words out of my mouth, Oz. How are you?"

"I'm fine," I say glumly. "I think at this point I'd be lightheaded if they put up a sign saying the lifts actually worked."

He laughs and moves towards the stairs. I shake my head and jump after him. "You're not carrying those," I say firmly. "Hand them over."

"You're a good boy," he says affectionately. "I said to your mum the other day what a wonderful son she'd raised."

"You're a bit biased," I say softly, taking the bags laden with groceries from him. "You've known me since I was twelve."

"Your mother showed me your childhood photos the other day. An uglier baby I've never seen," he says solemnly.

I burst into laughter. "Thank you. Don't be giving me a big head."

He laughs but then by common accord we both shut up and stick to inhaling through our noses shallowly, so the smell of urine doesn't go too deep.

By the time I've dropped him off at his door and made my way to my mum's flat, I'm panting like I've run the London Marathon and my legs don't feel like they work properly. I ring the bell and breathe deeply in an attempt not to throw up.

Quick footsteps sound and I smile as my mum flings the door open. She's tiny, but her Irish heritage shows in her hair, which is still black, and her bright blue eyes.

She looks me up and down. "You okay?" she asks immediately.

"Bloody stairs," I gasp.

She huffs. "I know. I've been up and down them three times today already. Bloody council."

"*Three times*. Why aren't you dead?" I gasp and she smacks my arm.

"Because I'm fit, Oz, unlike you who does nothing apart from wait for fat to find you."

"I exercise," I say indignantly but she shakes her head.

"Your jaw, mostly."

I pause. "Okay, that's probably true."

"Come in." She smiles and drags me in. She's freakishly strong for someone who is five foot four and eight stone. I smile affectionately at her as she pushes me down the hall chattering happily. I love her so much. She and I have always been everything to each other. My dad, who was a foreign student, cleared off pretty quickly once he'd managed the arduous task of impregnating her. Her parents were staunch Catholics so they quickly threw her out. Alone, she could have caved, but instead she stood as strong as an oak tree and promptly moved in with her sister and brother-in-law while she qualified as a nurse. When they came to London, she got on a ferry and followed them. We'd lived with them for another year until she got this flat which has been her home ever since.

We've always been a team of two and she's stuck up for me through everything. The word blindly loyal could have been coined for my mother because I was a right little shit growing up. It's only her and Shaun who kept me on a straightish path, a fact not lost on my mum who adores Shaun and won't hear a word said against him.

Even when I told her I was gay she never flinched. Instead she grabbed me by my face, kissed me and thanked me for telling her. She stared into my eyes and told me that she'd had the luxury of choosing an idiot for her partner and so why shouldn't I?

When the priest at her church gave a sermon about the horror of being gay she had stood up in the middle of it and called him a bloody old windbag. She'd then searched for a church where the priest would fall in line with her. She'd found one, and according to my auntie she now practically runs it.

I follow her into the small kitchen with its jaw-dropping view of the London skyline. People would pay a fortune for this view. I smirk. But only if they're prepared for the fact that they'd probably have a heart attack getting up here, not to mention the fact that one of her neighbours grows pot and the other has a fondness for loud rows and even louder make-up sex.

"What are you doing here?" she asks, the Irish brogue heavy in her voice.

"Oh, lovely," I huff. "Can't a son visit his mother?"

She pats my cheek. "He can and does. He's a good boy."

"Are you talking about Shaun?" I ask, and she laughs.

"Of course." She looks at me. "How's that James?"

That James, I mouth. She's referred to him as this after the one memorable time they'd met when he'd tried so hard to prove that he wasn't a snob by grafting an incredibly bad East End accent onto his rich educated drawl. We'd sat staring at him in wonder for far longer than we should have. It was like watching Dick Van Dyke in *Mary Poppins*, only far worse.

She shakes her head. "Arsehole," she mutters and goes to switch the kettle on. "What's he done this time?" she asks over her shoulder.

I slide into a chair at the table and look at the surface which is strewn with shiny travel brochures. "What's all this? You won the lottery?" I ask, prodding a cruise brochure. I pause. "Tell me you're not doing papier mâché again, because Simon at the travel agency is only just talking to you again after you got his hopes up by asking for all those luxury destination brochures."

"I haven't won the lottery," she scoffs. "But you'll never guess who has."

"Father O'Reilly," I say faintly.

She shakes her head impatiently. "Auntie Vera."

"Your sister has won the lottery?"

She smiles. "Not the full thing. She won fifty grand."

"Jesus. We're going to have to watch out for the men crawling out of the woodwork willing to do things I don't want to think about for a slice of that." My auntie has become man mad since her divorce.

"Don't spoil her fun," my mum giggles. I stare at her because there's a palpable air of excitement about her.

"What's happening?"

"Vera's treating me. We're off on a cruise," she shrieks.

"No," I gasp.

She reaches over and pats the magazines and there's something so soft and awed and almost reverent about the way she touches the expensive papers. Something that makes tears rise in my throat and sorrow in my belly because my mum should always have this.

"That's good, Ma," I say softly. "I'm so pleased you're doing this. You'll have so much fun." It's the truth and I worry slightly that the cruise liner system isn't quite ready for the Gallagher sisters. Then I stiffen and pull out a magazine. "Tell me you're not considering this one."

She nods happily. "That's the main one at the moment."

"It's the Wild Knights Cruise, Ma. I'm not sure about that. You do know there won't be any men in chainmail with swords." I pause. "At least I bloody hope not," I mutter.

She smiles. "Auntie Vera said it sounded so much like her, it's like it's meant to be." She crosses herself piously.

"Ugh," I groan. "Ma, please don't say things like that. I'm not sure this is for you."

She looks cross and picks up the brochure. "It says there are parties every day and it doesn't sound too posh because clothing is optional for the Captain's Dinner."

"Optional being the notable word." She looks at me, perplexed, so I try another tack. "The parties aren't your sort of thing," I say earnestly. "I mean, there are toys involved in this one."

She looks bemused. "That's nice. It'll be handy for the children."

"It's adults only, Ma. There's a reason for that."

She sighs. "Even better. I'm not a huge fan of children. Always shrieking and crying and making a fuss. I mean, I liked you," she says hurriedly, misinterpreting my look. "But not any other children. Anyway, it'll just mean there'll be more free sun loungers."

"It means more than that. Ow!" I mutter as she slaps my arm.

"Stop being so overprotective, Oz. It's time to let me be an adult." I open my mouth to argue more but she leans forward. "What's happened to put you in a mood?"

"I've left James." I give a wry smile as she tries and fails not to look ecstatic.

"Oh, mo stór. That's so sad."

"That'd be a lot more convincing if you weren't smiling like the fucking Cheshire Cat."

She grins, a wry quirky twist on her lips that I see on my own. "Okay, I'll drop the act. I'm so happy about that. He was bloody embarrassed of you, Oz."

"Well, he wasn't wrong," I say slowly, and she gasps with all humour gone.

"Don't you ever say that," she says sharply. "You might not have had his advantages in life but you're a wonderful person. You're clever and funny. A man would be lucky to have you, and the day you introduce me to a man who looks at you as if you're all his Christmases in one go then I'll be happy. You should look for one like that."

Concern suddenly clouds her face. "Does that mean you've lost your job? Oh my God, where are you going to live?"

She looks at the brochures. Determination and a soft sadness fill her face, and it's this that decides me.

"No," I say firmly. "You are *not* giving up the cruise. Not for anything and certainly not for me." I reach over and drag out the crumpled magazine from my jacket pocket. I never thought I'd look at it again. "Anyway, I'm applying for this job, Ma. I think it's just what I need."

CHAPTER 2

THIS IS GOING TO BE A DISASTER

Oz

A few days later I shift uncomfortably in my chair and look around. I still can't quite believe that I've been summoned to an interview in a suite at the Dorchester. Not with my CV, anyway. Even with the highly creative liberties I've taken with my job history, the holes seem very evident to me. Still, if all else fails, I've obviously got a lucrative career as a fantasy writer in my future.

I sneak a quick look around at the other applicants sitting near me. They're eerily similar, like they rolled off a production line somewhere for earnest posh people. They're dressed in variations of expensive suits, and a few of them seem to know each other judging by the muted exclamations about people called Piers and India and recitations of evenings spent at each other's country houses. They look sparkly and untouched, and I look down at my own outfit of black pinstriped trousers with braces and a white shirt. I fold my arms across my chest, feeling slightly self-conscious.

I've obviously been judged somewhat because most of them have taken a second look at my bright blue crocodile lace-up shoes and the tattoos from my sleeve that are peeking out from my shirt cuff. I cross my legs and try hard to look serious and focused. I think it probably comes off more as boredom, because that's what I am. Bored to fucking death.

It takes a second call of my name from a nervous-looking man to register that the tedium is about to end. I know it's probably going to be replaced with abject humiliation, but at least I won't be stuck in that room listening to what someone called Bunty did to Rupert while playing sardines at the weekend.

I leap to my feet with alacrity. "That's me," I say loudly.

The young man jumps nervously and waves me in.

I wander past him into the other room where a very good-looking blond man is reclining in a chair pulled up to a table. In front of him is another chair which is obviously where I'm supposed to rest my bum. I start towards the man, trying not to gawp too noticeably at the beautiful room and also trying not to notice that he has a copy of what looks like my CV in his hand and a smile playing on his full lips. *Shit.*

"Oz Gallagher?" he asks, getting to his feet and holding out his hand. "I'm Niall Fawcett. I'm the Earl of Ashworth's estate manager."

"Nice to meet you," I say lightly, shaking the hand before stepping back and sitting in the chair he indicates.

"I'm very pleased to meet you, Oz," he says deeply. "Was your mother a fan of the book?"

"*The Wizard of Oz*? No. She just really likes Ozzy Osborne."

"Oh, that's nice." He pauses. "I've been wanting to meet the author of this wonderful ... CV all day." The pause is noticeable, as is the smirk which is growing wider.

I raise my chin and sit straight in my chair and as tall as my body makes possible. If he thinks he's going to intimidate me he's going to be wrong. Better men than him have tried and been shot down in glorious flames.

I don't want this poxy job anyway, I remind myself. *I'll just head off to The Crown and Arrows and get a bar job from Chris the manager. He's been wanting in my undies for a long while.* As soon as I think that, I relax into the chair and smile at the man. *Time for some fun.*

Something must amuse him because his lip quirks. He sits back down and ruffles my CV rather dramatically. "So, Oz, I see that you have a first class degree in Fine Art and History of Art." I nod encouragingly and he strokes the side of his face contemplatively. "And can you say that you've used this in a productive manner?"

I shrug and smile earnestly. "It's allowed me to work on Bernie's Antique stall on Camden Market." I lean forward in the manner of someone imparting great knowledge. "So many people trying to fence shit these days. Always trying to pass off total tut for Titian." I smile and sit back. "My name wasn't Milo or Hilary and I didn't go to Eton or Roedean. Not many opportunities in the Fine Art arena for me."

He looks down at my CV. "And is it on that stall that you pursue what you say in here is your goal of preserving and defending the property of the aristocracy?" There's a tremor of laughter running through his voice.

"No. That's just a hobby."

He coughs and sits back, enjoyment of this showing clearly in his face. "And you're working where now?"

"Foxton, Brown and Associates," I say calmly. "Or at least I was until a few days ago."

"Oh, you've left?"

I nod happily. "I had a slight difference of opinion with my boss."

"Which was?"

"I said he shouldn't shag my replacement in our bed. He disagreed."

The pale young man chokes on the water he's just sipped, and Niall looks even more entertained. "That's unusual, Oz." Silence falls for a beat before he stirs. "Should I ask what your job description was, or would that be inappropriate?"

"Not at all," I say, waving my hand in a very cavalier manner. "Let's see. I organised his diary, booked his travel arrangements, made his coffee, and had sex with him whenever he wanted." I lean forward. "Mainly when *he* wanted, I'm afraid. I'm too much of a people pleaser. It's a problem."

The other man is staring at me as if I'm a mirage while Niall just smirks. "Interesting," he murmurs. "Not quite what you'll be required to do in this job, I'm afraid."

I seesaw my hands. "Swings and roundabouts."

He snorts. "Indeed." He flicks my CV up and down, fanning himself leisurely. "The position that you're interviewing for is that of the house manager of Ashworth House. Can you tell me what you think this entails?"

I shrug and smile winsomely. "I imagine it's a bit like being a tour manager, only with less drugs and hookers."

There's a stunned silence but then his face cracks slightly. His eyes light up. "Such an interesting description," he purrs. "Milo, make a note of that for the next job advert we run." At the sound of his name I shoot Milo an apologetic look, but he seems oblivious, ignoring the irony and writing busily in his notepad. I sigh sadly.

Niall leans forward, licking his finger and paging dramatically through my CV. "The estate you'd be working on is going through a bit of a transformation. The Earl of Ashworth is intending to open the house and gardens to the general public for six months every year. As you'd imagine, that entails a lot of building work and organisation to get it ready. The last manager left rather suddenly and under a cloud. Have you any experience in organising workmen?"

I lean forward and smile ingeniously. "If you look at my CV

you'll see that I organised the decoration of a flat in the Crandon Block in Tottenham."

He bites his lip. "I saw that. It was quite ... fascinating."

My lip quirks. *Bastard,* I think admiringly, but I lean back and smile calmly.

"So how is this experience going to help in this job, Mr Gallagher?"

"Well, it demonstrates patience," I say sagely. "Have you ever dealt with the council?" He shakes his head. "Well, I can tell you that after one and a half hours of a very tinny rendition of Adele's *Hello,* the fact that I didn't fracture my own skull with the receiver should tell you a lot about my level of patience."

Milo gives a choked snort but Niall smiles and rifles through to the last page. "And the owner of the flat who is providing you with a reference has the same surname as you. Is that a coincidence?"

"Not really," I say placidly. "That's my mum."

Milo stares at me in mute horror but Niall smiles. "Interesting. What does your mum say about you, Oz?"

"Have you ever worked for a five-foot-four Irish woman?" I ask, and he shakes his head. "Well, let me tell you that my mother is more demanding than Prince Charles but with better ears. If she was in heaven she'd be running it." I shrug. "She'll tell the truth."

Niall stares at me, his eyes twinkling. "Well, I think that's all from my side. Do you have any questions?"

I stare at him. No way have I got any chance with this job. Smirking slightly, I hold my hands out. "What do you think of my nail varnish?"

There's a stunned silence in the room before he leans forward. "I think it'll look good in Cornwall," he says deliberately.

"*What?*" I jerk out.

He smirks. "Welcome to the staff of Ashworth House, Oz. I think you're going to do well."

"Are you mad?" I demand loudly. "I just gave the worst interview of my life." Milo nods frantically and I gesture to him. "Yes. Even Milo knows this, don't you?"

Niall looks at him and then back at me. "Let me introduce you to the young man you'll be mentoring. Milo, meet your mentor, Oz."

The two of us exchange mutually horrified looks before I turn to Niall. "Have you been drinking?" I demand. "You're giving me a job and also the responsibility of moulding a young mind." I shake my head. "You're off your bloody rocker." I pause. "What will his lordship say about this?"

Niall smiles. "I think you're just what he needs, Oz." He mutters something about being bored but I can't hear him properly.

I shake my head. "This is going to be a disaster," I say in a very doom-laden voice and Milo nods emphatically, but Niall just smiles.

"On the contrary, I think you're going to be perfect."

∼

One week later finds me sitting on my suitcase in the dusty carpark which is attached to the extremely small Cornish railway station. It's like one of those stations you see in the miniature Lego village at Legoland. Perfectly proportioned, but small. I smile. A bit like me.

I stretch my legs out and enjoy the hot sunshine and the quiet. The two people that got off the train with me have long gone, leaving me alone and starting to wonder if all this has been a joke. I can't summon up the energy to be worried about that after the horrendous train journey here. If the job doesn't pan out I might just stay here and become some sort of monument to the folly of trusting in strangers.

My thoughts are interrupted by a dirty green Land Rover pulling up in front of me. The window rolls down and I look into Milo's anxious brown eyes. "I'm so sorry," he says immediately. "I got stuck behind a tractor and with these narrow roads it's impossible to get past and–"

I wave my hand and interrupt his anxious monologuing. "It's fine,

Milo. Don't worry about it." I stand up and watch as he vaults out of the car and scurries around to open the boot. I heft my case up, ignoring his outstretched hands. "I can manage it." I swing the case in and the car rocks slightly with the impact. He shoots me an uneasy look.

"What is in that?" he gasps and immediately looks worried that he's offended me.

I smile at him. "Mainly shoes and—" I pause. "No, it's mostly shoes. I'm like Paris Hilton but with far better hair and dress sense."

He shoots me a bewildered look but shows some sense in that he doesn't travel down my conversational cul-de-sac.

I climb into the car and pull my seatbelt around me, watching as he pulls off neatly onto the road. I sneak a look at him. On a second glance he's actually extremely pretty. He's tall and willowy with wavy hair that's the colour of dark muscovado sugar. However, the overriding impression is one of nervousness.

We drive in silence for a while until I start to fidget slightly. "So, tell me about the house," I demand. A bit abruptly, obviously, because he swerves slightly. "Sorry," I say. "Didn't mean to startle you. Tell me what it's like. Is it in a huge mess?"

He presses his lips together, but discretion evidently takes a back seat to indignation because his words come out in a huge rush. "It's a real mess. David left it in terrible order. None of the building work is on schedule. It's so far behind and the house is due to open in six months. Nothing is done. There aren't any staff being trained. The collections haven't been looked after properly and nothing is being done about setting the house up for visitors."

He stops to take in a much-needed breath. I whistle. "Wow. Okay, that sounds ... terrible." His lip quirks, the first display of humour I've seen in him, so I chance more conversation. "David was the previous house manager?"

He nods and shoots me a quick look. "He was a friend of the earl."

"Oh, okay, I get it," I sigh and pause for thought. "Actually, that makes it worse. He's a *friend* and he still left like that?"

He shifts in his seat uncomfortably and my interest sharpens. "I think they had a bit of an argument," he mutters, taking a deep breath. "And David walked out." He shrugs. "Good riddance. Lord Ashworth deserves a lot better."

I'm not sure whether he's putting down what I'm picking up, but I'm thinking the mysterious Lord Ashworth was sleeping with his house manager. "Ouch!" I say with feeling. "Been there, done that."

His lips twitch again. "Yes, I remember that bit vividly from your interview."

We share a look and as if synchronised we both burst into laughter. I shake my head. "I'm not normally that flamboyant." He shoots me a disbelieving glance and I capitulate. "Okay, I totally am, but I really thought I wouldn't have a chance at this job so I just relaxed."

"Relaxed?" he says doubtfully. "It was like watching a really easygoing car crash."

I grin and give him a gentle nudge. "Milo, you're so sassy. Who knew?"

"Not me," he says wryly.

I smile. "I think we're going to get along together, after all."

Lapsing into a comfortable silence, we drive down winding roads that look like green tunnels with trees hanging over them. Occasionally he pulls over to let a car or van past. This is always done with huge civility and smiles, and on one occasion we stop so Milo and the other driver can have a quick chat. He accelerates away, and I shake my head.

"What?" he asks.

"It's very different from London. We'd have had several rude hand gestures by now and a lot of bellowing and swearing accompanied by the utter refusal of both parties to move until the police have to be summoned."

He smiles. "It's the country. It's different here."

"I get the feeling I'm going to hear that sentence a lot," I say, and he grins.

We pass a high honey-coloured stone wall and the car slows.

"Is this it?" I ask, nerves suddenly fluttering in my stomach.

He nods. "We'll go in through the side entrance which is the way the visitors will enter. It'll give you an idea of what you're up against."

"Shit!" I say, and he smiles.

He pulls into a large grassy area. Ahead are some long stone buildings.

"This is the visitor's car park," he says, switching the engine off.

"I'm not a driver," I say cautiously, looking around at the overgrown area. "But isn't this more of a field than a car park?"

He shoots me a look. "Now you're getting it."

"Shit!" I say again.

We get out of the car and I stand for a second and breathe in. "It's so fresh," I say softly. "I swear the air tastes salty."

"It does. The sea is just over there on the other side of the house. You can hear it in all the rooms."

"How lovely."

He shoots me a funny look. "It's just background noise."

"Yes. Well, so are car alarms, fire engines, and police sirens. This is better, believe me."

He smiles. "We'll leave your case in the boot and come back for it later. You can have a look around first."

I shake my head and fall in next to him. "You think that I'll take one look at all the work needing to be done and run away as far and as fast as I can."

He shoots me a look. "Actually, I don't," he says slowly. "I'd have said it last week, but I don't think you actually run away from anything."

"It's better to face up to everything," I say staunchly. We approach a small, low, honey-coloured building, and step inside. I look around slowly. "Apart from this," I say faintly. "Holy fucking shitballs!"

He laughs in a startled fashion. "Welcome to the visitor's centre."

I shake my head. The room is stripped back to the bare brick and the floor is open, revealing wires and pipes underneath. There's no glass in the windows and no workmen in sight. "Is it a visitor's centre for visiting sheep?" He snorts, and we pick our way delicately over the floor to a door at the side. "And this has got to be ready in six months?"

He nods. "This is nothing. Wait until you see–" He stops abruptly, colour staining his high cheekbones.

I stop. "Milo, for your sins I'm going to be your mentor." I pause and shake my head. "You must have been incredibly evil in a former life. Miss Trunchbull level." His lips quirk in a bewildered fashion as I turn to face him. "First mentoring lesson. When you're dealing with me, I like the truth. I hate being blindsided by something. Remember, face on."

"Face on," he echoes dutifully. He makes a gesture as if he's thinking of going for his notepad so I divert him.

"Where are the workmen? Dare I presume that they're doing something dreadfully important somewhere else?"

"That would be a nice thought," he says solemnly. "But I think they're in the pub."

"In the *pub*? Have they had a long lunch?"

"Not so much a lunch as a whole day." He slumps slightly. "They haven't been here for three days."

"And no one's queried it?" I ask sharply.

He flinches and I make a shushing noise. "Not you. I wouldn't expect you to be doing this. What about that Niall?"

"He's busy at the moment." He shrugs. "Everyone's busy."

"Including Little Lord Fauntleroy?" I say sharply, hating that Milo's obviously feeling guilty. "Is he sitting on a velvet cushion eating foie gras and waiting for the peasants to turn up and pay him money to look round the aristocratic building site?" I stare around, feeling myself build up a head of steam. I'm not a fan of the concept of aristocracy after a few years of coming up short against them in job interviews, and this strange earl isn't endearing himself to me at the moment. "He didn't even come to London to interview for a house manager. Just got a minion to do it," I tut crossly.

Milo looks horrified. "Oh no, Lord Ashworth is actually–"

"Milo." The shout comes from the door and Niall appears. "There you are," he says abruptly and then notices me. "Mr Gallagher," he says, his lip twitching as he takes in my outfit of skinny jeans, battered old combat boots, and a yellow t-shirt proclaiming *In My Defence I Was Left Unsupervised*. "How lovely to see you. Settling in okay?"

"Like a bear for winter," I say sourly. Milo shoots me a horrified look but Niall just laughs. He turns back to my companion. "Can I steal you for a second, Milo? I need your opinion on these plans."

Milo flushes and stumbles over his words and I eye him surreptitiously. *So that's where the land lies*. I look at Niall, big and beautiful and arrogant, and feel a bit sad. Milo doesn't stand a chance with this man. He's the sort to go for confident and assured.

Niall turns to me. "Do you mind waiting for Milo, Oz? We shouldn't be more than ten minutes." He points to the door he came through. "If you go out that way and follow the path you'll get to the lavender garden. Wait there and Milo will find you."

I nod and wander out onto a shadowed white gravel path lined with bright rhododendrons. A tree lowers its branches gracefully over the path, shielding two blue tits who are quarrelling crossly over a bird feeder. I walk slowly, the only sound the crunch of my feet on the path, and then gasp as I come out into sunshine and the most incredible sight.

In front of me is an old Elizabethan knot garden formed by beds of bright purple lavender edged with white roses and bay trees. I step onto the white gravelled path that edges the beds and inhale greedily. The air is heavy with the sharp, sweet scent of lavender. I wander over to a black iron bench at the side of the garden and lower myself to sit.

The sun beats down and a mischievous breeze dances over me,

ruffling my hair and gifting me with the heavy scent from the blowsy roses next to the bench. When I look up I still at the sight of the house. I knew it was an Elizabethan manor house but my research didn't tell me how beautiful it was. Built of golden stone with ornate gables and mullioned windows, it seems etched against the cornflower blue of the sky.

There's something so utterly timeless about the scene. I could have been picked up and put down in Elizabethan England and not know it. The only sound is that of birdsong and a faint low buzzing. I cock my head to one side and lean forwards to look into the nearest lavender bush. For a second I just see purple but then I smile in delight as my eye adjusts and I see that the bed is actually alive with hundreds of bees busily hovering over the delicate flower stalks. It's like I've been allowed to look into a secret colony hidden away in plain sight, and I stare for long minutes feeling oddly fascinated.

Finally, I settle back, feeling the heat beat down on me. I breathe in and a strange sense of peace steals over me. I've always been fidgety and on the lookout for more, but for the first time I can remember I'm actually content to sit quietly. It's ironic that it's in an old garden heated by the sun with my only companions the busy bees and the silent stone presence of an old house.

I shake my head at the absurd feeling that this is my place, and become suddenly aware of another sound filling the air. Anxious bleating. I stand up and look around. Next to the knot garden are a few apple trees and an old wooden fence from where the noise is coming. I look around but there's no sign of Milo, so I amble over, feeling the heat of the sun on my back.

The noise gets louder as I near the fence and I can hear the low soothing rumble of a man's voice. Reaching the fence, I hang over it and find myself looking into a long, low field. A small sheep is dancing around agitatedly on the grass but my attention is all on the man muttering assurances to her and holding her tightly while he looks at her foot.

He's tanned with dark, almost black hair which forms messy

waves over his olive-skinned face. He's bearded and has high cheekbones and a sharp blade of a nose. He's dressed in old faded jeans and a red polo shirt that clings to his wide shoulders and long muscled arms. He looks up and starts.

"Shit!" His voice is deep and rumbly but I don't get the chance to say anything as in his surprise he lets go of the sheep and she seizes her freedom with alacrity, bouncing and hopping away startlingly quickly for an animal with a limp. "Shit!" he says again.

"Sorry," I say, jumping up and straddling the fence. "Let me help you."

"There's no need," he begins to say but I jump down on the other side and grin up at him. And I mean up. I only come up to his shoulder and he dwarfs me.

"No problem," I say. "She looks hurt and it's my fault anyway for creeping up on you." I grimace. "Like a great big sheep creeper." I wave my hands. "Like something mother sheep warn their babies about. Beware the London Sheep Creeper. He's a nose breather."

He stares at me for a second and I just have time to register how pretty his eyes are. Hazel coloured, they glow almost green in the sunlight, clear and limpid like a forest stream. Then he bursts into laughter and I stare, transfixed and probably not hiding it very well. His laughter is warm and rich and has an almost gentle air about it. Almost comforting. I shake my head. He's probably straight and I really don't need to perv over him. I might get my head kicked in.

Recovering, he looks at me. "Okay then," he says. His voice is deep and rich. There's a posh drawl to it but it's undercut by a local twang, as if the voice has a split personality. "Let's catch Kylie."

"Kylie? Who calls their sheep *Kylie?*"

"She's quick on her feet," he muses. "It's perfect."

"I'm not sure the actual Kylie would be flattered," I say dourly, and he laughs again.

At that moment Kylie darts out of a bush and runs at us. The ovine one obviously, not the Australian diva.

"Kylie," my companion shouts. "Who's a good girl? Come here, beauty."

Kylie shoots him a very old-fashioned look, tosses her head and bounces off as best she can with only three healthy feet.

"You've got a way with the women," I say dryly as we watch her little bum bounce up and down and her tail wagging furiously with the movement.

He shakes his head. "You have no idea." He looks me up and down slowly and time seems to slow like being caught in treacle. "With the men too," he says slowly and I actually shiver. *Wow. He's potent.*

I open my mouth to say I don't know what, but Kylie makes a running dart past me and before I can think, I reach down and grab her. She's surprisingly strong, and for a second I freeze as I'm not actually sure what to do with a sheep now I've got one.

However, Mr Tall, Dark, and Handsome has no problem. "Brilliant," he shouts enthusiastically. "Hold her steady."

"What for?" I ask, but it's to fresh air as he bends down and rummages through a huge canvas bag before coming out with a small silver instrument.

"What the hell is *that*?" I ask breathlessly. "It's like watching the film *Marathon Man*." He brandishes it, grinning, and I shake my head. "What are you doing to Kylie?"

"Getting a stone out of her hoof," he says and drops smoothly into a kneeling position at my feet. I swallow hard at the sight of that handsome face so near to my groin and I watch as the breeze blows the black waves around and the sun picks out gleaming red strands that glow like fire.

Kylie wriggles and bucks but I maintain a strong arm around her as the man forages quickly and deftly. Exclaiming in triumph, he grabs something and removes it, holding a small stone up to show me. "Teamwork," he grins, and I give a strained smile.

"You okay?" he asks, kneeling and looking up at me like the sort of wet dream I've never been lucky enough to have.

I swallow hard. "Peachy. This position is like most Saturdays for me." I pause before saying quickly, "Minus the sheep, obviously. I like animals, but I don't *love* animals if you know what I mean."

Silence lengthens and I mentally close my eyes and sigh. *Wow, Oz. A fit handsome man at your feet and you're talking casually about bestiality. I'm surprised he's not proposing already.* I might have to consider that my datable personality has finally deserted me.

I look down, startled as he breaks into loud laughter. Kylie, sensing escape, wriggles and I let her go in surprise. The man gives a startled huff as she jumps over him and runs quickly away, disappearing into the furthest reaches of the field. He carries on laughing and I grin down at him, taken by the laughter wrinkles around his eyes.

He sits up and offers his hand. "I'm Silas."

I look at it for a second, feeling an odd sense of trepidation that I dismiss with an internal huff. The quiet here is obviously affecting me. "Oz," I reply and touch his hand. A warm tingle runs through my palm and up my arm, and he looks up startled as if he felt the same.

As if by common accord we both step back and stare at each other. He turns slightly and puts his hand to the gate behind him.

The next second I hear my name being shouted, and when I look up I can see Milo rushing through the knot garden like the White Rabbit. "I have to go," I say and turn back before standing in surprise.

The field is empty, the only sign that anyone else had been there the pollen rising and glittering in the sun and the click of the gate.

CHAPTER 3

LORD ASHWORTH, I PRESUME

Oz

I follow Milo down the path as he mutters apologies and I look back, wondering for a wild moment whether I imagined that encounter. I brighten slightly. If I did, my imagination has gotten immeasurably better. I can't wait to have a sex dream about the stranger too.

We walk up the side of the house, stone mullioned windows looking down on us and glittering in the sun. Coming to an arched mint green door in the wall, Milo opens it and gestures me through. It's like going into the secret garden as we pass through shade and then onto what is obviously the front of the house. I look up and gasp. It's bloody huge. Wisteria grows over the honey-coloured stone and its sweet scent drifts down. In front is a grassed forecourt that leads down some stone steps to a long, gravelled driveway which is obviously the main entrance.

Milo doesn't give me much chance to look as he marches up to a huge studded door and beckons me through and into a whitewashed passage with ancient-looking flagstones that are worn smooth and shining with the patina of years.

"We've got to hurry," he says, opening a door and beckoning me through. "Lord Ashworth is here and wants to meet you."

"Well, we mustn't keep him waiting," I say wryly, trying not to gape at what is obviously the great hall of the manor. It's full of sunshine that pours through the two-storey multipaned window. It lays lazy stripes over a long oak refectory table, and when I look up I'm entranced with the white plasterwork ceiling. Oak leaves and patterns sprawl across it and I nearly bump into a suit of battered-looking armour while I stare. I look ahead at Milo. "So, let me get this straight. He's the Earl of Ashworth but we call him Lord Ashworth?"

He nods. "That's right." He hesitates. "Although he doesn't seem to like a lot of ceremony at the best of times."

He rushes through the great hall, going down some steps before knocking at a white painted door. He listens before opening it cautiously and looking round. His shoulders relax and he beckons me in. "He's not here yet. I'll leave you here and come back for you in an hour."

"An *hour?*" I ask but it's to thin air. I look around curiously at the room. It's obviously the man's study. Old oak bookcases rise to the ceiling stuffed full of books and I inhale the scent of leather from their jackets. The room is wide and graceful. A large stone fireplace is on one wall and an old velvet sofa sits in front of it looking insanely comfortable as do the tapestry chairs to either side, their material worn soft with the years. An oak desk sits at the other side of the room piled high with mountains of papers and a computer. The French doors are open letting in a soft breeze from the garden outside. The air is redolent with the scent of furniture polish and paper.

What look like family portraits line the walls, and I've just stepped closer to look at a particularly grumpy lady with two children in Stuart dress when a disturbance at the door makes my head shoot up.

"*You!*" I gasp and Silas pauses, giving me a curiously knowing look. "What are you doing here?" I ask, darting forward.

The look is immediately replaced by confusion. "I've come to talk to you," he starts to say but I hush him impatiently.

"We haven't got time for *that*." I feel faintly scandalized, like I'm being infected with propriety the longer I stay here. "You can't be in here," I say. "I'm expecting to meet the lord of the house any minute. How am I going to explain you to him?"

"You're going to explain me?" he says slowly and I wonder if he's had too much sun.

"Never mind," I hiss. "He's obviously a lazy rich old man who leaves his staff to deal with everything. But I do actually need this job as I don't think I've got enough money to get a train back to London." I'm struck by a horrible thought. "Oh, my God. I'll be stuck roaming the back lanes with my suitcase until I die of tiredness or boredom. Whichever gets me first." I pause. "Probably boredom. Then I'll be a ghost they warn people about. Beware the London Ghost. He's been wandering the roads for a hundred years and still doesn't know his way because all the fucking lanes look the bloody same here."

Incredibly he looks like he wants to laugh. He also doesn't look like he's moving any day soon and to my horror I hear footsteps approaching the room. I look around frantically and spying a half-open door, I drag him over to it. I open it and a cursory glance shows me a small cupboard being used to store stationery. I push him in.

"Stay in there," I hiss as I hear the door handle turn.

He turns to me, his face contorted with what looks very much like laughter. "Can I just say–" he starts.

"No," I snap, and slam the door. Just in time. The study door opens and I dart to the middle of the room, looking up as Milo pops his head round.

"Have you seen–" he starts to say and stops. "What are you doing?"

"Nothing," I say brightly. I probably look like he's caught me in the middle of stealing the family silver.

He stares at me for a long second and then shrugs. It's the sort of shrug that people tend to give when they've known me for longer than an hour. I'm glad he's getting with the programme. "Have you seen Lord Ashworth? We can't find him."

"No, I haven't seen anyone," I say quickly, hoping he doesn't see my glance at the cupboard.

He shrugs. "No one's seen him since lunch. He was in the first field helping with some sheep and–"

"What does he look like?" I break in, a horrible feeling settling in my stomach.

He looks startled but obliges. "Tall. Dark hair with a beard."

"Shit!" I say. He jerks and I shake my head. "Nope. Haven't seen him. I have never seen anyone who looks like that ... with a beard," I finish slowly, and I'm sure it's not my imagination that I heard a soft snort coming from the stationery cupboard.

Milo looks at me strangely but then shrugs. "Okay, I'll leave you to it. I'm sure he'll be in soon."

"Me too," I say emphatically. I wait until the door closes behind him before walking over to the cupboard slowly and opening the door. "Lord Ashworth, I presume," I say hoarsely.

He looks up from where he's perched on a stool reading a book. His lip twitches. "Oz Gallagher?"

I shake my head. "How lovely to meet you, sir."

He stands up and stretches and I gulp as the muscles move sinuously under all that lovely olive skin.

"Now, Oz, please don't be formal, and call me Silas. I'm sure I'm far too lazy and ancient and rich to get really aggravated."

"Shit!" I say with feeling, but to my astonishment he breaks into laughter. Loud and glorious laughter. The sort that comes from deep in your stomach and leaves you clutching onto furniture. I shake my head as he laughs like a drain until he's breathless and rubbing tears from his eyes.

"That's the best fucking time I've had in ages," he gasps.

"You should get out more," I say sourly, shaking my head as that causes more paroxysms of mirth. I make my way back into the room, settling onto the chair in front of the desk gratefully. I think we're beyond manners and waiting to be asked before seating myself.

He follows me, occasionally snorting until he's seated opposite me at his desk. He looks at me and gives another peal of laughter.

I hold up my hand. "Hilarious as this is and I'm sure we'll laugh about it when we're eighty, do you think I can get a lift back to the station?"

The laughter dies from his face immediately. "What? Why?"

I stare at him. "Well, I'm sort of presuming that you'll want me to leave."

"Why?" he asks, his face blank with astonishment.

I falter. "Well, because of what I said about you and then the inappropriate flirting and–"

He shakes his head, seriousness appearing. "I didn't mind."

"You didn't?"

He runs his finger contemplatively along the surface of his desk. I stare at his broad hands and long tanned fingers and swallow. "I think if you'd met my father you'd have got what you were expecting from a member of the nobility," he says slowly. He looks up and the faint cloud that had appeared over his face vanishes immediately. He shakes his head. "Never mind. I'm not like him." He pauses. "I know I'm not here a lot–"

"That's none of my business," I immediately say.

"Well, actually it is. If you're my house manager you sort of need to know where I am as you'll need my approval for a lot of things."

"You're still going to employ me?" I gasp, and he frowns.

"Of course. Why not?" He shakes his head. "I like you, Oz." He falters slightly. "I mean you've obviously got a sense of humour, which you'll need, and you're different."

"Different good or different weird?"

"Bit of both. Both of which I think we need here," he says tentatively and relaxes when I smile. He continues staring down at that restless hand. "Niall vouched for you, anyway."

"I'm not sure why," I say in a spirit of absolute honesty. "I think he might have had sunstroke or something."

He laughs. "Niall's a good judge of character. If he thinks you'll fit, you will. I wish he'd had a say in employing–" He pauses.

"The previous house manager?" I ask softly.

He jerks, looking awkward. "Yes," he says slowly. "But that's all on me. I think it speaks volumes as to why I shouldn't get involved in hiring anymore. And if I had any doubts I just have to look around and see the mess he left us in."

I shrug, feeling something twang in my chest at the look of disappointment on his face. I don't know why, but I don't like the idea of someone hurting this man. My earlier judgement is fast vanishing. This is not an uncaring posh bloke at all. He has a warmth and a genuineness to him that's almost palpable.

"Never mind." I make myself wave my hand carelessly and his gaze seems caught on the black polish on my nails. For the first time I feel almost self-conscious at what someone thinks of my eyeliner and nail varnish.

He looks up at me. "I like that black. It's glittery."

I stare back at him for a long second, feeling astonishment swirl through me before bursting into laughter. "Yes. It's as black as my soul and you'll be glad of it because I'm going to ride roughshod all over the arrangements here. It'll suit my image of being the Dark Destroyer."

He laughs, and when it dies away, we stare at each other. Then he clears his throat and gets to his feet. Offering his hand, he smiles gently. "Welcome to the madhouse, Oz."

I shake it, feeling that warm tingle run lazily through my blood again. "May God help us."

He chuckles and I smile helplessly as the sun lays lazy stripes over our clasped hands, making my polish sparkle and pop.

∽

The next morning, I wander out of my bathroom and over to the window in my bedroom. I switch the toothbrush around in my mouth and carry on brushing as I look down at my view of the lavender garden.

Milo had shown me to my room last night, apologising for its smallness and plainness in a way I can't comprehend. I grew up sleeping in a bedroom that was smaller than the en-suite bathroom I've been given, and the clean pure lines of the room and the large window showing a view of the gardens seem like something I've seen in a hotel brochure. Not to mention the softness of the mattress. I'd slept like a baby cocooned in a nest of soft, scented covers, the only sound in the night the rustle of the trees and the distant sound of the sea.

Ten minutes later, dressed in skinny jeans, an old denim shirt, and my navy Converse, I trot down the stairs. Ten minutes after that, I trot down another set of fucking stairs, and then another. The place is like a bloody rabbit warren. Staircases run here and there with no rhyme or reason. By the end of the six months I'll definitely have lost weight because I'll have missed every fucking meal.

Finally, I reach the ground floor and follow the scent of coffee and sound of clinking cutlery. It leads me to the dining room which is a light-filled room set at the back of the house. Sun streams through the tall windows highlighting the old furniture that looks like it's been here since the house was built. My eye catches on threadbare faded fabric and the thinness of the carpet.

At a huge oak table Milo is sitting eating toast and reading *The Times*. I mentally roll my eyes and saunter in.

"Sorry I'm late," I say cheerfully. "Took the wrong staircase a few times." I look at his paper. "You're like a walking, talking advertisement for private school, Milo."

He smiles up at me, which is a nice change from the startled rabbit look of yesterday. "Help yourself to breakfast," he says, pointing to a huge sideboard on which are set silver warming dishes. I lift the lids, seeing bacon and eggs. The bacon is grey and congealed in grease and when I prod the eggs with a fork they don't move.

"I'd have a better breakfast at a service station," I muse. I lift another lid and cringe. "What the hell is *this*?" I mutter, pointing at the offending item.

Milo obligingly cranes his neck. "Kidneys," he says happily.

"What the fuck?" I mutter. "*Kidneys*. Who eats kidneys apart from Hannibal Lecter and Jeffrey Dahmer?"

There's a low chuckle behind me and I don't need to turn around to identify who has just come in. I just need to feel the tightening in my balls to know Silas is standing behind me. I cast a look over my shoulder and see him there looking fresh and fantastic in battered old jeans and a green and white striped shirt that makes his hazel eyes gleam greenly.

Becoming aware that silence has fallen and his lip is twitching, I shake my head. "Kidneys," I mutter.

"They were my father's favourite food. I'm not actually sure why Mrs Granger keeps serving them unless it's tradition," he says, coming up next to me and grabbing some of the least charred toast.

I inhale his scent. It's sharply sweet and smells like the ocean. I then try to ignore the fact that I just did that. "Aren't you eating anything else?"

He shudders slightly at the limp breakfast offerings. "Fuck no," he mutters. "I don't need an ulcer on top of everything else." He smiles. "Anyway, I find the less I have to do with my father's habits, the better for everyone," he says solemnly which is slightly spoiled by the twinkle in his eyes. A twinkle that Milo obviously misses because he looks highly uncomfortable.

"Good morning, Lord Ashworth," he says quickly.

"Not Lord Ashworth," Silas says patiently in a way that suggests they've had this conversation a few times. "Please just call me Silas. Lord Ashworth was my father and we don't want a Lord Ashworth standing behind us."

"Oh, I don't know," I say flirtily and then want to slap myself as Silas looks at me assessingly. I catch and hold his gaze, but the moment is quickly broken by Milo choking slightly on his toast.

I pat him on the back and smile affectionately at him. He's growing on me very quickly. I look up to find Silas's eyes on me so I immediately grab some toast and pour myself a very large cup of tea.

I throw myself into the seat next to Milo and become involved in scraping the burnt bits. When I've finished, I look assessingly at the three-inch piece of toast I'm left with. "Hmm," I say and Silas coughs. I look at him suspiciously but he grabs one of the supplements from Milo's paper and buries himself in it.

I turn to Milo. "So, am I going to have the full tour of doom this morning?" I ask cheerfully.

Milo blanches slightly and shots a look at Silas who immediately pretends he isn't listening. "Oh. Erm yes, I'll show you around the house and you can get an idea of the scale of the work needed."

"I've already got that," I say darkly. "It's hovering somewhere between disastrous and utterly fucking calamitous."

"Oh no," Milo groans, but Silas throws his head back and laughs loudly.

"Surely there must be something worse on the scale?" he says.

I bite my lip. "I feel we'll all be inventing new names by the time these six months are finished."

He shakes his head and throws his napkin down before giving a low whistle. A few seconds later a shaggy golden retriever dances into the room. He looks fairly young and he prances about, almost dancing on his paws.

"He's lovely," I say, putting my hand out to the dog. "What's his name?"

"Boris Johnson."

I blink. "Pardon?"

He smiles. "Because he's blond and stupid and makes very questionable decisions."

I throw my head back and laugh loudly. "That's so good," I say, looking up and stilling because he's gazing at me in a very focused way.

Milo breaks in quickly. "I'll show you the house and the collections and the grounds."

"No need," Silas says casually, taking a sip of his tea. "I'll show Oz around."

Milo looks startled. "Oh, really?"

"There's no need," I say quickly.

I'm not sure it's a good thing for me to be near him. I seem to have a knack of opening my mouth and saying really stupid things around him. I'd be a lot more at ease with Milo.

"Not at all," Silas says slowly, his eyes sparkling with mirth at my probably poorly concealed horror. "I need to show you the awful story in all its technicolour glory."

"Lovely," I say faintly.

Ten minutes later, I follow him out of the dining room, trying not to look at his arse in front of me which is tight and rounded in his old jeans. There's a slight rip on the back of the upper thigh and it offers a tantalising glimpse of white cotton. I swallow hard and immediately try to look innocent when he turns back suddenly. I'm not sure I manage it, judging by the quirk on his lips.

I open my mouth to say something that will probably be very stupid, but I'm saved by the sound of heavy padding footsteps. The next second a huge brown and white dog comes around the corner and walks straight to Silas's side. He easily reaches Silas's hips and has massive paws. His face is mournful looking with long ears and a droopy moustache and his eyes look extraordinarily human. He looks up at Silas and gives what sounds like a miserable sigh before nudging Silas's thigh strongly enough to make him stagger.

"Oh my God," I breathe. "What is that?"

Silas grins and pats the dog affectionately, pulling gently on his ears and leaning down to drop a gentle kiss on the giant's nose. The dog looks even more mournful, if that's possible.

"He's an Italian Spinone," he says grinning up at me. "I know he's big, but he's a total sweetheart. He's really gentle."

I put my fingers out and the dog noses them before giving another sigh which is strong enough to be labelled a breeze. "What's his name?"

"Chewwy."

I look down at the dog's furry face, big bones, and depressed demeanour. "Oh my God. It's Chewbacca."

He laughs. "When he yawns he even makes the same noise."

"That's amazing." He smiles at me and he looks rumpled and handsome. Our eyes meet and seem to catch.

"Where do you want the public to go?" I ask quickly, and he looks startled. I pause before ploughing on. "What I mean is, in an ideal world, where would you like the public to be able to go because we both know they'll wander all over the bloody house regardless?"

He smiles. "I think the Great Hall. There's a staircase that runs from there to the East Wing of the house. We can close that wing off from the rest of the house. The King's Bedroom is up there."

"Won't he mind?" I ask faintly.

He grins widely. "Henry the Eighth. He's so dead, he won't give a toss."

He startles a laugh out of me and I look up to find him staring at me. "What?"

He shakes himself like a dog. "Nothing. Come on and I'll show you."

We move through the Great Hall which is no less impressive this morning with the sun pouring through the leaded windows and bathing the room in light.

"I'll show you the collections when we've done the house," he throws over his shoulder.

"The only person I've met so far with a collection was an ex who had all his baby teeth in a box," I muse. "Tell me yours is more interesting and a bit less creepy."

He laughs. "I'm sorry. I can't. There's a collection of letters from one of my female ancestors who was a mistress of Charles the Second." He looks back at me. "But unfortunately, not the type of mistress who did well financially. With our luck I wouldn't be surprised if she had to pay him. Other than that we have the Elizabethan Earl of Ashworth who was a huge fan of the theatre." He shrugs. "Either the theatre or the players, I'm not sure. Either way, he was a sponsor of a company of actors and there are letters from Elizabeth the First about the plays he put on for her when she came to stay. It's not teeth, but I suppose you could jazz that up."

"Jazz them up? Are you envisioning streamers and confetti?"

He laughs as we skirt a lady who is pushing a Hoover around in a rather dispirited manner. Silas grins at her and immediately her face brightens and she smiles back at him.

I try not to look at his bright face and pretty eyes and look up at the portraits hanging on the walls instead. "God, your family were a grim lot," I say without thinking and swallow in horror, but he just laughs. It seems like laughter floats around him like pollen round a flower.

"Yes. You should have met some of them. My grandfather would have chided Vlad the Impaler for being too good natured, and my father never met a smile he couldn't turn upside down. Milo's restoring a lot of the old portraits. I don't know whether to be thankful that I can see their faces again or horrified."

I laugh and follow him up the staircase tailed by the dogs. "Before I forget," he says over his shoulder. "There will be a party at the end of the summer. It's an annual event. A marquee goes up and we serve food and provide a band. It was always looked on as a chance for my father to sneer at the hoi polloi while taking their money to fund his hobbies. It's the house manager's job to organise it. I'll get Milo to give you the details."

I stare at him before shaking my head. "I'll think about it tomorrow," I say faintly.

"Okay, Scarlett O'Hara."

I grin. "Please don't carry me up the stairs."

"I'll try not to. It might put my back out," he says solemnly.

We come out into a small room with a half wall that has intricately carved openings. "Musician's Gallery," I say automatically and move to look through them and down onto the hall below.

He comes to stand next to me. "Musicians and children," he says. "Henry and I spent many happy times up here spying on the adults without having to make polite conversation with any of them."

"I don't think my family and I ever had polite conversation," I muse. "Who's Henry?"

"My brother." He smiles, tracing the carving with one long finger.

"Does he live here too?"

He shakes his head. "No. He lives in London."

"You must miss him."

He nods. "I do. Every day, but he's very happy. He visits a lot and he's only on the end of the phone." He shoots me a look. "How about you? Any siblings?"

"God no," I laugh. "My father would have had to come out of hiding and risk his life to impregnate my mother again."

He laughs but I feel a flush on my cheeks. I hate feeling embarrassed about my background because I love my mum fiercely and totally, but it's a fact that my childhood was nothing like his. I feel a divide open up between us that previously I hadn't seen, but I embrace it wholeheartedly because I'm very attracted to him and I really think that being sacked after shagging another boss would make me an idiot.

I dutifully step back and paste a distant look on my face. He seems to sense it immediately and for a second, a disappointed look crosses his face, but then he straightens and moves off. I follow, wondering whether he's glad I did it.

We walk down a long corridor lined with more grumpy-looking

ancestors until I stop. "Bloody hell, look at this one. He actually looks really cheerful. Who is he?"

He looks up at the rotund man with red cheeks. "Lionel. He was the earl during Charles the First's reign. Legend says he was an alcoholic and broke his neck falling down the stairs."

"Oh," I say faintly. "Well, at least his smile muscles worked. That must have been a novelty. He looks quite nice."

"You'll have a chance to see," he says casually. "He haunts the West Wing."

"Oh lovely," I say weakly and follow him into a room near the portrait. It's a bedroom with a huge bay window looking down onto the main drive and a massive fireplace with ornate carved plasterwork above it.

"This was the original solar chamber. Apparently, the entrance to the house would have been up some stairs outside and through this tall bay window. I think my ancestor blocked it up when Henry the Eighth slept here."

"Poor sod," I say idly, wandering over to the window. "Bet he wanted to barricade the front door too. Having the king or queen to stay wasn't exactly a blessing. With them came the courtiers, their horses, and the servants, all of whom had to be housed and fed and entertained. It could bankrupt a person." I run my finger down the stone mullion. "I imagine it must have been a bit like having five hundred Brian Blesseds come to stay."

He breaks into peals of laughter. "That would be the best." He shoots me a look and leans against the window, the sunlight playing over the dark waves of his hair. "You've got a degree, haven't you?"

I nod. "In Fine Art and History of Art."

I wander over to the huge four poster bed which is swathed in red velvet. I sit down and bounce slightly and a spring practically impales my thigh. "This must be the original mattress Henry the Eighth slept on," I say, eyeing him. "Do you think he's hidden some Hobnobs under it?"

He grins. "Probably too busy deciding which wife he was going to decapitate next. It was hardly *The Bachelor*."

He startles a laugh out of me again. "I don't know. Looking at some of those contestants I'd have decapitated myself instead of going on a date."

He laughs and flicks a look at me. It's almost shy and kindles something in my stomach. *It's probably that breakfast repeating on me,* I reassure myself.

"I'm surprised you're not working in Sotheby's or something. Niall said you got a first," he says curiously.

I bristle slightly. "I applied for loads of jobs, but the problem seemed to lie in the fact that an Irish boy from a council estate never went to Eton."

"Count your blessings. You didn't miss much," he says calmly. "Lots of waiting on the older boys, getting them food and doing their homework. Still, it equipped me for a life of dealing with the general public."

I stare at him. He's the first person I've ever met who doesn't make excuses, doesn't protest that I'm wrong and inform me that our society has free movement. I can tell you right now that those people didn't grow up where I did. I shoot him a look because he's not conforming to any of my stereotypes. It's almost like I'm going to have to get to know him. *Bastard.*

"I liked it though," I say, surprising myself. "I've always loved history. I think because I have a very colourful imagination. You need that."

"And the art?"

"Well, I love that," I say softly. "I love beauty and how the more you look at something, the more the small details jump out at you." I trail off when I see him staring at me. "Where next?" I say abruptly.

He shakes his head but goes along with me. "We'll go and have a look at the stables that are going to be lovely tea rooms."

"Don't tell me," I say sourly. "There aren't any walls."

"Certainly not," he says primly. "Of course there are walls." He shoots me a look. "Just no roof."

I laugh, but when we get to the stable block via a room that will be a gift shop, although no one seems to have the faintest idea what gifts they'll be fucking selling, I stare at the building. "Fucking hell," I say softly.

He snorts. "You can say that again."

"Why are you doing this?" I ask suddenly, turning to him. "You must know that this is looking pretty impossible to get done in six months. And even if I do get it done you'll have people trampling all over your beautiful house, disturbing the peace, dropping litter, and being rude and nosy."

He stares at me and then sighs heavily. "Come and sit down," he says softly and steers me to a bench by a high stone wall. It sits in a patch of warm sunlight. The only sign of life nearby is a fat tabby cat crouched peering intently at a bush. He settles next to me and for a brief thrilling moment I feel the warmth of his thigh. He clicks his tongue at the cat who immediately stops hunting and sashays up, leaping onto his lap and circling before settling down. Silas smiles affectionately and strokes the cat's back, and soon the sound of purring fills the still air.

I shoot him a look. "You like animals, don't you?"

He smiles. "I should hope so. It's pretty much a requirement for a vet."

"*What?*" I exclaim and the cat startles before relaxing when Silas strokes it again. "You're a vet? Why?"

"Because I like looking after animals," he says drolly.

I shake my head. "That's why you're not around a lot?"

He smiles. "My practice is very busy. I have a partner, and it's local, but it's still a lot of work."

"So, why take on more with the house?" I ask the million-dollar question.

There's a silence that lasts long enough for me to wonder whether I've overstepped my mark, but then he speaks slowly. "My father was not a nice man. He also had a lot of very expensive habits."

"Golf and hunting?"

He shakes his head. "Marriage." I stare at him and incredibly he laughs. "He liked the ladies, but after a few months they never really liked him back. So, what he loved to do best was to find someone really unsuitable, marry them immediately and then a few months later divorce them and give them a lovely present of money, also called maintenance."

I say nothing, staring at him intently, and he smiles sadly. "He almost bankrupted the estate, Oz. There's hardly any money left after the divorces, the death duties, and a multitude of his bad business decisions. And it costs a lot to run this place. At the very least it's two hundred thousand a year just for the upkeep of the building and the gardens. There's a very real chance that I could lose the house if I don't do something quickly." He pauses. "And I love this house," he says quietly.

"Ashworth House," I muse.

He chuckles. "It's not really called that. Its original name was *Chi an Mor*."

"What does that mean?"

"It means House by the Sea. It's Cornish."

"That's beautiful." I laugh. "It's just a bit understated for such a huge house." We smile at each other. "I prefer it though," I say slowly, and he nods.

"Me too. It's how I think of it."

I shift on the seat. "Does your brother know about the money?"

He shakes his head. "No. He suffered enough with our father. I'm not adding to it. This is my problem."

"Why are you telling me, then?"

He shoots me a look. "Because you need to know." He pauses. "There's so much work that needs to be done. And I think I can trust you."

"You don't know that," I immediately protest, but then shake my head. "But yes, of course you can trust me." I look at his kind face and suddenly I can see the tired lines around his eyes and the trace of worry on that open countenance that I'd missed while concentrating on his good looks.

I don't know why I like him. I try not to like too many people because it usually brings an obligation to please them, but him I like, and I can't explain it. It runs contrary to my organised and meticulous nature, but I decide not to think too much about it. Resolution fills me, and I turn to him. "I will do my level best to help you and get this house ready in the six months. I may make enemies. I may piss people off, but I'll get us there." He stares at me, something working behind his eyes. I pause. "Did David know this?"

He shoots his head up sharply at the mention of the other man's name. "Of course," he says. "He was–" He falters before finishing almost inaudibly. "David wasn't just the house manager. We were in a relationship."

"Hmm," I say noncommittally. Then I jerk. "He knew all this and still fucked off and left you in this mess?"

He shrugs. "He hated being here. Said it was boring. He also hated being told what to do. He was happy to take a wage but seemed to think he earned it on his back." He winces. "It was a bit messy at the end."

"Yes, I know that feeling," I say softly. He shoots me a look, realisation on his face, and I nod. "It's why I'm looking for a new job." I pause before saying firmly, "I won't do that again."

"Well, that's good, isn't it?" he says softly. "I think we can work well together, Oz. I've got a good feeling." His next words come slowly and almost reluctantly. "I suppose it's good that we're both on the same page about the inadvisability of workplace relationships."

And just like that, we both agree without too many words not to act on the attraction we can feel. I fight the instinctive urge I have to argue with our decision because I don't know where it's coming from.

"Same page, same paragraph, same word," I say slowly. I know that I'm lying. As for him, I have no idea.

CHAPTER 4

PICK OUT THE GEMS

Silas

I sit in my study, trying to attend to at least some of the paperwork, but my attention is drawn once more to the open French windows and the gardens beyond. Oz marched past the windows about ten minutes ago with Milo and Chewwy following obediently behind. Much to Oz's bemusement, Chewwy has become fascinated with him and follows him everywhere.

Oz was talking twenty miles a minute, his hands flying and his face alternatively horrified and amused. I'm embarrassed to admit that I crept over to the window and watched them have a very animated conversation about the siting of rubbish bins and the fact that the raised curb is a lawsuit in waiting if anyone trips on it.

I'd stood concealed by the curtains, utterly enthralled by him. He's very beautiful. That's an obvious fact. He has shiny hair that's as dark and glossy as the blackbird's plumage that waits outside the kitchen door every morning for toast crumbs. His eyes are a clear bright blue that reminds me of the bottle of Bombay Sapphire gin that always sat in my father's drinks cabinet. His cheekbones are high and his mouth is full and pink. He's slender and small but somehow the force of his personality makes him seem bigger.

I'd watched them for a while until they'd concluded their list of failings and moved onwards with Oz's low, slightly hoarse voice with its tinge of north London and a light Irish brogue sounding out above the more familiar tones of Milo.

I've then spent the last ten minutes reminding myself that, judging from my history, I am an appallingly bad judge of character and cannot be trusted to find a partner. I remind myself about the fact that Oz has obviously just come out of a relationship with his boss that ended badly. I then try to recall David and how fucking angry I feel at the mess he's made.

When that doesn't work and I find myself thinking about the sleeve of tattoos on Oz's arm and trying to remember what the pictures are on it, I give up and bring out the big guns. Picking up the phone, I dial a familiar number and settle back in my chair, one ear still out for the sound of Oz's voice. The phone rings a couple of times before a much-loved voice says, "Silas, is that you?"

"Henry, can you do me a favour very quickly?"

"Anything for you." My brother pauses and laughs. "Is it illegal? If it is, I'm definitely in. I'm getting very bored of defending the law."

"You make yourself sound like a knight," I laugh. "Rather than a rich ginger lawyer."

"Always with the ginger jibes," he says mournfully. "I'd have thought during the thirty-odd years you've been my brother you'd have thought up better insults."

I laugh. "Why bother when this one has always worked?"

"Well, my time is money. I've always wanted to say that. Makes me sound a bit like Michael Douglas in *Wall Street*."

"No, it makes you sound like an ageing old hooker. Stop it and focus on helping me."

"What do you need?" he asks immediately. "If I can't do it, then Ivo will."

"You'd bring your lover into this?"

He laughs. "Try keeping him out of it. You know how fucking nosy he is."

I laugh. "Okay, very quickly I need you to list the worst examples of partners I've picked from the beginning."

"Since the beginning of time?" he says doubtfully.

"I'm not that old, Henry. Just the twenty-odd years of dating. Pick out the gems."

"How can I do that? They were all bloody awful. That's like asking me to pick between Darth Vader and Donald Trump. Both terrible but for different reasons."

"Well, I know I'm a bad picker but I'd never have gone for Trump. That orange instant tan would have messed up my Egyptian cotton sheets."

He laughs and I hear his pen tapping. "Okay. How about Rupert? He drank all of Father's port and then passed out in his study and we had to hide him behind the curtain when Father came home early." He pauses. "Or Katy who got so drunk at Mother's third wedding that she threw up over the wedding cake?"

I think hard, trying to conjure up their faces. "Okay, this is good. Although the latent theme of alcoholism in my dates is *slightly* worrisome. Keep going."

"Phillipa, who you dated for a couple of weeks. She came for a weekend and left wedding brochures lying around everywhere. Beatrice, who didn't leave *any* wedding brochures around because she was already married and whose irate husband made such a wonderful addition to my birthday weekend. Or the charming

Freddie who took out a credit card in your name. If spending was an Olympic sport you'd have actually been able to claim that you'd slept with a champion." I laugh and he pauses for a second. "Why am I doing this?" There's a stunned silence and I know he's going to come to the correct conclusion. When he speaks again his voice has gone high. "You've met someone."

"*Henry.*"

"Oh shit. How bad is it?" He coughs. "Should I come down there and help? Wait. Wait. Don't let them meet Mother until I can witness it. I need a good laugh."

I shake my head. "Calm down. No one's meeting anyone because there's no reason."

"Tell that to someone who doesn't know you. Tell it to Mother."

"She's still in denial about my bisexuality. I'll be dead by the time she comes round to it."

"Or been eaten by feral cats."

"What the fuck? I'm not that old. Anyway, the only cat we have is Mabel and she's too fat and lazy to look at me as dinner."

"Seriously, Silas. How bad could it be? I mean, I know you've had some bad luck–"

"He's the new house manager."

"Well shit, you're fucking doomed then."

I laugh and shake my head. "I *know*. I absolutely know that. It's terrible timing and a shitstorm waiting to happen, but he's just–"

"Just what?"

"Funny and alive."

There's a long silence before he speaks. "I've never heard you talk like that."

"Pshaw. Of course you have."

"No. No, I haven't. You'll talk about their faces or bodies or how they need you and that you can help them. But I've never heard you talk about someone like that."

I shrug. "Well, nothing's going to happen."

He pauses. "Okay."

I'm startled and a little disappointed by his ready acquiescence but I remind myself again that he knows me. "Anyway, I'm going," I say. "How's Ivo?"

"He's fine." I can hear the smile in his voice and it warms my chest. He's been in love with our old stepbrother Ivo for years and they got together a couple of years ago. I've never seen a happier or more sarcastic couple. They make me smile.

"I love you," I say affectionately.

"I love you too," he says solemnly. "I'll see you very, *very* soon."

"In the blink of an eye," I return, the way we always used to quantify our separations when we were sent to different boarding schools.

I put the phone down, smiling, and look up as the door opens and Niall sticks his head round. "Quick, come on."

I stand up. "What's the matter? Where are we going?"

"Stable block. Oz has cornered Mr Johnson the builder. It's a bit like Tyson versus Holyfield."

"Shit," I say, crossing the study quickly. Then I pause. "Who's winning?"

He shoots me a look. "Who do you think?"

"Oz, of course." He laughs and I shoot him a look. "He's very different from the sort of person you said you wanted for the job, Niall."

He hums thoughtfully. "I know. But I sat in the interview room and it was like they'd all been made by Mattel. Perfect and plastic. I was *so* bored and then he walked in and the room came alive. And I thought how sick I was of public school Barbie and Kens. He's perfect for–" He pauses. "I just sat there and I thought, I want him."

"You want him?" My voice is a little sharper than I want but I can't backtrack because Niall knows me better than anyone. He should do. We were roommates at boarding school and all through uni.

He stops abruptly and turns to face me. "Of course not."

"What do you mean by that? What's wrong with him?"

He smiles while I stare at him. "Absolutely nothing. He's just not for me."

"Then who is he for?" I ask, but I'm distracted by the sound of raised voices and quicken my pace.

By mutual accord we stop before the door and poke our heads around.

Mr Johnson the builder is pacing agitatedly around the rubble-strewn room, pausing only to shout and wave his hands around. Oz, meanwhile, looks as cool as a cucumber. He's leaning against the wall, his ankles neatly crossed. I watch as he checks his nails and sighs resignedly while Milo, clutching an armful of plans, looks askance at him.

"Mr Johnson," Oz finally says, and although he isn't loud his voice cuts through the room and the builder stops. "Mr Johnson, can I call you Barry?" Milo mutters something and Oz nods. "Okay, I won't call you Barry because apparently that isn't your name." He pauses. "Although it would suit you."

I repress a snort of laughter and Niall turns a laughing face to me.

"What the hell are you on about?" Mr Johnson roars.

"Well, I like to be friendly," Oz says primly. He turns a warm gaze on the man that obviously startles him. "I'm just so *sorry* for everything."

"What?" The builder sounds worried now and his eyes are fixed on Oz who shakes his head in a very sorrowful manner.

"I'm sorry that times are so hard for you."

"Times are so hard for *me*?"

"Oh, I'm sorry." Oz puts a hand up to his mouth. "That's just what I've heard."

"Heard? Heard where? Who the fuck is spreading rumours about me?"

"I really don't know. Isn't it terrible?" Oz sighs. He moves closer to the man and lowers his voice. "They're saying you can't complete jobs anymore what with the problems with your workforce and everything."

"What bloody problems with my workforce?"

Oz looks at him confidingly and I want to shout with laughter. "Well, the rampant alcoholism amongst your men."

Milo stares at Oz and Mr Johnson goes slowly purple in the face. "What the hell do you mean?"

"Well, talk says they're always in the pub and a few people have seen the pig's ear here and–" He shrugs. "They put two and two together and made–"

"Seventeen," the builder barks but Oz slowly shakes his head.

"I'd have said four myself."

"What the hell would you know about it, you tatted-up bog-trotting Southerner?"

My fists clench and I go to push my way in but Niall grabs my arm. "No. Leave him."

"He's getting really offensive."

"So? Watch. Oz has got this."

His utter confidence makes me relax slightly and I peep into the room to see Oz shrug.

"Obviously nothing, Mr Johnson. Because, as you so astutely pointed out, I am an Irishman living in our great capital city and we don't know much about building work." The builder looks suspiciously at him as if he senses a piss take, but Oz carries on relentlessly. "However, I do know something about gossip and if this inadequate work rate continues and your firm doesn't complete the job in an excellent and timely manner, well," He shrugs. "I might just develop a drinking problem of my own. Of course, I'm too much of a flibbertigibbet and grow bored so easily that I won't just drink in the local. I think I'll spread my drinking around, and, Barry, when I drink I develop very loose lips." He turns to Milo who immediately looks worried. "At least that's what it says on the toilet walls in Tottenham."

I can't help my snort of laughter. The conversation automatically dies and Niall and I step into the room.

"Oh, Lord Ashworth," the builder immediately says. "How nice to see you."

Oz rolls his eyes and I repress a smile.

"The same to you, Mr Johnson," I say solemnly. "Has Oz been speaking to you about a way forward through this awful mess?"

"Yes. I, … yes," the builder falters.

"Yes," Oz says brightly. "We thought, or rather Mr Johnson thought, that the solution would be to put more men on it." He smiles winsomely at him.

"But won't that cost more money?" I cry out far too dramatically because Oz's lips twitch.

"Of course not," he says smoothly and turns to the builder who has the look of someone who's walked into a wall he didn't see. I'd be prepared to bet my house that a lot of people wear this look after misjudging Oz Gallagher. "I think that Mr Johnson was about to say that he'd carry the cost because of the mismanagement of the project." He smiles sunnily at the man. "And Mr Johnson himself is going to oversee his men. Isn't that lovely of him? We need him so much."

"How super," I cry out, and Niall snorts.

The builder shakes his head, his expression wry and almost admiring when he looks at Oz. "I know when I'm beat," he says.

"Never beaten," Oz says charmingly, putting out his hand to the man. "Let's just say we've come to an understanding."

"I understand it's best not to underestimate you, Oz."

Oz nods happily. "That's the best sort of understanding. Now, shall we get a nice cup of tea and walk through how much work there is to do?" He pauses. "And maybe how you should put some more workers on it."

The builder nods dazedly and turns to walk out. Oz turns back and winks at me and we share a smile of total understanding, mirth brimming in our gaze, before he leaves like a king followed by Milo clutching the plans and looking nonplussed.

Niall claps me on the back. "Shit, we might get this done in time," he says in an awed manner.

I shrug. "I haven't doubted that since I met him."

"You see? Perfect."

"What?" I ask absently but he never replies.

～

Oz

That night at midnight I sit at the kitchen table looking over the mass of papers and plans and sheets of paper covered with my sprawling handwriting. I lift my glasses and rub my eyes and look again. *No, still there.*

I look down at my current huge shadow who is sitting by my chair and watching me with mournful brown eyes. "Are you waiting for me to start screaming, Chewwy, or just bored?" I ask conversationally. He stares at me for a long second and then gives a huge yawn which shows off his massive teeth. I shrug. "Okay, just bored."

"I didn't know you wore glasses."

The deep voice coming from the kitchen door makes me jump. "Shit, you startled me." I take my black-framed glasses off, feeling slightly self-conscious at being found talking to the dog. "I took my contact lenses out."

Silas gives me an exhausted smile. "They suit you."

He comes into the room fully and I look at the tired slump of his shoulders. "Have you been out on a call?"

He gives a jaw-cracking yawn that almost sets me off. "Horse birth that looked like it was about to go pear shaped."

"Bugger. Was everything okay?"

He nods and grins. "One very pretty filly called Moonshine."

"Aw, that's pretty." I pause. "So, while we had dinner you've had your hand up a horse's vagina." He nods, biting his lip in an attempt not to smile, and I grin. "After the dinner we had, I have to say your evening looks like it might have been better."

A burst of laughter comes from him and I smile as he sinks into the chair opposite me. I can't help the warm feeling I'm getting in my chest at making him laugh. *Why, oh why, does he have to be so nice and sleepy looking?*

His voice breaks into my thoughts. "How bad was it?"

I shudder. "We had beef casserole."

He grimaces. "God, I feel your pain. Last time I forced that down I was ten and I had to eat it because my father believed in serving up leftovers until they were eaten." I stare at him and he nods. "I had it for breakfast, lunch and supper."

"Oh my God. Did you eat it in the end?"

"Did I, fuck. I gave it to Cyclops, our old bulldog. It made him sick, though, so I spent a whole night nursing him and mopping up vomit." He pauses. "Which was still better than eating that shit."

I laugh. "Is that where the desire to be a vet came from?"

He stares at the wall, deep in thought. "No. I just think that animals are better than humans for the most part. They're simple. You love them and they love you back, and no matter how you fuck up they still love you. That's loyalty for you." He seems to come to and gives me an embarrassed look.

I smile at him, touched but not saying anything. "So, that must mean the cook's been with you for thirty years. How the fuck is that possible?"

"Mrs Granger is actually lovely. She just can't cook. Although her baking is wonderful." He sighs. "Her cakes are so gorgeous and wait until you try her scones." He gives me an almost shy look. "She was always really good to Henry and me when we were little."

"Ah, that explains the longevity of a cook that can't actually cook." I pause. "I was starting to think she was a Borrower or something. I've never seen her. Just these meals appearing on the table." I think for a moment. "But a reverse Borrower because they're so awful. I looked up the nearest McDonalds tonight."

He grins. "St Austell. Mention my name and you'll get a good table."

"It's not what you know, it's who," I say piously as he laughs.

I smile at him and chuckle as his stomach gives a massive rumble.

"Sorry," he grins. "It's all that talk about cake."

I stand up. "Well, unlike Mrs Granger, I *can* cook. I'll make you something."

He looks startled, which he should be. I don't usually cook for men, only my mum. "Oh no, you don't have to."

"What do you normally do?" I ask curiously. "I imagine vets keep very late hours."

He nods. "If I'm not too tired I'll grab a sandwich. If I'm knackered I just go to bed." He shudders. "And look forward to breakfast."

"Well, I'm going to make you something and I don't want any arguments. They're so tedious and it gets boring when I win them."

He smiles with a devastating quirk of his lips, but then looks at his watch and frowns. "But it's so late."

"Pshaw. This isn't late. In London I'd only just be going into the clubs. Besides, I'm used to cooking at this time." He shoots a questioning look at me and I grin. "My mum's a nurse. I used to cook for her when she came in off a late shift."

"How old were you when you started doing that?"

I think hard. "I was about twelve when I picked up a cookery book. She used to be so bloody tired when she came in, literally dragging herself over the doorstep, and it was a way for me to help."

He gives me a soft smile. "You're close to your mum, aren't you?"

I turn to grab a pan from the cupboard and nod. "It's always been just the two of us so we're Team Gallagher. She's the best person in the world."

"She sounds it," he says softly.

"I'll make you a breakfast frittata," I decide. "It's her favourite."

He groans. "God, that sounds good."

I shift slightly at that low sound, my cock filling. *What would it sound like if we were lying naked together?* I push the thought quickly away and busy myself with grabbing the stuff I need from the fridge.

He prods the papers on the table. "Are these keeping you awake?"

I groan. "It's a mess. I can't lie."

He shakes his head. "I'm so sorry.'

"Why? It's not your fault."

"I did employ him."

"Did you know him from before?"

He nods. "He's a friend's little brother." He pauses. "Which has gone down as well as can be expected." I grimace and he nods. "Still, you make your bed."

"Seems to me he didn't help with the making of it or the tidying up in the morning." I shrug. "He's gone. We're here. This is the mess we have to deal with."

He looks startled. "Okay. That's blunt."

I smile at him as I fry the potatoes. "It is as it is. If I was nobility I'd have that as my heraldic motto." I pause. "What's on yours?"

He looks almost embarrassed. "Duty and love," he mutters, and I pause with the spatula held up. I don't know him well but already that seems like something he would try to live by. He has a very honest and earnest air about him. An air of capability and strength. I mentally shake myself.

"Shame it doesn't read, 'Ashworths. Making the money rain for centuries'."

He laughs. "That sounds like an insurance ad. Or a stripper's business card." He picks up one of the plans. "I was very impressed with you this morning."

I look up startled and feel a flush on my cheeks. I had no idea he was listening until he appeared and I'd spent a few hours afterwards trying to remember if I'd said anything outrageous. After that, I'd shrugged and accepted the fact that I probably had.

"Why?" I ask before I can stop myself.

"Because Barry–" He shoots me a glance and I grin. "Barry is a very tough customer. He's a really good builder but a shit judge of character, and the leader of the project on his side is his future son-in-law."

"Shit!" I say with feeling. "I'm amazed he gave in."

He laughs. "I don't think he had much choice with your not-so-veiled threat to chat shit about him all over Cornwall."

"Just South Cornwall," I protest. "And then only the pubs on a bus route. I can't drive."

His head shoots up. "You can't *drive?*"

"I also can't shoot aliens and ride unicorns if you want to say that in the same disbelieving tone."

He tries to stop his smile. "I'm sorry. It's just I thought everyone drove."

"Out here probably," I say mildly, dishing up his very early breakfast and placing it in front of him. Chewwy immediately sits up in an interested fashion and I shake my head at him. The frittata looks colourful with peppers and tomatoes gleaming like tiny jewels. "But we didn't have the money for either driving lessons or a car when I was of age so I never bothered. Besides, it's so expensive to have a car in London, and where would I keep it? It'd only have wheels for a few hours where I live."

A troubled expression crosses his face so I shake my head. "Don't feel sorry for me, for God's sake. London transport is cheap, and although not cheerful, it's plentiful. I don't need a car."

"You might struggle out here."

"You mean I haven't got my own chauffeur?" I ask, opening my eyes wide.

He laughs. "Of course. It's just that he's at the pub at the moment." He takes a bite of the frittata and moans under his breath. "Christ, this is lovely."

"I know," I say modestly.

He grins at me as I pour us both a cup of tea. "It's like a miracle. It's not cold or greasy and it even looks like food."

"Oh, stop it," I grin. "And by that, I mean do go on."

He smiles and falls on his food, eating with a healthy appreciation that touches me. I draw my pad to me and out of sight scrawl: *Employ new cook and do something else for Mrs Granger.*

He looks at me curiously. "So, you've sorted out the builders. Tell me what's next on your list of miracles."

I consider before shoving my master list towards him. "I think I'll start here."

He looks down and for the next hour we sit companionably, chatting over tea with our plan of action, and I wince as I realise that this job just got a lot more difficult because at the top of my plan of action I really want to write: *Make Silas smile and stop being so tired and worried.*

Shit!

CHAPTER 5

I NEED TO LET LOOSE

TWO WEEKS LATER

Oz

I look around the stable block and raise my eyebrows. "This looks fantastic, Mr Johnson."

"Oh, Oz, please call me Barry."

I laugh and push his elbow gently. "You're such a joker, Barry."

A couple of his men look askance at this, but he just smiles. "It has been said." He looks around at the room which looked like it belonged on the set of a disaster movie a few weeks ago. Now, it's freshly plastered with windows letting the sun stream in over the varnished wooden floors.

He gestures me over. "The counter will go here and the kitchen fitters come tomorrow. You happy with everything so far?"

I squint as I look around. "It's looking good." I shoot him a look. "So tomorrow it's on with the visitor's centre then?"

His lip quirks. "Yes, Oz, and not via the pub."

"Thank you, Barry," I say sedately, and he huffs a laugh.

Obviously feeling our conversation is at an end he turns to his men. "Okay, grab your gear. Next step is the visitor's centre."

They hasten to obey and within minutes they've cleared out, leaving Milo and me standing in the wide-open space. "What do you think?" I ask. "Have I forgotten anything?"

"Not likely," he says, staring around. "I can't believe it's done."

I shrug. "It's not exactly a miracle. Just people doing what they've actually been paid to do." I shake my head. "I sometimes think that people view that sort of thing as old fashioned and I can't work out why."

"Because you're very straightforward," he says simply and grabs the plans from the table by the door. "So, what's next?"

"Tomorrow we'll be here all day with the fitters." I grab my diary to leaf through the crammed book and check my watch. "It's nearly three. Why don't you finish early and bugger off?"

"Are you sure?" he asks, startled. "David didn't like me to finish early."

"I'm not David," I say grimly. "And it seems that's a good thing, as he apparently didn't like to actually start work at all. You've worked hard. Take off."

"But haven't you got stuff to do?"

"Yes, but it's just paperwork and I don't need anyone's help with that. I just like to get things in order for the next day." I look at his earnest face. "If it helps, I'll sit outside and go through it."

He smiles. There's very little trace of the worried man I'd met a month ago. "Okay, as long as we're in agreement. I'll drop the plans off in the office first."

"We are. Go. Off with you."

He pats my shoulder and is gone very quickly.

I gather my diary and look around again. It's amazing what a difference a few weeks have made. It hasn't been easy. The other builders are, by and large, fairly hostile at having their freedom curtailed, but after a few run-ins they now keep a wary distance, which suits me. I've got no patience with lazy people.

I nod with satisfaction and tick a few items on my main list. Then, shutting the door behind me, I amble out into the gardens with Chewwy at my heels. These are beautiful in the late afternoon sunshine. They spread and surround the house, but my favourite, apart from the lavender garden, is the Lady's Walk along the side of the house. This was used by the women of the house as a secluded place to walk and get fresh air, and it's a low-walled piece of paradise filled with scented plants that fill the air with perfume.

However, the real attraction lies in its direct view of the sea which lies to the west of the house. You can walk or sit on an old iron bench and watch the restless waves. Silas's land sweeps down to it and Milo told me the beach belongs to him too. Apparently, there's a path leading down, but I've not found that yet. Every evening before dinner I've wandered the grounds with Chewwy, taking any path that takes our fancy and getting a feel for the house and land.

I think I'm falling in love because it seems the most beautiful place on earth to me. Nestled in the green grounds, the windows are always open to the sound of the surf, and sand lays a gritty film over everything. The house itself seems to shelter me and I wander its staircases that take me here and there like a traveller that's come home after a long time away.

I shake my head. This is just brilliant. *All the feels for somewhere I'll be leaving in a few months.*

I traipse through the old wooden door set into the wall, pausing to blink as I come out into the full afternoon sunshine. Then I stop dead, staring with my tongue hanging out at the newest addition to my secret place.

Silas is there, pushing an ancient old mower up and down the grass. He's obviously been there a while because half of the walk lies in neat manicured lines. It's another hot afternoon as England basks in the heatwave that's been going on for a couple of months and shows no sign of stopping.

He's wearing tatty trainers and disreputable old shorts that hang from his narrow hips and show off the wonderful Adonis belt whose lines are so defined.

However, my attention is all on the fact that he's shirtless. My mouth fills with saliva and I swallow hard at the sight of all that olive-toned skin before me. He has wide shoulders and the muscles in his arms bulge as he pushes the mower. Sweat glistens on his skin and his wide chest which is covered in thick dark hair.

I resist the urge to either moan or touch myself because a hairy chest is my kryptonite. It's led me into many situations, some of which I won't discuss, but I can't deny the draw. I shake my head. This is like someone rifled my head for my best porny fantasies and set Silas neatly down in front of me.

I must have made a sound because his head shoots up and he jumps. "Shit! You startled me." He smiles, reaching and turning the mower off.

"You look hot," I blurt out, my voice thick.

An intense look crosses his face before he grins and strikes a pose. "Why, thank you, Oz. I can't deny it's been said before."

I shake my head, the heat thankfully banking a little at his humour. "Was that from the members of the idiot club?"

He throws his head back and laughs loudly. "Many, *many* members, Oz. If you're interested, their general meeting is next week."

"I'll make a note of it and bake some cheese straws. I don't want to miss that." I smile at his laugh before reason slowly returns. "Why are you mowing?" I ask. "Haven't you got gardeners for that?"

He looks a little embarrassed. "Sid's back was bad so I offered to do it."

"I bet his back was bad," I mutter, thinking of the lazy older man who can usually be found lying down in the apple orchard. "He spends enough time lying on it."

He shakes his head, looking earnest. "No, it really is bad and he's been with us a long time."

"Let me guess," I sigh. "He was nice to you as a child."

He nods, flags of red on his cheeks. "Yes, he always used to sneak me and Henry food when we'd been sent to our rooms."

I shake my head, wanting to both shout in frustration and also kiss him really hard. "This place is a little bit like a retirement home."

He immediately shakes his head. "Oh no, it's fine. I don't mind. Most of the staff are old and I don't mind helping out."

"Didn't you get in at one this morning?"

He shoots me a look because I know this. I did, after all, wait up for him. He doesn't know that, of course. He thinks I was doing paperwork. However, as I've done for the last few weeks, I cooked him something and we sat talking and laughing for an hour. It's become our routine and it's something I secretly look forward to far too much. I've grown to love that late dead time when the whole house is quiet and it's just us. To have his attention on me, his tired face lighting up when he comes through the door, is too much. I know I'm storing up trouble but I can't seem to stop.

I shake my head to clear my thoughts. "I'm going to get you a drink."

"Oh no, you don't have to," he immediately and predictably protests.

"I know I don't," I say patiently. "Please allow people to do something for you."

I wander off and add another item to my master list: *Figure out the gardener problem to stop Silas from killing himself.*

Silas

A few days later I wander reluctantly down to the dining room.

Last night's dinner had been stupendous in its awfulness. Mrs Granger had made a shepherd's pie, but I think even a starving shepherd would have struggled with it. The meat was half cold, the gravy congealed, and the potatoes hard. I'd taken one bite and switched to drinking my dinner in the form of red wine.

Oz had blanched and caught my eye in a moment of shared hilarity. He'd then stuck to bread and butter. Milo had eaten the whole thing placidly and with no sign of discomfort. However, I've eaten at his family home and their cook makes Mrs Granger look like Delia Smith.

I look up as Niall falls into step beside me. "I haven't seen you all day. Busy one?" I ask.

He grunts. "The busiest. A meeting this morning with the tenants, and this afternoon the fence came down in the bottom field and some of the deer got out."

"Did you get them all back?"

He nods. "After an hour chasing them. They were like Bambi on fucking acid."

I laugh but then we come to the door and by mutual accord we both stop and draw in deep bolstering breaths. "You ready?" he mutters.

"No," I say honestly. "But it's got to be done."

We both square our shoulders and walk in. Oz looks up from his seat where he's been staring at that bulging diary of his with Chewwy at his side, as normal. He offers us his wide smile that always seems to me to have the sweetest edge to it. It's almost lost in the wicked sparkle of his eyes, but the soft curve of his lips gives it away every time. I falter slightly, and Niall gives me a very knowing look.

"Alright there, Silas, or did you start drinking early tonight?"

"All the better to eat dinner," I mutter and Oz shudders.

"Last night was bad," he whispers.

I nod emphatically. "You can say that again."

"Last night was bad," he dutifully says, and I shake my head at him.

He grins and gets up. Chewwy immediately leaps to his feet like they're connected by an invisible rope.

"Wait. Where are you going?" I ask in a far too panicked voice.

He looks at me strangely. "To tell them they can serve dinner."

"Oh. Okay," I falter. "Yes, that sounds good. Thank you."

Niall snorts and I send him a death glare. "Shut up," I mutter.

"I certainly will. Not talking will allow me to enjoy this whole thing so much more."

"What whole thing?"

"You two. It's like watching elephants mate. Dangerous, messy, and uncomfortable, but ever so slightly sweet."

I shake my head, but the door opens and Milo appears holding two plates, one of which he slides in front of me. I cross myself. "Deliver me from–" I begin to say and stop dead. "What the hell is this?" I breathe.

Milo looks in a puzzled fashion at my plate. "It's seafood pie," he says in the manner of a person talking to someone slow, or in the manner of Oz. He then blushes profusely. "I'm so sorry, Lord Ashworth. I mean it's seafood pie."

I smile up at him. "Silas please, Milo. What I meant to say is this looks like–" I look towards the kitchen door. "It looks edible," I whisper.

He looks even more confused. "If you say so, Lord... I mean S-S-Silas. I suppose so."

I look down at the dish where the pie sits steaming fragrantly. The fish is cooked in a creamy sauce packed with prawns shining pinkly, while the piped potatoes are topped heavily with cheese. Then I look at Niall. "Is this some sort of alternate dimension we've entered?" I hold up my hand. "No, don't say anything. You might yank us back to the dimension where Mrs Granger can't cook."

"Oh, Mrs Granger didn't make this," Milo says happily.

"Who did?" I ask.

"Maggie," comes Oz's voice from the door. He hands Milo a plate and sits down with his own.

"Maggie, the maid?" I ask, suddenly realising that she isn't serving dinner.

He nods and takes a bite of his food. He gives a low groan and I shift in my chair slightly while ignoring Niall's raised eyebrow.

"Wait. Maggie can cook?"

He nods slowly.

"But what about Mrs Granger?" I stiffen. "You haven't sacked her, have you?" I whisper.

He immediately shakes his head. "Of course not. I wouldn't do that." He pauses. "Well, I would totally sack people and I did sack two of the cleaners when I found them eating biscuits in one of the beds upstairs and watching *The Jeremy Kyle Show*, but no one else at the moment. Anyway, that would always be up to you." I relax back into my chair and he smiles. "Mrs Granger is going to head up the baking in the kitchen in the visitor's centre."

"Oh my God," I breathe. "That's fucking genius."

He nods. "I know," he says modestly. "She's very happy. She makes wonderful cakes, and homemade baked goods go down really well with the general public. We can offer cream teas and things like that. We should make a mint. Meanwhile, Maggie has taken over in the kitchen. I've been watching her and she cooked lunch for us once when Mrs Granger had gone for a lie down." He shrugs. "It was an easy decision to make. Mrs Granger will stay on her money but I've offered Maggie some more." He looks at me quickly. "Was that okay?" he whispers.

"It was genius," I say again. "Of course she should have more."

"I was worried," he says, darting a glance at an oblivious Milo.

"It's fine."

Niall snorts. "I'll say so. I knew you were the one for the job when you mentioned guarding the aristocracy's possessions."

"What?" I ask, but Oz chuffs slightly.

"Nothing. Dinner's getting cold."

We all immediately turn back to the food. Silence falls for minutes while we eat and then gradually conversation starts up again the way it has since Oz came. He'll mention a TV programme or a film or relate some humorous incident from the day, and everyone will spark off it.

I sneak a look at him sitting in a pool of evening sunshine. The light enhances his dark hair and plays over his high cheekbones, making them look like they're washed in gold. At that moment he looks up at me and for the life of me I can't tear my gaze away. Our eyes hold and time seems to slow around us.

Milo breaks it by asking a question, and when Oz looks away I notice his chest rising and falling sharply. I look out of the French windows, endeavouring to control my breathing and trying hard to think of something terrible that will make my erection go down. I think of last night's dinner and feel my cock wilt. *Thank God for Mrs Granger's cooking.*

The next second all my thoughts fly out of my head when a man wanders past the windows. "Who the fuck is that?" I ask and everyone looks up.

Oz immediately jumps up. "Oh, that's Josh. He was supposed to go home hours ago."

"Who is he?" I persist, looking at the young man who's bending over my flower beds.

"That's the apprentice gardener," Oz says and walks out of the doors to speak to the lad.

I turn to Niall. "*Apprentice gardener?*" I mouth.

He shrugs. "I don't know." He turns to Milo, who immediately blushes bright red. "Who is he?" he asks.

"That's Josh. Oz contacted the local agricultural college last week and enquired about apprenticeships and whether they had any keen young gardeners." He looks at me. "He said something about Sid's bad back."

My mouth quirks. "Clever bastard," I say admiringly.

Milo blinks and looks up as Oz comes back through the door.

"He's really keen," Oz says, sitting down at the table again. "He says Sid's taught him loads already. Apparently, he knows lots about rare types of plants." He looks at me and winks. "Maybe he found them while he was lying on them in the orchard."

I can't help my grin and I shake my head. "Are there any other staff here that I don't know anything about and don't appear to be paying much for?"

"Well," Milo starts to say, "there's—"

"Nooo," Oz interrupts somewhat unconvincingly. "Not that I can think of."

"Well, you'd know," I say slowly. "You know everything."

"Do you mind?" he asks, his expression serious for the first time.

I shake my head. "No. That's your job, after all." I look at him. "I trust you."

"You do?" He seems almost startled.

"Yes, you're still here after a month and we're not sleeping together and you haven't thrown crockery at me yet," I laugh.

He laughs too but the flash of heat in his eyes kindles the one in my balls.

Oz

Later on that night I close my bedroom door and collapse on the bed. The scent of lavender fills the air in the room from the open windows, but I feel stiflingly hot. Sitting up, I tug off my shirt and throw it across the room. It's followed quickly by my jeans and briefs. Naked, I spread out on the bed, feeling the heat run under my skin like a river. I open my legs and feel the cool air wash over my balls. They're tight and high and I feel one stroke away from coming already.

I sat across the table from him tonight and every time I looked up I'd feel his eyes on me, the look in them dark and hot. I'd fought a hard-on all night and now I need to let loose.

I reach over to the bedside drawer, and, rooting around, I draw out a bottle of lube and my trusty companion, Ted. I look at the flesh-coloured dildo glistening in the moonlight on the mattress and swallow hard.

I grab the lube and pour a stream into my hand. Coating my fingers liberally, I reach down and send them flirting round the edge of my hole. I screw my eyes up tight and moan harshly. The touch feels incredibly good on the nerve-rich exterior. I rub against the opening, teasing myself and hearing my breath heavy in the air. Finally, unable to wait any longer, I tap the hole with my index finger and wriggle it gently. I work it into the hole, screwing it gently against the tight opening.

A moan sounds in the dark room and I realise it's me. Panting, I add another finger, enjoying the burn and hearing the slick sound of fingers in my arse. Before I know it, I have three fingers up there and I'm writhing on the bed. I feel heat and electricity in the base of my balls and I know I'm close.

Taking my fingers out slowly, I gasp and reach for the dildo. After coating it with lube, I stand up and head towards the low table by the window that I'd earmarked for this a while ago. I attach the suction base of the dildo to it, and after checking to make sure it's secure, I crouch over it, feeling the head against my opening. I wiggle it into position, and then slowly lower myself down, gasping loudly as I feel it slide into me, the slight curve of the dildo hitting me just right.

Fumbling for the remote control, I turn it on and the buzzing is loud in the room. It almost sounds like the lavender bushes out there at midday. I gasp and give a thin cry, throwing my head back at the feelings coursing through my passage. I click the button a couple of times to get the speed I want, then widen my legs and lean back so it sits full in me.

I close my eyes as the dildo goes to work exerting wonderful vibrating pressure on my prostate. The breeze is cool on my body, but my attention is between my legs. I search for the trusty go-tos in my spank bank, but instead, Silas is there front and centre. I jerk my eyes open immediately. *Shit no, that's a step too far.*

I arch my pelvis and the toy kicks against the space inside me, rubbing and rubbing deliciously and lighting me up.

"Yes," I gasp, kicking my head back and reaching up to twist my nipple sharply. The pain makes me cry out, a thin high sound in the dark, but all modesty and caution has gone. Instead I ride the dildo, one hand on the table by my side for balance while the other pinches my nipple and occasionally lowers to cup and tug at my sac and fist my cock.

I rut down hard, feeling the flare and burn, and finally let my thoughts go. Silas lies under me naked, all that olive skin shining. Sweat glistens on his lip and amongst the chest hair. In my mind I lean back and rest my arms on his thighs, and the dildo becomes his cock forcing his way inside me, thrusting deep and battering against my prostate.

In my head he writhes underneath me and I see myself slamming onto him faster and faster as his big hands grab my cheeks and pull them downwards to make the penetration deeper. I feel his whispers of heated praise in my head as his fingers travel between my cheeks and taps my hole full of his cock. He ruts deep and heavy, his beard harsh on my face as I kiss him and he pounds up and into me, panting and groaning.

I jerk my cock hard, the slick sounds loud in the silence of the room, then give a choked scream of "*Silas*" as all the pressure races down my cock and I clench my buttocks around the shaft inside me and shoot streams of come over the worn floorboards in front of me.

For a long few minutes I hover over the dildo, panting and feeling the sweat and come cool on me, until I rise up gingerly and my body pushes the toy out almost pettily. I breathe in, and for the first time I notice a sweet scent of pipe tobacco and leather in the room, but when I stand up it vanishes. I shake my head and, picking up the dildo, I move towards the bathroom, intending to have a shower and wash the toy.

Something makes me deviate to the window and I stand in front of the tall mullioned window looking down onto the dark garden and enjoying the breeze blowing through. Then I stiffen as a shadow detaches itself and I gasp as I look down into Silas's face.

He's standing below my window and I have no doubt that he heard everything. It's so quiet here that any sound travels. I stare at him. Moonlight conceals most of his features but I can see his chest rise and fall quickly and the breath falling heavily from his open lips. He raises his fingers to his lips and the red end of a cigarette glows like a firefly.

We stare at each other for a long moment and for some reason I make no attempt to hide myself from him. The moon shines full on me and I wonder if it's affected me the way peasants in the Middle Ages used to claim that they'd been moon addled. It must be that, because I display myself openly in the moonlight to him while he looks his fill until finally he catches my eye and raises his fingers to his temple in a sort of salute.

Then he's gone, and I stand there for long moments watching the garden fall back into stillness and wondering if I just imagined that encounter.

CHAPTER 6

YOU ARE IN CONTROL OF THE CAR

Oz

I don't see anything of Silas for the next few days. I'm not sure whether it's him or me, but we seem to be assiduously avoiding each other. Whenever I've entered a room it's to find that he's just left it. It's like he's an anti-homing pigeon. I tell myself that I'm happy with this. I don't get attached to many people. I've always thought of that as my superpower, because in my experience people invariably let you down. Far better to avoid nasty words and bitterness by just not being bothered.

Anyway, if I shag another boss I'm sure I'll be qualifying for a spot on *The Jeremy Kyle Show*. I try to imagine what the banner heading for my appearance would be, and I've just settled on 'Can you believe what a fucking idiot this man is?' when Milo coughs.

I start and look up. "What?"

"The fitters want to know where you want the counter and workspace and shelves?"

I shake my head. "Sorry, I was far away." I step over to the waiting men and point out where I want everything situated. As they unpack the boxes I look around at what will be the gift shop. The small room near the tea rooms was once an office for the old stable master. Now, freshly plastered and decorated and with the sun streaming through the new long windows and onto the flagstones, it looks lovely.

It also looks very empty. I pull my diary out and leaf through the pages looking for the date of the county show. "When is–?"

"Next Friday," Milo replies, watching the men work.

I stare at him. "How do you know what I was going to say?"

He smiles. It's a full smile, unlike the nervy ones he used to offer. "I'm starting to know your mind." He gives a mock shudder. "Down there be monsters."

I shake my head, trying not to laugh. "You're too sassy, that's your problem." I turn to him and lean against the wall. "You sure this is the right way to go?"

He nods confidently. "The house is a local landmark. Lord Ashworth needs to showcase local products and this county fair is the best around for local craftsmen."

"I suppose it'll make him popular with the locals," I muse.

He looks astonished. "He couldn't get any more popular. He's always the first one to put his hand in his pocket to help someone. And it's not just money. He's always the first to help. When Mr Brown's tree fell on his farmhouse, Lord Ashworth turned up in the middle of the storm to help and then he put him and his wife up in this house until the repairs were done. When Bob Richardson, one of the tenant farmers, broke his leg, Lord Ashworth drove him to physiotherapy every week for months."

"That sounds like him," I muse, and I don't need Milo's sudden stillness to know that I sounded too fond. *Motherfucker*. "I mean, good on him. He seems like a good bloke," I say heartily, feeling a flush rise on my cheeks while Milo looks at me like I've grown a second head.

"Who's a good bloke?"

The deep voice comes from behind me and Silas tries to repress a smile as Milo and I jump like little old ladies.

"Lord Ashworth," Milo stammers, but I put my hands on my hips. My heart is hammering, not just at the shock, but at seeing him up close. I drink in his appearance in faded jeans, navy Vans, and a white polo shirt, like he's a bottle of cold beer on a hot day.

"What are you doing sneaking up on people?" I demand. "I could have a weak constitution."

He bites his lips, his eyes brimming with humour. "That makes you sound like an extra from *Wuthering Heights*. Still, as long as you're not wandering the moors in a nightie I think we'll be safe."

I shake my head. "That's my Saturday night plans ruined, then. Feel bad, Silas. Feel *really* bad."

He laughs loudly, then looks at Milo who is standing with his mouth slightly open. Silas coughs and rubs the back of his neck awkwardly. "So ... what's happening here?"

We both stare at him. "Erm, the workmen are fitting the counter and shelves," I say, looking round at the men who are being very obvious in what they're doing.

I watch in fascination as colour floods over his high cheekbones. *I don't find this adorable*, I say to myself. *I definitely do not find this adorable*.

I give in to my softer, more stupid inclinations and give him an out. "Did you need us, Lord–" I stutter slightly, and equilibrium regained, he smirks at me.

"Are you alright?" he asks.

I shake my head. "I can't. I'm sorry. I probably should be able to call you by your title, but I just can't."

Milo looks both horrified and titillated and I shoot him a scowl.

Silas smiles. "Are there too many syllables, Oz?"

"How many are in fuck off?" I ask pertly, and he laughs. I sigh loudly. "Have you come to oversee the work?"

He looks startled and shakes his head. "No, of course not. I trust you to do it properly."

I don't feel happy because he approves of me, I tell myself sternly. *I don't need anyone's approval.* I pause. *Except my mum's, of course.* I pause again. *And Auntie Vera.*

His voice breaks into my thoughts. "I need to borrow you, Oz, if you're free for a couple of hours."

"Borrow me?" I stop to clear the Mickey Mouse squeakiness from my voice. "I mean, why do you need me?"

He bites his lips. "Well, you'll find out if you come with me."

Our eyes meet and tangle and everything seems to be muffled around me. The only thing I can see are the warm depths of his hazel eyes. They're clear and limpid today like a shallow stream where the water runs clear, but they darken as the other night seems to rise up in front of us like a hologram in *Star Wars*. Only that film never had holograms of a man anally pleasuring himself with a dildo. I think even Darth Vader would have been a bit startled by that.

I swallow hard and he licks his lips almost nervously. Milo coughs and shifts and we both start as if he's woken us up.

Silas looks at me questioningly and I abruptly remember what he's just said. I don't want to be alone with him. I'll either say something really fucking stupid or crawl onto his lap and beg him to fuck me. Or both. He looks at me expectantly, and for just a second, I think I see worry in the soft depths.

I immediately smile at him reassuringly, watching him relax almost instantly. I then compound my stupidity by turning to Milo and saying, "Are you okay with me pushing off?"

He takes the plans from me. "I'm fine. It's self-explanatory."

I turn back to Silas and gesture. "Well, lead on then."

He smiles before turning to Chewwy who has sat up and is

watching our movements. "Stay," Silas says to the huge dog. Chewwy gives him a face that implies Silas is torturing him and then collapses onto the floor next to Milo with a long and disgusted sigh. I turn and follow Silas, trying hard not to look at his arse in the faded jeans he seems to favour. They're mostly worn to within an inch of their life with interesting holes, and they hold his lower body shape like a lover. He looks back suddenly and missteps almost comically as he catches me looking at his arse.

I flush and instantly burst into talk. *Hello stupidity. Here you are again, my old friend.* "Don't you own any new clothes?" I come to a dead stop. "Oh my God, that was really tactless. I'm so sorry. I know you don't have much money and–"

He looks startled but then follows my glance to the holes in the knees of his jeans. When he looks up his eyes are soft. "Oh no, I'm okay for money myself, Oz. I'm sorry if I gave you that impression. I earn a good living with my practice, but it's the house and the estate. The figures involved in that are way out of the park." He pauses. "And a few other parks too." He shrugs, looking almost bashful. "I just like being comfortable, and I like jeans best when they're–"

"Almost on the verge of extinction?" I say sympathetically and smile as he laughs.

He shakes his head. "I like old things."

"Please don't ever say that if I take you to leather daddy night in Camden. They'd eat you alive."

He grins. "You do make me laugh," he says almost impulsively and then blushes again.

"Well, it's nice I can do that. I think my humour is slightly lost on Milo. He hovers between a twitchy smile and horror."

"He likes you. He doesn't say boo to a goose normally."

I shake my head. "What does that even mean? Why would anyone go around saying boo to a farmyard bird? It's not like they're going to turn around and engage you in conversation."

"Swans are birds and they've been known to break people's arms," he says casually.

I stop dead. "*What?*"

He turns back. "They are not good-tempered birds, especially if you get near them during spring nesting. They can hurt you if they're defending their nest."

"You're joking."

He grins. "Nope. There was a swan called Mr Asbo on the River Cam. He got the name because he kept attacking the rowers."

"But you've got swans in the lake," I splutter. "Shouldn't they be behind bars?"

"They're not Charles Bronson, Oz. Just don't say boo to them."

"You're so funny," I mutter, following him down past the tea rooms to the private car park. "Where are we going?" I finally ask.

He comes to the concreted area and stops by an old red Volkswagen Polo. "Voilà!"

I stare at him and then at the car. "Voilà, what?"

He smiles. "I'm going to give you your first driving lesson."

I hold my hands up. "Oh no. No, thank you. It's very kind of you but I don't think that's a very good idea."

"I think it's a really good idea," he says firmly. "This isn't London. The nicest thing you could say about the transport service around here is that it's sporadic." He looks at me. "We're far from anything, Oz, and I don't want you feeling trapped. If you can drive, you can go where you want."

"You are aware I have a lot less than six months now to complete a task that Jesus would have baulked at in his miracles phase? I barely have time to sleep, let alone jaunt off to the seaside and have some fish and chips."

He immediately looks worried. "Have you had a day off since you came here?"

I hesitate. "That's not the point," I start to say, but he groans.

"Oh my God, that's terrible. You'll be burning out."

"Slow down. I think that happens to hedge fund managers, not building site organisers."

His lips quirk. "Is that your new job title?"

I put my hands on my hips. "Does it suit me?" I turn around. "Does my new job title make my bum look big?"

There's a protracted silence and I suddenly realise that I'm actually talking to my boss and not flirting in a club. He's so lovely it's hard to remember. I turn slowly back and swallow hard as his eyes seem to cling to my arse.

"Sorry," I mutter and he jerks and looks up.

"Why?"

I shrug. "You're my boss. I keep forgetting it."

He stares at me and suddenly smiles. "I have the same problem, Oz. Why do you think that is?"

I open my mouth and shut it quickly because I cannot think of a thing to say that wouldn't land me in worse trouble than I've just got out of. For a second, disappointment seems to flit across his face, but then he clears it and claps his hands together.

"Well, shall we do this?"

I breathe in deeply, trying to dispel the strong urge I have to fall on him and kiss his face off. "There's nothing I can say that's going to change your mind, is there?" I say resignedly.

He smiles happily. "Nope."

He presses the button to open the locks and gestures me sunnily into the driving seat. Climbing in next to me, he turns to face me. "First lesson. When we're getting in and out of a car what should we be looking for?"

"I'm thinking serial killer swans now," I say morosely and try to stop the uptick of my lips at his laughter.

"Apart from swans, what other disasters should we avoid?"

"Disasters? It's not *The Towering Inferno*. Oh, my God," I say, starting to panic. "I haven't started the engine yet. What's going to happen?"

He snorts. "I'm thinking maybe just look around so you're not going to open the door and bang into a cyclist or pedestrian."

I subside. "Oh. Okay, that sounds doable." I wave my hand. "Carry on."

His lip twitches. "Thank you." He straightens up in his seat, the leather creaking, and I try to inhale his fresh, sweet scent without being too obvious or looking like I'm having an asthma attack.

He pulls out an old book and starts to thumb through the pages.

"What's that?" I ask.

He cradles it protectively as if he thinks I'm going to rip it from his hands and feed it to the thuggish swans.

"It's a book on teaching driving. I found it in the study."

"How old is it?" I marvel.

"It's not *that* old," he says defensively.

"I bet there's a chapter in there on how not to run over the man walking in front of your car with a flag."

He snorts. "Shut the fuck up. I just want to do this right."

I shake my head while melting inside. "Okay then." I wave a lordly hand. "Proceed."

"Thank you," he says dryly and touches his forehead in a salute. "Okay, the first thing you have to be aware of is that *you* are in control of the car. The car is not in control of you."

I nod. "Like BDSM."

"Pardon?"

"Like BDSM. The person on their knees is the one with all the power, not the person spanking them." He stares at me and I cough. "At least so I've heard."

He looks at me, biting his lip before obviously deciding not to venture down that conversational bypass. "Okay, let's start with the pedals. First, can you reach them?"

I push my foot out and flush. "Not exactly," I say through clenched teeth. If he says how cute I am or sweet, I'll smack him one. Most men when confronted with my size tend to think it makes me the adult male equivalent of a Pokémon.

Silas, however, is smarter. Hastily looking at the pedals, he avoids my irate gaze. "Pull your chair forwards if you want. Or backwards," he quickly adds. "I mean if you haven't got enough leg room."

My lip twitches. *He's so adorable.*

He watches while I grab the lever and pull the chair forward. "You can go up and down too," he mutters.

I turn to wink at him. "I know I can. It's one of my specialities."

He swallows hard. "No, I mean the chair goes up and down if you can't see over the wheel." He falters slightly when he catches my steely gaze and settles for pointing aimlessly across the car park ahead of us as if I'd somehow mistakenly thought that I'd look out the back window when driving.

I bite my lip. "I'm just a bit sensitive about my size," I say in a low voice. "Too many years of having the piss taken out of me or being spoken to like a child."

He smiles at me and says hesitantly, "I think the problem, Oz, is that you look delicate but that's not who you are. You're actually really fierce."

I stare at him. No man who's not a friend has ever said that about me. "My mum used to say that my spirit animal was probably something small with sharp teeth."

He looks me up and down. "Like a hamster?"

I glare at him. "I was actually thinking of a fox but you're saying I've got a big belly and round cheeks."

He breaks into a fit of what can only be described as giggles. To see a big bearded man giggle is oddly awesome. "Like a mutant hamster," he gets out between laughter and holding his sides.

I shake my head, trying not to smile and failing. "If you've quite finished insulting me, can we get on with this terrible driving lesson? I'm sure no one at a professional driving school would have called me a hamster and made BDSM jokes."

"I didn't make them," he says indignantly. "That was you."

"I can't hear you," I say loudly. "I'm concentrating on my pedals."

He shakes his head, grinning. "Okay, back to business, Pika."

"What the fuck is that?"

"It's a little animal that looks like a rabbit."

"Oh my *God*." I throw my arms up. "I don't need second sight to know that nickname's fucking sticking."

He laughs. "You're so talented you should have a stall at Blackpool Pier and read some palms."

I shake my head as he sobers up from the next fit of laughter. "Okay," he finally manages. "Okay, I'm ready." He looks at me and snorts again but composes himself and checks his book. "Can you get your hands all round the wheel?"

I smile salaciously at him. "I can get my hands around most girths. It's like a superpower."

He sighs. "*So* many innuendos. It's like teaching David Walliams to drive."

I laugh. "Okay, I can manage to handle the wheel. What's next?"

He flicks a page in the bloody book and consults it. "Make sure the doors are shut," he reads aloud. "Any idea how we can tell?"

I shake my head. "If there's a bit of a draft and I fall out, they must be open."

He flushes. *He's so earnest and adorable. Who knew that would be my kryptonite?*

"Stupid fucking book," he mutters and chucks it in the back seat accompanied by my laughter. He twists round. "Okay, we'll do it my way."

"Be still my heart," I mutter.

He grins. "You should be worried. I failed my test three times."

"*Three times.* Who the fuck fails *three times*?"

"Says the man who's never taken a test."

"Even so, I know enough to know you'd have to be seriously bad to fail a driving test *three times.*"

"They're very harsh in their judgements," he says primly. "I felt they were being far too picky."

"What did you fail on?" He mutters something and I grin. "I'm sorry. What did you say?"

"I crashed the car the first time," he mutters.

I start to laugh, holding my sides. "Oh my God, this is so good. And they failed you for that? Judgemental arseholes."

"The instructor used very harsh language. He swore at me."

I laugh harder. "Poor baby," I gasp. "What happened the second time?"

"I reversed rather than going forward."

I snort. "Did you hit anything?"

"No. Luckily with the dual controls the examiner was able to swerve and miss the old lady."

I'm crying now. "Shit. This is brilliant. So, crashing the car and a near flattening of an OAP. These tests are so fucking *harsh*. Who could pass with those unattainably high standards? What was the third?"

He shakes his head. "I don't want to tell you."

I grab his arm. I'm laughing so hard I can't speak properly. "Please, you have to."

A grin flirts across his lips before he quashes it. "You have to do an emergency stop. The examiner signals it when he slams his clipboard down on the dashboard."

"And?"

He shrugs. "You have to understand I was quite jumpy by then. I was a bag of nerves, really. Anyway, he slammed his hand down very loudly." He pauses. "Much too loudly and extremely forcefully, if you ask me."

I bite my lip. "And?"

He shoots me a dark look. "I jumped and broke his nose with my elbow."

I'm howling with laughter now and holding my sides. "Oh my God, *I* should teach *you*."

He watches me, grinning ruefully. "It's not funny. I had to go and take my test in St Austell because the examiners refused to have me."

I laugh for ages while he grins at me. Finally, I sober and I think a lot of that is to do with the soft way he's looking at me. No one has ever looked at me like this. Soft and brimming over with humour and warmth. For a long second, we stare at each other, the laughter dying and heat replacing it.

I wipe my eyes and straighten and for a second disappointment flits across his face before he schools it.

"Okay, let's show you the controls."

He painstakingly shows me the foot controls, explaining everything very clearly and banging on about mirrors and blind spots while I stare at the side of his face and sniff his aftershave.

"Oz, are you listening?"

I jerk and look at him to find him examining me with a quizzical expression on his face.

"Sorry," I say.

He smiles. "It is pretty boring, but it's got to be done. Here, this is the gearbox. Push your foot down on the clutch and feel the stick moving through the gears."

I hesitate and he grabs my hand, putting his own over the top of it. He counts out the gears but my whole attention is on his hand. The calloused palm and long, almost artistic-looking fingers spread over mine. I look at the spray of freckles on the back of his hand like it's hypnotizing me, and all I can think about is standing at that window fresh from coming and letting him see all of me in the moonlight.

I suddenly become aware that he's stopped talking and the resulting silence is heavy. I can almost feel it on the air.

"Oz," he says hoarsely.

I look up and I'm done for. He's staring at me, his pupils big and dark and his expression wrecked, and without another word we fly at each other. Teeth clash and lips bang together in our rush, but then we're really kissing. Kissing as if we've been doing it together all our lives. Our tongues meet and lips suck and cling and we twist together as if synchronised, all our movements designed to get closer. He eats at my mouth, giving choked groans, and I can hear my panting breaths loud in the silence. One of us moans and he raises his head.

"Oh my God," he whispers, his mouth shining. His lips are gorgeous. Thin on the top and lush and pouty on the bottom. I reach up and send my tongue languorously over that full curve and he moans deep inside his throat.

"Yes," he gasps and takes my mouth again.

This time it isn't enough and I lunge at him. I need pressure and weight. Without taking my mouth away I reach and unclip my belt. The sound attracts his attention and he pulls away, looking blearily at me, his eyes half-mast and his lips spit-slick.

"Oz," he says and I come up onto my knees and scramble across the handbrake, landing in his lap and quickly straddling him. "Oh fuck, yes," he calls out. His big hands seize my hips and he pulls me further into him.

We both groan as our cocks meet hard and ready, and I start to writhe on him. All I can see is the sun beating a red haze behind my eyelids. Sweat runs down my back and I feel almost crazed with the need for more. More kissing, more touching.

"Fuck, I need more," I gasp, pulling away from his mouth as he follows mine with his own almost drunkenly.

"Come back," he whispers and, grabbing my arse cheeks, he pulls me forward so I rest all along his chest. I cant my hips and start a slow hard grind, crying out as I feel the denim of his jeans rubbing against my cock behind its layer of fabric.

"Yes, Silas. Yes," I groan and push my hands into his hair, feeling the dark strands slip through my fingers like silk. I throw my head back and gasp as he nips and suckles at the tendon, sending fire and sparks through my blood.

"Don't stop," I mutter, pulling his face harder into my neck. "Right there. Oh God."

"Yes," he groans and I feel his fingers at the zipper of my jeans. "I need you now," he says fiercely.

"Yes." I lean up on my knees and start to unbutton his jeans as I sway faintly from the movement of the car.

I just have time to realise that the car shouldn't be moving when there's a bang and we come to a stop.

"What the *fuck*?" I breathe.

Silas looks around dazedly. "Erm, I think you took the hand brake off when you crawled across," he says slowly. "We're in the Buddleia bush at the moment."

For a long second, we stare at each other. Expressions pass too quickly over his face for me to analyse, but I see heated longing and warmth before he shutters them and then all I can see is caution.

I take his cue instantly. In films the retreat is always graceful and it fades to black. That's not possible with two men in a Volkswagen Polo, so instead, we treat ourselves to the full quiet and awkward rezipping and tucking back in along with the scrambling back over the gearbox that he has to help with a quick boost of my bum.

When I'm back in my seat I look at him. "I'm sorry," I begin.

"So am I," he says instantly and I flinch. *Wow! Regrets after twenty seconds. Must be a new world record.* He carries on talking. "I'm sorry you had a shitty time with your last boss. That's not the sort of man I am, but I don't expect you to believe that given the way I've just behaved." He sighs. "I just want you to feel okay here. I don't want you to feel like you have to leave, and I never want you to be put in a position where you feel you have to do something you don't want to."

"This isn't *Upstairs Downstairs*," I start to say but he shakes his head.

"Can we go back to normal, Oz?" He looks hard at me. "I really want that. I've grown to consider you a friend and I'd miss the us that we are now if you decided to leave."

My heart melts because not many people want to keep the real me. I'm too abrasive, too forceful, too flippant. You name it, I'm too much of it. But this kind, clever man wants my friendship, and looking at the vast gulf between the two of us, maybe I should have this rather than trying for more, which would probably be ridiculous anyway. Why would he settle for me of all people, when he could have anyone? Someone clever and wealthy. Someone who could really bring something to help him in his life.

I make myself smile. "I'm not going anywhere, Silas." I pause. "It was an eventful driving lesson anyway. I'm sure not many people end up in a Buddleia bush." He looks slightly embarrassed and I can't help my laugh. "Oh my God, you did. You're terrible."

He laughs and starts to tell me the story, but even while he's talking our eyes are meeting and catching and neither of us mentions the sudden silences as he forgets his words.

Surely friendship will get easier.

CHAPTER 7

HAIRY PEOPLE PLEASER

ONE WEEK LATER

Silas

I straighten from my crouched position on the floor as the boy I've just given a balloon to runs back to his mum. "Christ, remind me why we do this," I ask my partner, Theo.

He looks up from his slouch on the counter and grins at me. "Because it's very good to interact with the general public. Because we might pick up more business. And because we're two of the on-call vets for the show." He strikes a pose. "Helping to guard against the spread of infectious diseases and biohazards."

I grin. "You just want to wear pants over your tights."

He laughs. "Can't fool you." He shrugs. "Anyway, it's a nice day for handing out balloons with our logo on them."

I look around at the bustling grounds in Wadebridge that are currently hosting the Royal Cornwall Show. Crowds move and surge past us, stopping to look at the stands all around us, or moving to the central ground where there's an equestrian show on. The sky is a bright clear blue and when I inhale I can smell straw and hot dogs cooking.

"It is a good day," I say and then stiffen as a small dark-haired man pushes his way through the crowd. I straighten and watch intently until he comes into full sight and then I slump as I realise it isn't Oz. I know he's here today and I'm ridiculously nervous.

I look up and flush when I catch Theo's very knowing gaze. "Not him?" he asks mock-sympathetically.

"Fuck off!" I whisper as another family moves towards our stand.

He laughs. "No, really. When am I going to meet the almost mythological Oz?"

I shake my head, but I'm prevented from answering him when the family reach me and I'm swamped with answering the mum's questions about what qualifications her son will need to become a vet.

I answer her questions as fully as I can while casting glances at the boy who is currently in his pram and fast asleep.

"Of course, qualifications might have changed by the time he's ready for university," I say smoothly and stiffen as I hear a familiar low chuckle from behind me. I spin around quickly and find Milo and Oz standing with Theo.

Oz is grinning at me. His eyes are covered with dark sunglasses, and he's wearing bold black and white striped shorts with a tight black t-shirt that proudly shows off his sleeve of tattoos along with tatty black Converse Chuck Taylors. He manages to look out of place, yet completely at home, which to me is one of his most endearing qualities. He's the most real person I've ever met in my life.

I become aware that I'm staring at him and his mouth is tightening in concern the way it has the last week whenever we've met and I've become as fucking tongue-tied as an awkward teenager. He always manages to look both nonplussed and sympathetic and I hate the idea that he might be pitying me, or even worse, humouring my crush.

I shake my head and walk towards them. "Hey," I say. "It's good to see you."

I don't need the quirk of Theo's lips to know that came out as appallingly hearty and I flush, but incredibly, Oz's lips relax, and he raises his glasses and gives me a soft look.

"It's good to see you too," he says. For a second time seems to still as we stare at each other. Then Milo shifts awkwardly and I snap back into the moment.

"Afternoon, Lord Ashworth," he says.

I shake my head. "It's Silas, Milo." I smile at them. "Going to find yourself some good suppliers?"

Oz gives his low chuckle that always without fail hits me in my balls and my heart simultaneously. It's like rough velvet. "That sounds like a line from *Sons of Anarchy*."

I grin at him. "Did Charlie Hunnam go shopping for local honey and tea towels too? I must have missed that episode."

"It was in the deleted scenes in the extras," he says demurely.

Theo laughs and Oz turns to him and smiles. I feel a flare of something hot in my chest. *Does he fancy him?* Theo's attractive and single. He's also not paying Oz's wages. I swallow. I want to bewail that fact, and I would if it hadn't been responsible for bringing Oz into my life in the first place.

I can't quite believe that I've only known him for a couple of months. He fits so easily in my life, like there's always been a corner carved out for a small fierce man who waits up for me at night to cook and talk. Who, when he knew the financial mess I was in, has thrown himself into making the house ready, like a knight riding to the rescue. I smile. A small, very feisty knight whose armour wears thin at the oddest times. I try to imagine the house done and him not there anymore, but my mind shies away from that like a tongue from a wobbly tooth.

I become aware of Milo looking at me in a bewildered fashion while Oz and Theo talk. I shake my head. "Sorry," I murmur. "I've got a lot on my plate today."

He shoots me a sharp quizzical look that's so like Oz, it's startling. Even here he's made his mark. Milo has worked for me for two years and no matter how hard I tried to put him at ease, he remained tongue-tied. I know and understand the reasons for his shyness, but Oz has been here for a few months and Milo's already showing a sassy side. Only the other day Niall had rather autocratically told him to pass him something and Milo had asked whether he wanted him to tie a broom to his arse and sweep the floor while he did it. It had quite put Niall off his stride and I hadn't missed the way he'd looked at Milo after that. Curious and wide eyed and almost proud.

Oz stirs at my words. "We ought to get going," he says, and I hope I'm not imagining that he sounds reluctant. "We've got honey to buy and you're working."

"Not all day," I blurt. I can feel Theo's laughing gaze burning into my head but I ignore him. "I've got to take a break. Do you want to meet me at the show ground at four? There's an exhibition of junior horse jumping."

I actually want to punch myself in the face at that extremely lame invitation, but to my astonishment his face lights up.

"I'd love that," he says softly. He gives his wicked grin, the arch of which I want to lick so badly. "Are they providing alcohol?"

"Fucking hope so," I mutter, giving him a swift grin, and watch as his smile turns wide and warm.

He and Milo exchange goodbyes with Theo and walk away, leaving me with a silence that is pregnant with mirth.

"Well?" he finally says.

"Oh, look," I say quickly. "Is that family coming over for a balloon? I think they are and it's your turn."

He stares at the family who are moving past us and heading

towards a giant robot who appears to be spitting water at people. "Nope," he says happily. "We are quite alone."

"You sound rather creepy at the moment."

"I should sound ecstatic and brimming with happiness."

I turn to him in surprise. "What?"

"Yes, it's like watching one of my grandma's afternoon films. Heartwarming and almost tragic."

"Shut up, you knob."

He bursts into very loud laughter, looking more like the eighteen-year-old student I met at Edinburgh University than a thirty-seven-year-old partner in a vet practice.

"Oh, shut up," I say sourly and give him a shove which makes him upset a case of cat collars.

We bend to pick them up and after a few seconds I give in and look up at him. "I looked like a fool," I mutter.

His face softens and he smiles. "Yes, that's true." I grimace and he grabs my arm. "But you weren't alone in it, if that's any consolation."

"What?"

He nods. "He's as interested in you as you are in him. It's as obvious as the fact that Chris Hemsworth is attractive."

I shake my head. "I don't know."

"How can you say that? He's extremely good looking."

"I'm not talking about Chris Hemsworth with you. It'll take ages."

He relents. "Even you, who is as blind to interest as a dead person, must recognise that Oz likes you."

"But I'm his boss." I hesitate. "He didn't have a good experience last time he got involved with someone."

"Please. Niall's his boss. You just pay the wage packet. Anyway, he's only here for a few more months."

"Don't mention that," I mutter and he rubs my arm. I look at him. "Anyway, we all know what a terrible picker I am. Henry reminded me a few weeks ago."

He laughs but then sobers. "I think you're getting better at it, son."

"Why?" I ask, startled.

"He's brilliant and somehow just perfect for you." He stares blindly at the crowds. "When I first saw him, I thought you were as different as anything."

"We are," I say wryly.

He shrugs. "Hmm, maybe. I don't think so. You actually seem very similar. You both have that very warm, settled air about you." He bites his lip in deep thought. "You're constant, Silas. I thought it the moment I met you. You have this air of loyalty and dependability."

"You make me sound like a Golden Labrador," I say sourly.

He laughs. "It's nothing to be ashamed of. Labs are lovely. Although inclined to be weighty. I'd watch that if I were you."

I shove him, but gently this time so he doesn't damage another case of products. "I'm not worried about my weight, thank you very much." He laughs but stares at me. "What?" I ask.

He smiles. "He's the same. You might have very different backgrounds and personalities, but underneath that air of *I don't give a shit* that he has, is actually a man who cares very deeply. I just think you have to work to get in that group. I bet it's small."

I shrug and smile as a couple with a small pug interrupt us, but my mind returns to it as the time moves as slowly as a snail to four o'clock. I want to be in that group that Oz guards so closely. I want him to look on me as something precious and dear, the way he does his family and close friends. I want to matter to him, and that desire is steadily eclipsing all my doubts of the wisdom of doing anything.

Oz

The lady in front of me drones on about her honey. She has dozens of jars open and Milo is dutifully trying some and making noises of appreciation. I edge slightly to the right so I can see beyond her and into the stand where Silas is currently charming a woman with a Chihuahua.

I stare at the wide smile on his open tanned face and watch as she shakes out her long auburn hair. She's very pretty. I can see appreciation on his face and I remember suddenly that he's bisexual.

I frown. I've nothing against bisexual people at all. The only thing it means to me in connection with Silas is that there is suddenly another section of the population who might be better for him than me.

I wonder why my heart isn't obeying the urgings of my head. I'm entirely wrong for him. His partner should be someone upper class, someone with effortless charm. Someone who can greet his guests and family properly. Someone who he can be proud to stand next to. That someone surely isn't me.

I look up and see the woman touch his arm and an adorably confused and panicked look come over his face. He looks beseechingly towards his friend Theo, who shakes his head but wanders over to join their conversation. They talk for a few minutes and then she leaves after touching her hair about thirty times and then his hand.

When she's gone, Theo says something and Silas shakes his head at once, giving that lopsided quirky smile he has. I close my eyes in resignation. That smile and the slightly lost air about him are the reasons I can't listen to my brain.

I've escaped heartache all these years because of that trusty organ, and right at the moment I need it most, it's faltering, helpless against the power of … Silas. I grimace and look up to see the honey woman and Milo looking at me aghast.

"Sorry," I say quickly. "I was just thinking–" I falter slightly. "Erm, I was just thinking about how much I love bees," I finish. Milo gives me a knowing look, but the woman smiles approvingly. This leads to a long and very intense conversation about bee habits and her extracting a promise to visit her hives.

Saying goodbye, we walk away from the honey stand. "Lovely," I sigh. "Now, I've got to go and put my hand in a hive and I'm far too pretty to wear a net over my face."

He snorts with laughter. "I hope the white outfit doesn't make you look plump."

I nudge him admiringly. "So pert."

He shakes his head. "It's nearly four, you know. Haven't you got a date?"

I look at my watch and curse. "Is that the time already? It isn't a date." I open my diary and thumb through the pages. "Okay, we've got honey, local candles, and the pottery from Boscastle. We've just got to put the book order in for the shop from the wholesalers. Anything else?"

He looks down at his list. "I think that's it for today. Don't forget that we also made the deal for those hand-carved walking sticks. And it is totally a date."

I elbow him gently. "No, it isn't. He's my boss and you and I have a fond memory of why that isn't a good route for me."

He makes a scoffing noise and I stare at him. "Oh, please. I never met your ex, but Silas isn't that wanker you were going out with before. If you can't see that, then you're an idiot."

I stare at him. "Where is all this coming from?"

He gives an embarrassed smile. "I like you, Oz," he says in a low voice. "You're my friend, even if your mentoring skills aren't fully developed." I shove him gently and he smiles. "I just think Lord Ashworth really likes you and you'd be good for him."

I rub his arm. "Was that uncomfortable?" I ask sympathetically.

He gives a big sigh and grins. "Sooo uncomfortable. Can we please move onto the not talking about feelings portion of the day?"

I laugh. "Okay. Are we done here, because I need to get a seat for the horse racing."

"It's children's horse jumping, not Formula One." He nods. "See you tomorrow. I'm going to ask for samples from the handmade chocolate stall."

"But we don't need them."

He smirks. "*We* know that."

"See, my mentoring skills are actually pretty good," I shout after him as he disappears into the crowd. "Get me some," I add as an afterthought.

I look down at my watch and curse. I'm going to be late if I don't hurry. Looking at the signs, I take a path to the right and follow it, dodging around the slow-moving crowd. I pass stalls selling cheese and scented candles and rather incongruously a steel drum band made up of very enthusiastic old ladies.

When I arrive at the showground the horses and their riders are just coming out. I look around and then see him as if he's got a spotlight on him. He's leaning against the fence sipping from a plastic cup. His navy polo shirt pulls across his wide shoulders and his navy shorts cup his arse lovingly.

A man leading a horse stops to say something to him and he throws his head back and laughs, and I stare because he's so beautiful.

At that moment he looks up and catches my gaze before I can shutter it. Surprise spreads across his own, along with something that looks like happiness. Then he smiles at me and the feelings have gone, leaving only his tanned open face and his eyes which are almost green at the moment and still with a vestige of that warmth lingering.

Becoming aware that I'm not moving, I make my way towards him. "Sorry I'm late," I say, edging past an old couple who tut at me as I squeeze in next to him.

"Doesn't matter," he says easily, handing me the twin of his cup.

I sniff and smile. "Cider?"

He grins. "Cornish cider."

"Well, I suppose I must, if it's tradition."

He laughs, and we turn to face the arena which is now filling with small children on sleek-looking ponies. I watch one little girl walk her horse past us. Her helmet is on too far forward, giving her a truculent look. I look at her horse who's trudging after her and snort. He looks at me enquiringly and I nod towards them. "Don't they say you start to look like your pets after a while?"

He grins. "It's actually truer than you think." He turns to me. "Who do you think I look like?"

I stare at him and smile evilly. "Probably Chewwy."

"Why?"

"You're both hairy people pleasers."

He laughs loudly, and I smile at him. I look around as the first competitor is announced and begins his assault on the brightly coloured jumps. The air is full of the smell of horses and leather. "I suppose this is what you grew up with," I say idly. "Did you or your brother compete?"

He laughs. "You must be joking. I could barely manage a car. Who the hell would put me on a fucking horse?" He pauses. "Henry liked the outfits, but he couldn't stay on a horse for more than ten seconds, so an equestrian career was ruled out pretty early."

I grin and look around as the Tannoy splutters into action announcing the next competitor. We watch as a young girl sits slumped on her horse who looks pissed off, to put it mildly. At her urging the horse canters slowly and reluctantly around. She aims his nose at the jumps and we watch open-mouthed as he proceeds to annihilate the entire course, balking at some rides, riding blatantly round jumps or kicking his way through the others.

Silas grins. "He's like the Sid Vicious of the riding fraternity." I laugh and he turns to me. "Want to take a walk?" he asks in a low voice and I swallow hard before following him out of the arena.

As if by mutual consent, we turn to our right and amble aimlessly along. The late afternoon sun beams down on us. His arm brushes me, and I fancy I can feel the heat from his skin. Occasionally his hand brushes mine, and although we're walking amongst a crowd, it feels like we're in a bubble of our own, full of warmth and light. I feel as aware of his body in this minute as I've ever felt while someone fucks me. It's just one more example of how he fucks up my status quo.

We wander along, talking in low voices with frequent pauses as our tongues still and our eyes tangle. He buys me a tub of strawberries and cream and we amble along eating them and sipping cider as the crowd thins and the stalls start to pack away. For the first time I don't want a time with a man to stop. Usually I'm eager to leave, my feet itching to move and go. But now it feels like I'm in one of the legends that talk of humans walking into fairy rings and being caught.

I slow, and it happens quickly. He stops to say something, but he must catch something on my face because he raises his hand and grabs my arm gently. For a second we lock gazes and then he moves fast, pulling me off the path and round the back of an empty stall. We're in a tiny corner boxed in by the back of a tent and surrounded by empty boxes, and I stare at him in the dim light.

I take a long shuddering breath at the look of incinerating heat on his face and he gasps before grabbing my head and pulling my face to his. At the first touch of his lips my eyes slide closed and I melt into him as he groans under his breath.

His hands slide down and he cups my arse, lifting me and pushing me into the back of the stall. I moan low in my throat and wrap my legs around him, feeling the heft and steely hardness of his cock as he starts to grind at me.

He tightens his grip and we eat at each other's mouths, rubbing our tongues together and suckling on lips. I gasp as he pulls away and then give a much too loud cry as he lowers his face and I feel his mouth run along the sensitive tendons of my neck. He rubs his beard there and finding my pulse he sucks gently, wringing another cry from me.

"Fuck!" I whisper. "Oh fuck, I need you inside me." I reach down and fumble with his belt buckle, but still in surprise as his large hand stops me.

"Wait," he mutters. "Wait, Oz."

I look up and groan. "Are you having second thoughts?"

I'm gratified to see the speed at which he shakes his head. "No, of course I'm bloody not. Jesus, can't you feel how fucking hard I am?"

I wriggle and we both groan, but then I pull back and try to regulate my breathing and get some control. To do that I fall back on my default setting of flippancy. "Then what's the problem?" I look around. "Is it the slight tackiness of the area in which we're going to consummate our passion?"

He snorts and starts to laugh. "It might be." His face turns serious and I swallow hard, my flippancy falling to pieces like an old tissue. "I don't want to do it this way with you." He breathes in. "I've had sex in many places and with many people, but I've never met anyone like you and–"

He pauses, and I shake my head fondly. "What are you trying to say?"

He bites his lip. "I want to take you out on a date. I want to get to know you."

I run my hand through his wavy hair and watch as his eyes lower sexily. "Why?"

"Because you're different. Nothing I've done before has ever led to anything good and I don't want that to happen with you. I want to try something new. I want to take you out."

I lower my face into his neck, feeling him sigh as I inhale the scent of him. "Have we got time for a date?" I ask. "There's so much still to do and I made you a promise that it would get done." I pause. "And aren't you still my boss?"

I feel his chuckle as I rub my face into his neck. "I think that ship has sailed. I don't care anymore." He pauses. "Do you?" A faint thread of worry seeps into his voice and I immediately raise my head.

"No, of course I bloody don't," I say sharply. "I went into the thing with my old boss on a whim and because I was bored. It got shitty, not because he cheated, but because he was a wanker. I don't think you are. Anyway, this isn't a Catherine Cookson novel where you're an evil mill owner seducing and abandoning your innocent worker. I'm well aware of what I'm doing and in full control. I never do anything I don't want to."

A wry look crosses his face. "I think I'm well aware of that fact," he says tartly. An amused look crosses his face. "A *Catherine Cookson* novel? Oz, you're so full of surprises you should have been a cracker."

I laugh, feeling my cheeks heat. "My mum liked them and I used to get bored when she was on nights."

"Okay," he mutters. He pauses. "So, if I were to say something in a Yorkshire accent you'd melt?"

"Try it."

"Eeh, by gum, missus," he starts, and I break into peals of laughter.

"Oh my God," I gasp. "Yorkshire people do *not* sound like that. Please don't consider a career on the stage."

His laughter dies and he rubs his hand gently through my hair, watching his fingers move through the strands as if fascinated. "So, a date? How about tomorrow?"

I swallow and nod. "Okay. I haven't been on many," I confess. "So, don't worry because I'll never spot it if you've got it wrong."

"Thank you," he says seriously. "That's made me feel so much better."

"You're welcome," I say demurely and he laughs. "Where are we going and when?"

He grins. "I've got the perfect idea and just know that it's both practical and functional. You'll feel like you're still working even though we're not on the premises."

I stare at him. "Yeah, no. I don't think that's how dates go," I say dubiously and smile as he hugs me tight, his head lowered over my own in our tiny hidden corner of the county fair.

CHAPTER 8

LAST TIME I WENT ON A PROPER DATE I THINK I WAS SEVENTEEN

Oz

The next morning, Chewwy and I clatter down the stairs and come to an abrupt stop. "What are you doing?"

He grins at me from his position on a stepladder. "Sorry. I'm just getting these cobwebs. They're getting bad."

I fold my arms. "Don't tell me. You are doing this because Martha, the housemaid, is frightened of heights and once smiled at you when you were five."

He grins and carries on swiping the duster over the ceiling.

"Actually no, smart arse. Martha has a headache." He pauses. "And yes, she was very smiley when we were children."

The stepladder wobbles alarmingly and I shake my head. "Okay, enough. Come down before you break something we might need on our date." He looks down at me and I nod emphatically. "I'll look into getting Martha to do something else." I reach for my diary. "Surely we've got a member of staff who used to be a stuntman."

He laughs and gives another few swipes of the cloth and then comes gingerly down the ladder. Once he's on the floor he lopes right over to me, stepping close as my pulse thrums. "Good morning," he says softly and kisses me. It's a soft kiss, barely there, but it feels like he's marked me. No one has ever done that before or looked so pleased to see me. Normally it's a quick 'thanks, was it good for you' and a hearty slap on the arse.

I swallow hard. "Good morning," I say softly. I step back to get my equilibrium and his lip quirks as if he knows. "Well, are we ready for our practical work date?" I say briskly.

He strokes his beard contemplatively and I swallow at the rasp of those long fingers against the hair. *I want to rub my face in it*, I think dreamily and then start as he speaks.

"Not work," he says firmly. I look dazedly at him, my mind still so full of face and beard rubbing that I'm not following. "It's a date," he says clearly. "I'm even buying food."

I make a face of amazement. "Wow! Food too."

He nods. "I know. Last time I went on a proper date, I think I was seventeen. We do kiss at the doorstep and go home, don't we?"

"We do," I murmur, stepping close to him. "But we live in the same home so I think we can do more kissing to fill the time."

"You strumpet," he says admiringly, and I laugh.

"Why haven't you dated?" I ask as he gestures to me to follow him. Chewwy gives a long-suffering sigh as if pondering the whims of humans and follows us. I look at Silas as he hasn't given me an answer.

He shrugs awkwardly. "I've been with a lot of people, but they usually started with sex. By the time we looked at actually getting out of bed they invariably discovered they couldn't cope with the isolation of living here. The fact that I was never here didn't help either."

"You are here. You're just here at different hours," I say crossly. "Why didn't they adjust?"

"What? Stay up to eat dinner at two in the morning?" He smiles at me. "I think you're the first."

"Did you date morons?"

He considers. "Probably in a few cases."

"And what gender were the morons?" I ask the question that's been in the back of my head since the woman at the county show.

He shoots me a look and then I gasp as he grabs my arm and shoves me through a door to our right. I look around. We're in a little lobby leading to whitewashed old stairs. "Oh, this is what you meant by a working date." I get my diary out. "What needs doing here?"

He grabs the diary, pulls the rubber band around it and puts it under his arm. "You won't be needing that," he says smartly.

"Why are we here?" I ask plaintively. "Because I can actually at the moment understand why you're single."

"Ssh," he says, his voice laced with laughter. He opens the door a crack. "Niall's coming."

I wriggle round until I'm in front of him. He groans under his breath as I get comfortable, my arse banging into his crotch. "Where?" I whisper.

Then I hear the voices of Niall and the builder. "Mr Johnson, I'm not really sure what the problem is here."

"Oh no," I whisper and go to open the door but he stops me.

"Ssh. Stay right where you are."

Mr Johnson says something and Niall's voice comes closer. "Well, there's an easy way to settle things. We can find Oz."

"No, no," the builder says quickly. "There's absolutely no need for *that*."

Silas gasps a laugh and I elbow him.

"Why is Chewwy sitting there?" Niall ponders and clicks his tongue. "Come on, boy. Let's go and find your beloved."

"Is Lord Ashworth around?"

"Oh, I wasn't talking about him," Niall says in a very dismissive voice. "Chewwy has a very pronounced attachment to Oz. I think it might be because he's actually taller than Oz. He enjoys the feeling of superiority."

"Cheeky twat," I hiss and Silas pinches me to be quiet.

The voices move on and the next second I'm spun around, and he kisses me. He takes his time, sucking on my lower lip and rubbing his tongue against mine while he pins me against the door. When he pulls away I feel almost dazed and follow his lips for a second. "What?"

He pulls back. "I didn't say good morning properly," he says simply. "You ready?"

"For what?" I ask faintly, but he grabs my hand and pulls me towards a door set under the stairs. I follow him through, looking around as I do. "This house is like fucking Hogwarts. Every time I think I know everything, I find something else. Where does this go?"

"Behind the stables. We can cut around to the car from there."

I follow behind him. "Why did you hide?" I hear myself say. I almost want to look behind me because that nervous voice surely doesn't belong to me.

He stops abruptly and turns back, grabbing my face in his warm fingers. "Not for the reason you're thinking. I just didn't want anything to stop us going out." He sounds horrified and I relent.

"Okay, that's fine."

He doesn't let go. "Did you think I was ashamed of you?" He sounds so incredulous I relax.

"I didn't know. It wouldn't be the first time. Wait, where are you going?"

He's turned and is walking back, still holding my hand. He stops and looks back at me. "I'm not ashamed of you. I'm *proud* to be seen with you. Come on. We'll go through the front door. I want everyone to see."

I laugh and tug free. "No. If we go through the front everyone will see us and someone will magic up thirty problems instantaneously. Silas, stop, it's fine."

He turns back reluctantly. His kind face is clouded. "Who treated you like that?"

I smile. "No one, and I mean no one. Don't worry about it." He opens his mouth, but I forestall him and turn back towards the car park. "Come on, for goodness' sake. I want to start the date."

"Now, it's a date," he says dolefully and makes me laugh.

We climb into his old Land Rover. It's battered, with dog hair on the back seat and a strange smell that seems to be a mingling of some sort of antiseptic and wet dog. However, for some strange reason I feel utterly at home.

I stay quiet for a few minutes while he drives and then turn to face him. He's sitting comfortably in the driving seat, the breeze from the open window making his hair fly around. This close I can see the laughter lines at the corners of those amazingly coloured eyes. He turns, and I don't even try to pretend I wasn't staring.

"What?" he asks, a smile tugging at his lips.

"Just surprised we've not driven into a bush yet," I say, a smile tugging at my lips.

"Fuck off," he laughs. "I'm a good driver. I was just a nervous wreck when I was a teenager. I just covered it well, unless you were a driving instructor. It was harder going back and telling my father I'd failed than it was breaking that poor bloke's nose."

I examine his face intently. He's given that information away so casually but I know I'll store it away like there's a worldwide embargo on Silas details. Things are starting to become clearer about him. He looks sideways and catches me watching him. "What?"

I shrug and give voice to the question that's been in the back of my mind for a while. "I was just wondering what your childhood was like."

He shoots me a glance that's heavy with something I can't put a name to. "Why?"

I hesitate. "You seem to have been very reliant on the staff."

To my amazement he laughs. "You're right. It's a good thing too, because if we'd been reliant on our mother then Henry and I would have died from neglect." He sobers. "While with my father, I'd have rather explored that option."

"Was he one of those helicopter parents the media keep going on about?"

"Only if the helicopter was an Apache helicopter and it was crashing on you."

"Oh. Oh shit!"

He nods and carries on talking slowly. I think it helps that he's not looking at me. "He wasn't a nice man at all. You'd have hated him. He was every preconceived idea of the aristocracy that you came here with. He was arrogant and petty, narrow minded and petulant. He thought he knew more than anyone else, which is why you're working yourself into an early grave trying to do up the house."

"Not an early grave. You make me sound like I've got cholera." He laughs. "Would he approve of all this?"

He laughs. "Fuck no. The thought would have given him apoplexy. We opened the house twice a year to let the peasants see how wonderful we were and then it was just us again trying to survive the guerrilla warfare he thought was child raising." I swallow hard at the shadow on his face. "He was terrible to the staff. They'd do some small thing and they'd be out on their ear, and as they lived in the house they'd lose their home as well as a job."

"What was he like to you and Henry?"

"He wasn't ... nice," he says slowly. "He was homophobic, which gave him a great deal of scope for parental angst seeing as Henry is gay and I'm bisexual." He pauses. "He was so cruel. He could cut you down in seconds if you disappointed him, not to mention using his fists." He sounds far away and then he shakes himself and shoots me a weak smile. "Look at me spoiling our date. This is why I'm single."

I shake my head. "I asked, so that means I want to know. I don't usually fake interest because my lack of attention gives me away every time. How did you cope?"

He shrugs. "I was away from it a lot. I was the heir, so I was sent away to boarding school very early. That made me feel worse though because it left Henry with him, and Henry is …" He smiles. "Well, Henry is lovely. He's dreamy and kind and very warm. Which made him perfect for pissing off our father. I intervened as much as I could."

"How?"

"I'd divert his attention and take the punishment or hold him back." He jerks as if he's said too much and smiles. "Needless to say, Henry and I had a very outdoor sort of childhood and if you were kind to us we remembered it."

"I get it now," I say softly. "I'll remember."

"Thank you," he says gratefully.

Silence falls for a second and then I stir. "So, you're bisexual?"

It doesn't come out as casually as I intend and he shoots a grin at me. "I am." He pauses. "Wait. Are you bothered by that?"

He looks anxious and I shake my head quickly. "Not at all. Should I be?"

"Other people have been," he says grimly. "If it's worth anything, I'm attracted to a person. I like a good sense of humour, nice eyes, and intelligence. I don't like labels."

I shrug. "I just like honesty," I say firmly. "As long as people are truthful, I'm happy."

He stares ahead at the road. "I will always be truthful," he says quietly and I nod.

He steers the talk into general getting-to-know-you chat then, and the mood lightens. We cover favourite bands and books while he steers the car adeptly down the narrow lanes. London Grammar's *Hey Now* is playing low and I hold my hand out of the car window feeling the wind buffet it and watching the rolling fields eagerly for a sign of the sea. Everything I see looks brown from the heatwave and the sky is a clear denim blue. I close my eyes and tilt my face into the breeze.

The car slows, and I look up as he flicks the indicator and turns down a long winding drive. "Going to tell me where we're going?" I ask, smiling at him.

He grins. "We're going to view a competitor."

I sit up, excitement coursing through me. "Is this a house?"

He nods. "Open to the public. Alexander, who is Lord Branton, lets a manager do it all, but it's very established. He's also the most pompous twat I've ever met. Niall and I were at boarding school with him and our fathers were close friends. I thought we'd scope out their operation, pick up some tips if we need them, and then tell him I'm opening to the public too. By five o'clock my father will be spinning in his grave."

The barely concealed glee makes me laugh. "*That's* your date?" He looks nervously at me and I stop and grin. "This is *epic*. Have you got my diary?"

"Of course," he says solemnly and, following the signs, he parks where a man in a reflective jacket signals him to. He switches the engine off and we both look at the man who is officiously pointing at a family in a Ford Focus.

"Do we need one of those people?" he asks dubiously.

I look at the man waving his arms around. "I don't think we need a human windmill, exactly." He snorts and I smile at him. "But we will need someone to direct cars. And a shed," I say as an afterthought. "And a portable radiator for when it's cold."

"My father would have expected him to burn his own belongings to keep warm."

I laugh. "I don't think your father would have got on with the European Court of Human Rights."

"He'd have been horrified that they recognised anybody below the aristocracy as human, let alone having rights."

I grab his hand and squeeze it. "Well, luckily I'm here with you today. I don't think your father and I would have got on."

"I'd have paid money to see it though," he says, lifting our hands up and dropping a casual kiss on mine. "One can understand people seeing gladiators if it had been you and my father in the Colosseum."

I stare at him, lost in the casual intimacy he shows, and in the fact that I just willingly picked his hand up. I never do that. Being cautious, I always wait for the other man to make overtures of affection. Which is why it's completely alien to me when it actually happens.

"You okay?" he asks and I smile.

"Absolutely. Let's go and steal secrets. It'll be like *Mission Impossible*."

"Weren't a large number of them massacred in that film?"

I laugh. "Yes. But that's not what's happening today."

Following the many signs, we walk to the visitor centre. "It's like he got these signs on special offer," I whisper to Silas. "Do you think he's got a man in the shed whose job is solely to make them?"

"Knowing Alexander, he's making him do it in his dinner hour."

I grin and move close to him, feeling warm inside when he maintains his hold on my hand and completely ignores the scandalized look on the woman's face at the ticket office as if she isn't there.

"Will that be for the two of you?" she asks in a frigid tone.

"It certainly will." Silas's voice is normally a rich warm drawl that combines a tinge of Cornish in it along with the upper-class tones of his upbringing. Now, however, you could cut glass with it and the woman responds like one of Pavlov's dogs, instantly straightening and smiling ingratiatingly.

"And would you like a guidebook?"

"I don't know. Darling, do you want a guidebook?"

There's a brief moment of silence before I realise that he's talking to me. "Oh. Oh, yes, that would be lovely."

Her nose wrinkles in consternation when she hears my accent but she scurries to get one and practically bows us out of the door. We find ourselves on a gravelled path and he stops and turns to me. "You okay?"

I look at him in consternation. "I'm fine. Why?"

"That old woman's attitude. It was horrible."

I laugh. "I've had worse and I'm sure you have."

He shrugs. "Not much."

I smile. "Well, of course you wouldn't. You're the son of an earl and you're very masculine. I, however, am small and not, so believe me, I've heard worse." His brow furrows with concern and I shake my head. "Let's move on … darling."

He laughs and moves closer. "I saw your face when I said that."

"I didn't realise you were talking to me."

"Yes, but when you did, you liked it." He grabs my shoulders and brings me into him. "Admit the truth."

I laugh. "Okay, I might have liked it a little bit," I admit. "But don't go getting a big head."

"It's unavoidable around you," he says solemnly, and I shove him.

"Come on. Mission Nosy Git is a go."

We turn and walk towards the house. I have to admit it's impressive. The grounds are immaculate and glowing green, even in this heatwave. The house sits in an Elizabethan 'E' shape, covered in ivy and looking down on the sweeping hills full of grazing sheep.

We crunch over the pea gravel and even that sounds expensive. I nudge him. "What do you think?"

Silas looks around dismissively. "Those sheep don't look very well fed," he says judiciously.

I shake my head. "Hand me my diary."

"Why?"

"I'm making a note to put the anorexic sheep out of the sight of the general public."

He snorts and throws his arm over my shoulders affectionately. "Come on, sassy boy. Let's go and criticise the house." He looks at the Aston Martin parked at a rakish angle on the forecourt and sniffs. "Bloody Alexander. Such a show-off."

I nudge him. "I'd rather have your Land Rover."

He looks at me doubtfully. "Really?"

I nod. "It's got character, like you."

He smiles helplessly. "Well, that's the one thing that can be said for me. No money and a house falling down, but I've got character." His face clouds slightly as he looks over the immaculate house.

"Can we be really mean when we judge him?" I whisper and his face clears.

"Only for you."

I laugh, and as he guides me to the house, I take a second to relish the moment. The sun beats down on us and his arm is a wonderful weight. His hair blows in the slight breeze, and I can smell the scent of apples from his shampoo along with his cologne and a trace of clean sweat.

Then we cross into the shadowed depths of what I have to say is a very poky lobby. It's flagstoned like Silas's house, but where his is an open, sun-washed space, this is dark because of the carved oak wood panelling.

"That's fake," I whisper.

He's instantly diverted. *"Really?* How do you know?"

"It's from a different period and if you look up, it doesn't reach the ceiling."

He looks at me admiringly. "You're going to be of so much use today."

Guides dressed in navy skirts and white blouses that make them look like air hostesses wait by the door, and as we queue I look idly over a display case full of family silver which is engraved with a crest that looks very much like a budgie my auntie had once. I snort, and he looks at me curiously, but we reach the front of the line so he turns to the woman.

"Ticket please," she snaps and waits with a very impatient air as he rummages through his pockets to find them. She sighs heavily as she accepts them and casts a sour gaze over him, pausing when she takes in his arm around me. Her lips tighten but she says nothing. Instead, she gestures at the rucksack on his arm.

"That will have to go in the lockers we provide, I'm afraid." She doesn't sound afraid. She sounds happy. "We can't have people walking round with bags that size." I hate women like this and I hate that her horrid gaze is still locked on Silas's hand on my shoulder.

"Why?" I ask blandly and Silas's arm tightens. I look up to find him studying the floor with a quirk to his lips.

"Well, I erm–" She hesitates, obviously unsure of calling someone a possible thief.

"Oh, is it because you think we're going to steal the family silver because he's hugging me?" I lean forwards. "If it's anything like the tut in that display case over there, you've no need to worry. I've seen better imitations on Camden Market."

"It's not imitation," she says crossly, and I nod.

"Yes, it is. So, we won't be pinching it today. We'll stick to cuddling and having the tour we've paid for."

"I would never accuse people of that." She wavers. "It's because he might knock something over."

"I don't think he's done that since he was five," I whisper back. "When he developed his spatial awareness. But maybe you want to give this lecture to that lady over there who appears to be carrying a suitcase on her shoulder. After all, it's only fair."

She hesitates but then accedes with bad grace and stalks over to the woman.

"Is it imitation?" Silas asks, lively curiosity in his voice.

"Probably," I say cavalierly and grab his hand to lead him on. "Quick, before the Bride of Dracula comes back and demands you change your underpants in case they knock something over."

"It's what's in my underpants that could cause a problem," he says wryly, and I laugh far too loudly, if the glares from the other guides are anything to go by.

As if by mutual accord we fall silent and join the group of people who are clustered around a woman wearing the uniform of a guide who has very large hair. Following Silas's guiding hand, I move to the back of the group.

He leans forward and I shiver as he talks into my ear. "I don't want her noticing me. I think she knows my mother."

I nod, and we move with the group into a superb wood-panelled dining room. A ten-seater table is laid with the finest china and glassware, and a large vase of flowers spill their opulent scent into the room.

Silas looks around the room and I'm sure he's comparing his own house with this richness. His gaze falls on the table and the glasses and silver cutlery that catch the sunlight. "That's ironic," he sniffs. "When we were at school I don't think Alexander even knew how to use a knife and fork."

I stare admiringly at him. "This date is bringing out an unexpectedly bitchy side to you." I nudge him. "Carry on. I like it."

He smirks and then looks up as the guide begins her spiel. "As you may have noticed, the house is built in the shape of an 'E'. This is because Lord Branton's ancestors were very canny courtiers and it was a sure way of getting Elizabeth the First to grace your home and favour you."

"Why isn't yours like that?" I whisper. "Were your ancestors not canny courtiers?"

"No, we were the complete opposite. If our house had been built in the shape of a yawn, it couldn't have been any clearer. We were the type to stand at the back and hope nobody noticed us."

I laugh and cover it with a cough when the guide glances at us. She carries on talking.

"The land came to Lord Branton's ancestors by his marriage to the daughter of a very well-known landowner," she carries on. "The men in this family had a knack of marrying very well and having land and houses practically thrown at them."

I look at Silas and raise an eyebrow but he shakes his head. "Not us. We married badly and had crockery thrown at us."

I can't help my laugh this time and the guide glares at me. We quiet and follow her from one sumptuous room to another. The house is certainly gorgeous. Everything is well maintained and smells of furniture polish and beeswax. It seems to bask in the sunshine like a very sleek Siamese cat, while our house is more like an old bulldog. Very British, but fleabitten and struggling to keep up.

The group drifts into a library and I inhale automatically. I love the scent of old paper and leather. This is gorgeous, with tall stained-glass windows and shelves that reach to the ceiling. The shelves are crammed with leather-bound books. As the guide begins her chat I edge closer and bend to look at the titles. I wrinkle my nose.

"I think *Georgian Birds of England* might not be as interesting as it sounds," I say dolefully, and he grins widely before turning back to the guide.

"This room has over ten thousand books," she says admiringly. "The works may be collector's items, but rest assured that this is still a working room. Lord Branton still gets his reading material from here."

"Does he, bollocks," Silas whispers. "Not unless they've shelved some copies of *Penthouse* and *The Beano*."

"In this very room," she continues, "Winston Graham wrote one of his famous Poldark novels. He was a guest of the family and composed the work on this very desk."

She moves over to show the group some ancient maps and Silas shakes his head. "Every guide in every old house in Cornwall claims that Winston Graham wrote a book there. He must barely have had time to go to the loo."

I laugh. "Why didn't he write a book in your house?"

He shrugs. "Probably couldn't get a minute's peace there. Too occupied with finding a chair that wouldn't collapse when you sat on it, or a mattress that hadn't been there since the time of William the Conqueror. He must have been a terrible guest anyway. Descending on people with his notebook and pen and then writing a book in the study at all hours. My forebears would have needed the room to look at porn."

We drift further and further behind the group until we're alone, meandering along into one gorgeous room after another. I look up at a picture of a very strange-looking woman.

"She looks a bit bonkers," I say dubiously.

He looks up. "That's not even one of his ancestors," he says disapprovingly. "This whole room was broken down and shipped here when a local family died out. Alexander bought the room lock, stock and barrel."

"So, this madwoman who looks like a sheep isn't even his family?"

He shakes his head. "Nope. At least my family portraits are my own family."

"I wouldn't be too proud about that," I say judiciously. "They all seem either congenitally depressed or like they're on the brink of serial killer fame."

He laughs and drags me into another room.

"I hate to say it, but it is a gorgeous house," I say quietly as we linger by a display of armour.

He sniffs. "It's okay, but it's like a bloody film set."

He carries on talking but I'm not listening anymore, struck dumb by a blinding idea.

"What are you thinking about?" he asks curiously. "You look in a daze."

I shake my head. I'm not getting his hopes up so instead I look at the armour and read the label. "It says this was used by Lord Branton's ancestor during the Battle of Bosworth."

Instantly diverted, he looks at the battered armour. "I doubt he did much fighting. He probably wore it to bed if he was anything like his descendant," he says sourly. "I've never met a lazier man."

I snort with laughter. "Yes, if you look closer his visor is very shiny where it rubbed on the pillow." I look at the note again. "I take it he was on the winning side?"

"He'd have been on the side that was in power when he got out of bed."

I look around. "It's so well organised. And he must be raking it in.

There were at least four groups waiting to be shown around and it's only ten o'clock. If each of them pays a tenner he'll have made four grand before lunch."

He looks around. "I'm not keen. I don't like the way the guides are wearing invisible jack boots. That woman almost had you shot at dawn in the Queen's Room."

I think of our guide who had reacted violently when I touched a curtain to marvel at the needlework.

"I thought she was going to rip my bloody hand off," I sniff. "And holding the sign up that said 'do not touch' and making me read it was overkill." He laughs and I look at him. "I don't think we want anyone like that, do you?"

He shakes his head. "Fuck, no. Have you ever been to Salisbury Cathedral?"

I blink at the change of subject but nod. "Yes, why?"

He shrugs, looking a bit awkward. "I just thought it was lovely in there. There's such a feeling of ownership and pride in the people that show you around there that makes it feel accessible and welcoming."

I nod slowly. "You're right." He smiles, and I carry on. "I hadn't thought of it like that apart from remembering it as a lovely place, but I think you're onto something. It's because everyone is so warm and interested." I think hard. "How about going to the next parish council meeting and the diocese meeting? See if there are any local older people around who worked in the house in the golden days before the war. They'd make fantastic guides. We could also look at staging a few plays in the grounds during the summer to celebrate that actor-obsessed ancestor of yours. Let everyone bring a picnic and sit on the grass. It would be amazing."

He grins at me. "You're so brilliant," he says softly.

I flush. "In the spirit of honesty, I have to tell you that I'm really not."

He looks around quickly and comes to stand in front of me. He raises his hands and cups his palms around my cheekbones. "You're brilliant and sharp and fierce," he says quietly. "And you fascinate me, Oz."

I stand caught by his eyes that are a clear green gold in this light. I open my mouth to say something flip, but something real and raw in his face and voice stays me and instead I cover his hands with my own. "Thank you," I whisper.

He nods and, lowering his head, he takes my lips in a soft kiss. Our lips rest against each other gently before his tongue slips into my mouth and I melt against him.

Goodness knows what we'd have done then, but we're saved from having possible intercourse in front of a suit of armour by an incredulous voice.

"Silas?"

Silas stiffens and turns around, and I can almost taste his next word on the air before he says it. "David."

CHAPTER 9

DAVID WAS THE PENIS WRANGLER

Silas

I turn with a sense of utter resignation to find David standing in the doorway. Of course he would be here just when everything is going okay. He's dressed in beige chinos and a white polo shirt, his blond hair looking perfect as usual. I look at those blue eyes of his that I've stared into so many times as I've moved inside him.

I thought if I met him again I'd be angry. He left in a fit of petulant rage because I wouldn't go up to London for a party. Never mind that I'd worked a straight fourteen hours. When he'd gone I started to look around and I could hardly comprehend the mess he'd left me in. Builders doing whatever they wanted, staff on the brink of leaving, and nothing arranged. I'd been so furious I could have spat feathers. Whatever that actually means. Why would anyone spit feathers? It doesn't make sense unless they were interrupted while eating a chicken. I become aware that I'm starting to think like Oz and shake myself.

At one time I'd wondered whether I'd found in David someone I could actually settle down with, but now when I look at him I feel nothing. Absolutely zero. Not even anger. Apart from the strongest desire to shove him out of the room and lock the door because he's disturbed a moment I was having with Oz.

At the thought of him, I turn to find him examining David with a very intent look on his face that I've learnt doesn't bode well. At that moment he looks at me and grins. When he's in a certain mood those smiles of his have a very wicked curl to them. It always makes me want to touch the arch of his lip with a finger, feel the softness and then slick it with my tongue.

His stare intensifies and his eyes darken. Then David's voice breaks the moment. "Why are you here?"

I turn back to him and sigh. "I'm juggling and driving a clown car. What does it look like I'm doing, David?"

Oz snorts, making me smile, but David frowns. "How did you find out where I was working? Are you stalking me?"

"You're working here?" I shake my head. "I hope it's not the same work you did for me. It figures you'd have something set up before you left. You're a bit like a cat in that respect. You always land on your feet."

He huffs. "Don't try to tell me you didn't know. If this is some attempt to get me back—"

My laughter breaks into his sentence. "I'm sorry, *what?* Have you fallen and hurt your head today? Why would I want you back?"

He folds his arms. "Oh, please. I'd bet money you've needed me."

"For what?" Oz's voice breaks into the conversation like a shot even if it was spoken softly.

David turns to him. "I'm sorry. Do I know you?"

"I'd be sorry if you did." Oz looks hard at him. "Why would Silas miss you?"

"Well, we had a long relationship."

"We were together for six weeks," I break in, but he huffs indignantly.

"Time doesn't matter." Oz raises his eyebrow but David's on a roll. "All the work I put into your place, Silas. All the backbreaking hours and did you care? Did you, buggery. We never went anywhere. You were always fucking working. I was left in that fucking crumbling monstrosity on my own trying to do everything with no help."

I open my mouth but Oz steps forward. "Weren't you employed as the house manager? Didn't you have an assistant and staff?"

"That's not the point." David looks at him in irritation. "Do I know you?"

"Oz Gallagher. But don't bother remembering the name. We won't talk again." David opens and shuts his mouth like a fish, but Oz carries on remorselessly. "I've seen the work you actually did, and it just seems like you were being paid a wage to lie on your back." He shrugs. "Or your front. Whatever floats your boat. Whichever way you did it, there's another job description for that and it's not house manager."

"Penis manager?" I enquire and Oz laughs.

"That's it. David was the penis wrangler."

"He wasn't very good at it," I say coolly.

"Who are you?" David asks in a frigid voice.

"I'm your replacement," Oz says sweetly, moving closer to me. David doesn't miss the movement and his eyes sharpen.

"Oh, my God, Silas. Why don't you just go on Grindr, for fuck's sake. Life would be a lot easier if you didn't keep getting your bed partners from the job pages." He smiles condescendingly at Oz. "Don't worry. You're just the latest in a long line. Silas here can't keep a man or a woman to save his life, not that he'd want to keep you."

"I really don't think you should smile," I mutter, massaging my temples with my fingers. Oz steps forward and I turn to David.

"Don't say I didn't try to warn you." I move back and look at Oz and wave my hand. "Go ahead."

Oz smiles at David and it's a smile with a lot of teeth. "It's a shame Grindr doesn't do a profile for your work as well as your sex life. What would yours say? Profile name would be Whinging Little Bitch. A chronic fuckwit who will spread his legs quicker than margarine. Likes lying in bed and being serviced. Dislikes any form of work at all." He shakes his head. "It's taken me two months to try and clear up your mess. You should be fucking ashamed of yourself."

David looks a little pale, which is normal when Oz is on a rampage, but to his credit he rallies. "You couldn't hope to understand what you're doing. Listen to you speak." He laughs. "Someone with your accent couldn't hope to understand the demands and needs of a house like that." He turns to me. "Where did you pick this one up? Did you abandon The Lady this time and just cruise King's Cross?"

I step forward with my fists curled but Oz, incredibly, laughs. "Mate, a hooker could do better than you at your job." He shakes his head. "Even Chewwy could do it better." I grin, and he smiles at me before turning to David. "You had a good bloke here and just because he wanted you to get out of bed and do the job he was paying you for, you fucked off." He shakes his head. "If you ask me, you could teach the girls and boys at King's Cross a thing or two about prostitution." He looks searchingly at David. "I may not have your upbringing and it may make me very common, but if I care for someone I make them happy. I don't take money from them and fuck them over when an easier job comes along. I cling on in the rough seas as well as the calm waters because I'm loyal. You should look that word up in a dictionary. They obviously didn't teach you it at public school."

David flushes. "And where did you go to school, Oz, or did you even bother?"

Oz nods and smirks. "You're so right. I never went to school. My first in a Fine Art and History of Art degree is an example of skiving at its best."

"What did you get, David?" I ask. It's unbecoming to be spiteful but I can't help it. "Wasn't it a third?"

David glares at me. "Good luck with this one," he says with a smirk. "Just count the silver before he goes."

"You'd be better employed doing that," Oz says sharply. "The cutlery on the dining table is fake. It's proper tat."

"It is not."

"It is. You couldn't give that shit away in a cracker."

"And on that note, we're going to complete our tour," I say smoothly, becoming fed up of this. I hold my hand out to Oz and see David's brow furrow as Oz smiles and complies.

"You're *really* with him?" he says in a tone of disbelief. "Your father would turn over in his bloody grave."

"I look on my father as an arbiter of taste," I say coldly. "If he liked someone I instantly knew that person was a total cunt." I pause and look him up and down. "He'd have really loved you, David."

We sweep out of the room and Oz starts to laugh. He bounces up and down on his feet and does a quick dip and feint with his fists. "Did you see his face? Pop, pop, you told him."

I shake my head and look around quickly. Spotting a door whose opening is barred by a red rope, I hop over and open the door and then reach back and grab Oz. He comes easily like he's my partner in crime, his eyes wide and his smile wicked.

"We're not supposed to do this. I bet David put this rope up himself specially. Whatever are you doing, Lord Ashworth?"

I pull us through and we find ourselves in what I'm sure is Alexander's private drawing room. I cast a cursory glance around to check for observers, and when I don't find anyone I slam the door and push Oz up against it. "This," I say gutturally and take his mouth. He tastes of mint and seems to melt into me like butter, his whole body moving sleekly as he falls into me.

I kiss him hard, rubbing my tongue over his and mauling his mouth. His breaths puff against my cheek and he moans deep in his throat.

I pull away, ignoring his grunted protest, and frame his face in my hands. I look at his swollen lips and pretty eyes that are lazy with heat and lust. "You annihilated him," I gasp. "So hot!"

He stares up at me and grins widely. "My being sharp-tongued turns you on." He laughs. "Oh my God, this is epic. You're going to be hard most of the day and night." He looks upward to the ceiling as if searching for inspiration before grinning wickedly at me. "Well, I've created this problem. Never let it be said that Oz Gallagher doesn't clear up his own messes."

"What–" I start to say but it dies away to a groan as he lowers himself gracefully to his knees in front of me and reaches for my belt. "What is–" I stop and clear my throat. "Oz, I'm not sure this is the right place for this."

He looks up, and he would appear angelic if he didn't have such an evil expression. "On the contrary, this is the perfect place for it."

He unbuckles my belt and nimbly unzips my jeans. "Oh well," I say faintly. "Never let it be said that I get in the way of a workman."

"You know what they say," he mutters, grinning. "A good workman loves his tool."

"That's not what they–" I start to say but my words die away to a moan as he reaches in and draws out my cock and licks up the length of it. *Oh shit.*

Oz looks up, his eyes so blue in the light that they seem to shine. I reach my hand down and tangle it in his hair, feeling the silky waves run through my fingers. He waits, his mouth open and a wicked sparkle daring me to go further. He doesn't wait long.

Fisting my cock, I drag my hand down my length, drawing out a fat drop of pre-come. Then I rub the tip of my cock on his lower lip, seeing it glisten and shine before he moans under his breath and takes me down the back of his throat.

"Motherfucker," I hiss, arching my back and banging my head into the wall at the feel of that hot, tight grip on my cock.

He pulls off slowly, letting me feel my cock bathed in that wet tunnel, before he levers up from his knees and grabs my shoulders, taking my mouth in a hot kiss. I taste the tart tang of my pre-come on his tongue and grab the back of his head to keep him there as I tongue his mouth. I breathe hard through my nose, feeling him writhe against me, his cock a solid, rock-hard length against my hip.

He pulls away and kisses my neck with soft, suckling kisses, detouring to the lobe of my ear where he plays, making me fist my hand in my mouth to stop myself from shouting out. I shudder and grunt as the delicate kisses send cold shivers down my spine and my cock throbs wetly in the cool air between us.

His hands go down the back of my jeans, grabbing my arse cheeks in his callused hands and beginning to rub his groin against me, canting his hips and groaning.

I push my head into the plaster and moan. "So good," I whisper and he nods, the blue in his eyes already nearly eclipsed by his excited pupils. He pulls back and slowly raises my shirt until it's scrunched around my neck. He nestles his nose into my armpit hair and inhales deeply, his eyes closed in concentration, then tracks kisses across my chest, nuzzling into the hair there with a dreamy look on his face. I groan quietly and he nips my right nipple, looking up from underneath his lashes and biting down gently, making me squirm and moan.

He lowers gracefully to his knees and I watch with avid eyes as he unbuttons his jeans quickly and fists his cock. It's long and slender and as pale as he is with a ruddy, slick head. He groans long and low and I feel my cock harden even more at the sound. Starting to tunnel into his closed fist, he nuzzles into the neat thatch of hair around my cock and inhales deeply.

He looks up. "You smell so good," he says hoarsely, and then rises up and takes me down his throat, swallowing and licking the sensitive underside.

Kneeling there, he looks like a debauched angel with that high-cheekboned face flushed and dreamy, his lips swollen and stretched around my cock and his chin damp with spit. Abruptly I feel my balls tighten.

"I'm close," I grunt, and he blinks before pulling off my cock with a wet pop.

"Fuck my face," he says hoarsely and I nod, taking the sides of his head and pulling him back onto my cock. At first, I go slowly but he makes frantic noises of encouragement and soon I'm fucking his mouth frantically, feeling his suckling pulls drawing my come out of me. "Oh *God*," I whisper fervently.

He moans and as one hand frantically wanks himself, he reaches the other up, splaying it over my chest and pinching my nipple. The tiny bite of pain makes me jerk and before I know what I'm doing, I grab that hand and hold on tight. He looks up, almost startled, but then he groans and squeezes my fingers while sucking frantically and messily. Saliva drips over his chin, and the noises are obscene in the room.

"Oh fuck," I mutter. "So fucking *close*." I look down at him. "Don't swallow and don't come," I command. He looks up blearily at me, and the sight of those eyes clouded with lust and the red mouth around my cock sets me off. I clench my buttocks and unload spurt after spurt into his mouth. He chokes slightly and some escapes, flowing over the sides of those full lips.

Instantly I drag him up against me and kiss him, taking my come from his mouth and swallowing the salty liquid. I grab his cock in a firm grip and he shuttles through my fist, making choked, desperate noises as I suckle on his tongue. It isn't long before he goes rigid and groans deep in his throat, and I feel wet heat flowing over my fingers.

He rests against me for a long few minutes and then he moves back slightly, watching almost dreamily as I raise my hand and lick my palm clean. He shudders slightly and moans under his breath and for a second I consider round two, but quickly discount it as I'm amazed we haven't been caught this time.

Reading my expression, something passes over his face too quickly for me to analyse, and then it's gone and his face clears. He pulls back, breathing heavily, and leans against the wall next to me companionably. When my head finally stops spinning, I reach out and caress his cheekbones. He's looking at me with an inscrutable face and he seems to glow in the shafts of sunlight from the large window opposite us.

"Come back here and kiss me," I say hoarsely.

His expression lightens a little and he moves into me and takes my mouth, giving me his weight for a second. I groan under my breath at the feel of his tongue.

He pulls back and that expression has returned. I'd almost call it worried until he smiles gamely. "Come on," he says in a hearty voice. "Let's go and compare notes."

"On the *blow job?*" I say in a stunned voice, feeling myself reel at the way he's so swiftly shifted gear.

He laughs. "Of course," he says through his chuckles as we right our clothing. "We should always judge our performance. No. I meant our critique of this place."

He's still laughing when he opens the door and we find ourselves face to face with the second-to-last person I want to see. *It isn't my day today.*

"Alexander," I say resignedly.

"Silas?" he asks incredulously. "Is it really you?" He's dressed in navy chinos, a white shirt, and a navy sports jacket. He looks pompous and slightly ridiculous in this heat and he even has a cravat on, for fuck's sake.

"It's me," I say dryly. "In the flesh."

"What are you doing here?"

I flush a little because this is terrible manners. I've inveigled my way onto a tour, had a stand-up argument with his estate manager, and got a blow job in his drawing room. Then, I remember the time he held me upside down out of a window at school for not doing his homework properly, and I straighten.

"Just looking around," I say, waving a hand casually.

"In my house?"

"Isn't it open to the general public?"

"You're not the general public." Then his expression clears and he smirks. "Were you looking for David? Sad to say he's working for me now."

"It is sad, but not in the way you're thinking. But never mind. I'm not looking for him. This is Oz, and we're here–" I hesitate and Oz shifts.

"To look around the house. I'm very interested in old properties," he says smoothly.

Alexander looks Oz up and down so dismissively that my blood boils, then he laughs. "How about ruins? You'll love Silas's house, then. Make it quick, though, before lack of money sees it crumble into the ground. Still, at least you've seen how it should be done." He grins unpleasantly. "Silas never could keep his balance, let alone balance his chequebook."

"Not when someone was holding me out of a window," I say flippantly. "It tends to upset one's equilibrium." I'm aware of Oz stiffening and then he smiles at Alexander. It's not a nice smile.

"I'm so sorry about that suit of armour," he says.

"What? Why?"

"It's a fake."

"Of course it isn't," he says bombastically. "How the hell would you know that?"

Oz grins. "It's got Made in China on a label inside it." He tuts. "I'd remove that before someone sees."

He grabs my hand and tows me out of the room. When we're a good distance away I hiss, "Has it really got a Made in China label?"

"*No*," he scoffs. "But it'll take him ages looking for it."

My laughter is loud enough to be heard all over the house.

Oz

Once we're back in the car, he drives off without saying anything. The quiet feels ominous and I shoot him a nervous glance. *Was that too much?* I'm floundering here. Usually when I meet someone there isn't any of this getting to know one another. Shit, I can't remember the last time I was even on a fucking date. Usually it's just a quick chat, a grope, things get heavy, and both of us come.

This is outside of my experience. I'd somehow thought that Silas would be his usual self during sex. Calm and kind and funny. I thought I'd control the sex like I normally do and keep it light. Well, the joke's on me, because it was very far from that. He was intense and demanding and so fucking hot that I thought I'd burn up. I remember him instructing me not to swallow and then gulping down his own come while kissing me, and my cock stiffens. Then I remember his hand squeezing mine when he came, and I wriggle and feel something heavy in my stomach.

He's been so quiet since we left, and for the first time I worry about what another man thinks of me. *Have I put him off me, blowing him like that in another man's house? Has he lost interest now I've been on my knees for him, like so many others have?* I think of him moving on and I actually feel sick.

I hate this. I hate feeling so unsure about another person. This is why I avoid liking people. They bring ties and awful things like being bothered what they think of me and living up to their expectations.

I try to relax into my seat and stare out of the window watching the green fields fly past. *I'll just sit here,* I decide. *Let him speak when he wants to. I'm not begging someone to talk to me.*

"You're very quiet." The voice that just spoke sounded very much like me, but I'm so stunned at what my mouth just did that I actually look around for the someone else who just spoke. He turns to me and I blanch at the look of anger on his face. "What's the matter?" I ask before I can stop myself.

He sighs and his fingers flex on the steering wheel. "I'm just so angry at the way they spoke to you. Sneering at you like you were less than them."

I stare at him, feeling disconcerted by his answer. It wasn't what I expected. "People see me and make a lot of misconceptions. It doesn't bother me anymore, to be honest. People can think what they like. The only people whose opinions I care about are very few in number." I smile. "The rest can go fuck themselves."

He looks quickly at me before returning his eyes to the road. "I wish I could be like that," he muses softly. "But I've always been bothered."

"That's because you hate letting people down," I say sagely. "It's your curse to want people to be happy." I shake my head mournfully. "What a terrible person you are."

He laughs and something inside me unfurls a little bit, like a plant seeking the sun. I love making him laugh. To see him smile makes me incredibly happy, especially now. That feels like something I should be bothered about, but I tell myself that I can't be concerned about it if I don't think too hard about what it means.

"I'm glad you're okay," I say impulsively.

He looks at me quizzically. "Of course, I'm fine. Why wouldn't I be?"

I flounder slightly. "Well, after the blow job I thought you might be a bit cross with me." I shrug. "I mean, I did force it along and it would have been really embarrassing if someone had found us."

"You think I'm angry about you giving me a *blow job?*" he asks incredulously.

When he puts it like that, it does sound ridiculous. I laugh. "Ignore me. That was stupid." I look around as he pulls into the opening of a field and turns to me. "What are you doing?" I ask. "Is there a problem with the car?"

"There's a problem *in* the car. Why on earth would you think I'd be cross about you giving me a blow job?"

I shrug awkwardly. "I don't know. In my experience, men usually fuck off after we've both come. I just don't want you feeling awkward about having to still be on a date with me afterwards. We can go home now if you like."

Something flares in his eyes at the word home, but then a curious mix of anger and what looks like tenderness fills his eyes. He reaches out and cups my chin and turns my face to his. "Oz, that blow job was wonderful. I came so hard I saw stars. However, you're missing something very important."

"What?" I whisper.

"Most of what made it brilliant was because it was you. You make me hard when you smile at me, and when you get fierce I could drill stone with my cock. However, that's all tied up in you. I asked you on a date because I'm fascinated with you. You make me laugh, and there's something so vital and alive about you. So, the blow job was just icing. The real sweet stuff is being with you, talking together and making you laugh. If you never blew me again I would still want to be with you."

I try to swallow the stupid bloody lump in my throat. No one has ever talked or looked like this at me before. It's incredible and humbling at the same time, and I instantly try to dissolve the tension.

"So, you're saying you never want a blow job again, then?"

He smiles. "Of course I want one. I'm stupid for you, Oz. I'm not stupid in general."

I sigh. *Feelings are back again. Damn them.*

He looks at me determinedly. "I can see I'm going to have to up my game. This wasn't so much a date, as a farce." I laugh and he smiles. "Be ready tomorrow afternoon at four. And be prepared to be wowed."

I swallow hard.

CHAPTER 10

DID HE JUST RUFFLE MY HAIR LIKE I'M SEVEN?

Oz

I come into the breakfast room the next morning and stop dead. Silas looks up from his breakfast and I see a flush dapple the high planes of his cheekbones that's mirrored on mine. The last time I saw him he'd had me against the front door, kissing and grinding together. I'd thought his next move would be a bedroom somewhere, but no. Instead, he'd given me one last kiss and promised to see me the next morning in a hoarse, gravelly voice that hit my balls dead on.

I don't mind admitting that I'm confused. I've never got a bloke that hard and then had him wish me a good night's sleep. *Never.*

Ever. It's like meeting a fucking dodo or Britney Spears' dress sense. Both incomprehensible.

I'm also a little hurt. It brings back too many memories of other men who, if they could have got away with it, would have walked twenty paces away from me because they were so embarrassed to be seen with me. *Is Silas the same?* I know he'd protested it, but he'd still hidden us away yesterday before anyone could spot us.

I shake my head and walk towards the side table, an act that no longer fills anyone with dread because you can actually eat the stuff on it without a packet of Rennies and a glass of Milk of Magnesia nearby. I freeze when Silas jumps up, the scraping of his chair sounding loud in the room.

"Let me get you a cup of tea," he says, the words coming out so fast that they're almost jumbled.

I stare at him open-mouthed. "Sorry?"

"A cup of tea. Erm, I mean you need tea. I'll get you a cup."

Milo looks up from his toast, his eyes practically crossing, and Niall laughs and doesn't even try to cover it up. Silas directs a killing glare at him and moves over to stand next to me.

"Did you …?" He stops and clears his throat. "Did you sleep well?"

"What is happening right now?" I ask faintly, and Niall laughs loudly.

"This is Silas going a courting. It's like watching a Jane Austen film. So slow." He pretends to mop his eyes. "My boy's all growed up."

Silas sighs and closes his eyes. "Niall, I could do without your help, thank you very much."

He laughs, and throwing his napkin down on the table, he stands up. "You could actually do with my help but it's far more entertaining to watch you flounder." He shrugs. "*Love Island* just finished on TV. I'm bored."

"Wait a minute," Silas says firmly as Niall goes to leave the room.

Maggie comes into the room and hovers, obviously realising that she's interrupting something. I smile at her and wave her in. She moves past Silas and Niall quickly and puts a fresh pot of coffee down.

"Something you need to tell me, Silas?" Niall purrs.

Silas shakes his head and I suddenly realise that all my muscles are tense. I breathe in quietly and take a sip of my tea and relax. I don't know why I'm so tense. It's not like anyone ever laid claim to me and …

"Oz and I are dating now," Silas blurts out and I choke and spit my tea straight out onto his shirt. I can't believe he just admitted that in front of Niall and Milo, not to mention Maggie.

"Sorry, sorry," I say and try to brush the liquid off the fabric. My cheeks are burning, and I can feel Milo and Maggie's gazes hot on my face. Niall just looks at Silas and smiles.

"Okay. Thanks for telling me."

"That's it?" I blurt. "You do remember my interview, don't you?"

"Oz, it's ingrained on my brain, dearest. I try to forget. I try to drink the memory away. But every night when I close my eyes it still comes back to me."

Milo snorts. "Me too."

I glare at him and he just smirks. *Cocky little shit*, I think admiringly. I turn back to Niall. "Surely as his best friend you should be advising against it. It's not exactly conventional behaviour and it hasn't worked out well before."

He shrugs. "I'm his friend, not his lawyer." He sighs long-sufferingly. "Oz, when I'm breeding the pigs–"

"What you get up to in your private life is your own business, sweetie," I say faintly, and Silas laughs loudly.

Niall carries on as if I'd never spoken. "When I'm breeding the pigs, if it doesn't take the first time, I just make them try again and again. If I gave up at the first hurdle, the world would have no baby pigs."

"You're like a pig pimp," I say admiringly.

Silas flings his arm around me and kisses the side of my face affectionately while he laughs, and I look at him out of the corner of my eye. *What is happening here?* His arm is round me as if it means nothing to stand there boldly and declare that he's with me. *Isn't he worried about things going badly?*

He turns his head slightly and smiles at me. His eyes are warm and clear and untroubled. *Obviously not.*

"I'm taking Oz out this afternoon," he says to Maggie. "So please don't cook for the two of us." He shoots a look at Niall and Milo. "In fact, don't cook for them either. Take the night off."

Maggie smiles and exits the room quickly before he can take it back.

"Lovely," Niall snorts. "Fish and chips again." He looks at Silas. "Where are you going?"

"Mind your own business," he says serenely and Niall laughs.

"I just want to know so I don't make the mistake of doing the same thing. I do want to get laid in the next millennium."

"Surely your personality would interfere with that," I say smoothly, and he laughs.

"I'm off. See you later."

He moves through the door and Silas jerks. "Oh, wait a minute. I need a word with you about the top field." He grabs me closer into his side. "Be ready at four," he whispers. "Dress casually."

"Why? Are we raiding another stately home?"

He laughs and kisses me lightly. Or at least I think he means to do it lightly, but as soon as our lips touch he groans under his breath and licks into my mouth. I raise my hands automatically and thread them through his silky hair, but Milo coughs and Niall shouts through the door, "Not at the breakfast table."

Silas pulls back. His lips look full and slick. "Sorry," he says breathlessly. Then he ruffles my hair and darts out of the room after Niall. Their voices echo down the corridor and then silence falls.

I turn to Milo. "Did that just happen?" I ask faintly.

He nods, looking slightly astonished. "It did. I'm quite surprised because he isn't a terribly demonstrative person. I never saw him kissing David."

"Not *that*," I interrupt. "Did he just ruffle my hair like I'm seven?" I raise my fingers to my head. "It took me ages to get this quiff straight." I pause. "Although okay, let's go back to what you just said. That was much more interesting."

He grins. "Nope. You had your chance and it's long gone now. The pair of you will just have to muddle along and I'll watch."

I shake my head and butter my toast. "You're an enigma, Milo, I don't mind telling you."

"Why?"

"Because you seem so shy, but you're actually not."

He shrugs. "I was very shy as a child and had a really bad stutter. I'm better now. But if I'm nervous then it all comes back and I tend to get self-conscious and stuttery."

"But why would you be …?" I stop. "Niall?"

He flushes. "No, of course not."

"Don't take that hearty tone of voice with me, Milo," I say sharply. "We're friends, aren't we?"

"I always imagined that would be said in a much softer tone of voice than that of a wing commander," he muses, and I throw my napkin at him. He dodges it laughingly and smiles. "We are friends, Oz. I'm *so* glad you came here."

"I'm glad I'm here too," I say, but my mind is on him. I hesitate. "Niall's a hard one to summarise." He smiles, and I stare at him. At first glance they don't go together. Milo is slim and dark while Niall is big and bold and blond. However, I've noticed a few intense glances that Niall's thrown at him since he's become a bit more confident. He's also extremely protective of Milo and watches over him like a mother hen.

Milo shakes his head and throws his napkin down on the table. "Niall is very confident," he says quietly. "And I'm not. He goes for men like him who are confident and mature. Not the younger brother of one of his close friends."

"Niall is in no way mature," I say. "But I think you're wrong. I've noticed–"

"Can we not talk about it," he says quickly. I open my mouth, words tumbling on my tongue, but I still at the look of panic in his eyes.

"Okay," I say quietly. "Let's just eat breakfast and then we've got to unpack the book order for the shop." I pause. "And while we're doing that, I'd like to schedule a time for me to freak the fuck out about Silas."

He takes a sip of his tea. "Why?"

I stare at him and when Chewwy puts his head on my thigh, I scratch behind his velvety ear. "This has got disaster written all over it. I'm actually living with Silas. The last time I fucked my boss, he moved me in and threw me out within three weeks. I haven't exactly got longevity written over me."

"Silas has," he says quietly, watching me with those wise eyes of his. So clear and all-seeing, the product of a quiet man who sits back and watches before he engages.

"I'm not used to this," I mutter, rubbing Chewwy's head and feeling the hot moisture on my jeans from his sigh. "It always starts fast and furious and ends even faster and angrier. I don't really do relationships now. I just fuck and leave. It's way easier to do that than–"

"Than what?"

"Than watching them go," I say and smile. "Shit, this got serious quickly. Let's go and mock Barry." I push Chewwy gently until he moves and scrape my chair back, but Milo reaches over and grabs my hand to stay me.

"Why not give it a chance?" he says softly. "I think Silas might be very different from the men you've met before."

"Well, the same goes for me. I bet he's never met anyone like me before."

"I somehow know that's negative in your mind, but I also know that's true in a different way. He's never met anyone like you, Oz, and that's a very bloody good thing. Do me a favour?" I look up at him and he smiles. "Give it a chance. Go with him and see where he leads you." He pauses. "After all, it's just for the summer, isn't it?"

I nod and smile. "You're right. I'll be back in London by the autumn."

I can't even summon up the energy for fake enthusiasm.

∼

Later that afternoon I come down the stairs to find Silas waiting in the hallway. He's wearing jeans and a forest-green polo shirt, and he looks gorgeous. He looks up and, seeing me, a wide smile crosses his face.

"You look amazing," he murmurs, coming towards me as I reach the bottom step and pulling me into a kiss. The step puts me almost at his height and I look into his warm eyes, a clear green this afternoon, and smile.

"Thank you." I look down at my outfit of skinny jeans, motorcycle boots, and a cornflower-blue short-sleeved shirt. I tug at the shirt. "Is it okay for where we're going?"

"It's fine," he says soothingly.

"Eyeliner okay? I don't want to shock the locals."

"I don't think you'd shock anyone where we're going. All their attention will be elsewhere." He pauses and strokes my cheekbone. "Anyway, I've discovered that I'm very partial to your eyeliner. It makes those pretty blue eyes pop."

"They're going to pop out if you don't tell me where we're going."

He laughs and stands back, and for a second I mourn the loss of his warm arms. But then he grabs a backpack and slings it onto his shoulders before taking my hand and leading me out of the house.

I look down at his tanned large hand holding mine and look up as he steers us towards the private carpark. "So, we're fully public?" I ask wryly. "No hiding in cupboards for us."

He stops and turns to me with a troubled look on his face. "Did you mind? I've been a bit worried all day that I've forced you into something you didn't want."

I laugh. "*Force* me? I don't know if you've met me, Silas, but while I may be small I'm not exactly built of obedient material." He smiles a little, worry easing from his eyes but not enough, so I reach up and stroke his face. "It's fine. I was just surprised, that's all."

"I got that from the way your mouth opened and shut like a fish."

I grin lasciviously at him. "My mouth opening and closing should be a cause for celebration."

He shudders and his eyes darken. "I'll be sure to let off fireworks," he says slowly, and I grin.

"The stars will burn and the heavens burst."

"Happy as I am that you don't lack confidence, could we please stop talking now?" he says wryly and adjusts himself.

My mouth waters at the large bulge and I shake my head. "You know we don't have to go on a date, Silas. I don't usually need wining and dining. Just a name and a cock."

"Well, I know your name and I have a cock. But unfortunately, you're still going to have to wait for it."

"Why?" The bewilderment is strong in my voice and he smiles and tugs me into a hug.

His warm breath smells of mint and I can smell the scent of his aftershave in the sweet arch where his neck meets his shoulder. "Because in the past I've always jumped straight into bed," he whispers. "And it never ended well. We got to know each other after our bodies, and not before. I want something different this time. I don't know why, but I want to know you before I stick my cock in you."

"But you are going to do that, as well?" I confirm, and he pulls back and gives me a wry smile.

"Of course I am. I can't keep away from you. Haven't you noticed?"

I mull this over as he opens the door of his car and gestures me in. I'm still mulling it over ten minutes later. He sits quietly, seemingly happy to let me have my thoughts, which is a rarity in my life.

Normally men jump in, eager to hear their own voices and stories. My voice and thoughts are secondary and unimportant. I enjoy the silence which is strangely peaceful. Eventually, I sit up.

"Okay. I can do that," I say, and he reaches across and squeezes my hand. He keeps hold of it for a while, and when he has to change gears he lowers my hand to his thigh. It isn't a request for me to grab his dick. I've had enough of those to recognise the move. Instead, it's like a simple desire for contact between him and me, and when he turns to face me, for a second I see contentment in his eyes and I leave my hand there.

It stays there as we drive down the A30 and he starts to question me. Not my CV. Not my number of sexual partners. Instead, he asks about my favourite films and foods and anything else I could possibly have a favourite in. I'm still bewildered, but we find that we share a love of classic horror films and cold pizza, but while he loves blue cheese, I would rather eat vomit.

"It's disgusting," I protest, laughing as he turns an indignant face to me.

He shakes his head. "And you'd rather eat a grilled Babybel cheese and pickle sandwich? It's incomprehensible."

"Don't knock it," I advise. "It's the quickest cure for a hangover I know."

"God, I haven't had one of those in ages," he says wistfully.

"Why do you sound regretful?"

"Because I haven't been really drunk and let go in ages." He shrugs. "There's just so much to do with the practice, the building, and the house accounts." He shudders, and I wince sympathetically.

"Are you worried?"

He looks at me and grins. "It's probably bad form to introduce darker subjects on a second date."

"I just think–" I run out of words and he looks at me curiously.

"What?"

I shrug. "To me, if you're going to know someone, you should know everything. All the dark bits, all the sunny bits, because they add up to one person's whole. I don't ever shy away from problems. It's not in me."

He nods as if he's having something confirmed for him. "I think I sensed that in you from the beginning." He sighs. "Okay. I'm worried all the time because if the house thing doesn't work then it's not just me. *Chi an Mor* may be my inheritance, but I look on it as being shared with Henry and I can't let him down."

"Does he own it too?"

He shakes his head. "It's left to the eldest son. There should have been money left for Henry, but my twat of a father left everything to me because on a few occasions I enjoyed a vagina." I gasp and he grins. "I split the money immediately but the estate is entailed, so it falls to me."

"Could he give you the money back?" I ask tentatively but he shakes his head vehemently.

"No. I'd never ask him. That's not fair."

I stare at him, but he seems obdurate on this so I settle for a quiet okay.

"It's not just me though," he says as he navigates the narrow Cornish lanes adeptly, his hands relaxed on the wheel. "There's all the staff. If I lose the house they'll lose their home. I couldn't bear that."

"What about The National Trust and English Heritage?"

He pulls the car to a stop behind a long line of other cars waiting on the narrow country lane and then shoots me a look. "They've come calling but I'm not there yet." He winces. "Not quite yet."

I think hard. "Okay, let's be honest. If you open the house, the money will be good but it's probably not going to allow you much leeway with bills." I hesitate. "I have an idea, but I don't want to tell you. Do you trust me to put some feelers out?"

I know he can't or won't be able to. I would find it impossible to put my fate in a stranger's hands.

"Okay," he says softly and I jerk.

"*Really?*"

He laughs. "The incredulity in your voice is worrying, Oz." He smiles and squeezes my hand on his thigh. "I trust you. You have an air of trustworthiness about you. I know you care about *Chi an Mor* and the people and I know you won't jeopardise that." I open my mouth but before I can speak he exclaims in disgust. "What on earth are these people doing?" He unbuckles his seat belt and opens the door.

"Where are you going?" I ask.

He grins. "We'll be here forever if we wait for people to sort this out. There's obviously a bus or a motorhome trying to get through. This lane is notorious for it. If we leave it we'll still be here at night-time waiting for someone to have an idea, and we haven't got time. We're on a deadline."

"A deadline. What are we doing?" I ask, but it's to open air as he ambles round the car and moves over to the vehicles stuck in front of us. He bends down and says something to one of the drivers and the man immediately gets out. I watch them idly as they stand together pointing and talking. Two more men join them and Silas gestures at them and to a field on the left. They nod, listening intently, as I admire the late afternoon sun shining on his hair.

His shoulders are wide in the green shirt and his arse in those old jeans of his that he favours is a thing of beauty. He laughs at something one of the men says and I smile. That wide grin and the lines at the sides of his eyes attract me madly and resonate somewhere inside me deep, like someone is striking a bell in my stomach and chest.

His words ring in my ears about me caring and I shake my head and rub at my eyes. I do care about the people in the house and the beautiful dilapidated building that calls to something in me, but my deepest, most incomprehensible feelings are for him. It scares me, but I know I'll stay and I will do anything to help him keep his birthright.

I will stay and I will see where this thing leads me. I've never shied away from a challenge, but this might be my biggest one yet.

CHAPTER 11

THERE'S A THEATRE RIGHT AT THE EDGE OF ENGLAND

Oz

For the next five minutes, I watch bemused as he stands in the middle of the road and directs cars left and right into fields, along with a great deal of laughter and that wide, friendly smile on his face. A few times the driver of a vehicle has lowered his window with a frown, but each time Silas smiles and says something and the result is laughter and an easy-going acceptance of his requests.

When he gets back into the car I grin at him. "I really don't know why I'm here. You've got an arsenal of your own with that smile and the understanding that people will just do as they're told. Why haven't you pointed it at the house?"

He starts the engine and we move off. "I'm glad I didn't," he says. "Look what I got."

I shake my head. "Where are we going? Your date shouldn't be kept in the dark unless you've blindfolded them." He shoots me a look and I smile lasciviously. "Not that I'd know anything about that at all."

He groans and reaches down to rearrange himself. "Thanks for that, Oz." I laugh. "Anyway, we're nearly there now so your curiosity will be satisfied."

I look out of the window as we climb a steep and narrow sloping road and obey the directions of a man in a fluorescent jacket to park the car in a car park with a stunning view of the sea.

I open the door and slide out and immediately walk over to the fence. All I can see is the wide, glittering expanse of the sea. "It's like we're at the end of the world," I exclaim, turning to him as he locks the door and comes towards me.

He slings his rucksack over his shoulder and stands next to me. "Not the end of the world. Just the end of England," he says quietly. "Land's End is a few miles over that way." He grabs my hand. "Come on or we'll be late."

I turn to see people getting out of their cars and starting to flock towards an entrance to my left. They're grabbing bags and even blankets.

"Are we going camping?" I ask doubtfully. He laughs and I turn back. "Not that I'd mind, but the last time I did that I was with Shaun. The tent got flooded and we ended up sleeping in his car on the beach for a week."

He tugs me after him. "Who's Shaun?"

His voice is rich and even but there's a slight undercurrent to it. I want to say jealousy, but I'm probably wrong.

"He's been my best friend since school. He and his boyfriend Richard are my closest friends."

It's not my imagination that his body relaxes. He flashes me a smile and comes to a stop.

"Ta da!" he says, indicating a sign with a flourish.

I lean forward. "The Minack Theatre," I read. I look up. "There's a theatre right at the edge of England. That's cool."

"It's amazing. But it's not an ordinary theatre. Minack means rocky."

I nudge him. "Like the boxer?"

He grins. "Yes. At the end of England there is a small theatre dedicated to Sylvester Stallone, that brilliant classically trained actor of stage and screen. Don't tell anyone or we'll have a cult."

I laugh, and we join the throng of people moving down a winding path. The borders are full of fragrant plants and the air is full of excitement. We join a queue and I wait patiently as he pays for some tickets at a booth, then grabs my hand and pulls me after him. I look down at his fingers clasping mine and just have time to think how much I like this, when he comes to a stop and I look down and gasp.

The theatre is actually an amphitheatre set into the rocks. Rows of seats carved from stone and set into the side of the cliff tier down to a stone stage. People are moving and settling into their seats, their clothes a colourful exclamation mark to a place that belongs to a three-tone colour scheme with the green of the grass, the pale stone, and the deep blue sea that stretches out as far as I can see.

I turn to find him looking at me with a soft expression on his face.

"This is amazing," I say quietly. I look down at the sea breaking onto rocks. "It's almost like being in Ancient Greece."

His face breaks into a wide, relieved grin. "Really? I'm so glad you like it. It's not to everyone's taste."

"Why?"

"Well, because it's a bit rustic. You're out in the open so if it spits with rain you get it. There aren't cushioned seats and curtains."

I shake my head. "Have you tried bringing people here before?" I hold my breath because I don't want to know I'm not the first.

"No," he says, staring down at the busy scene. "I knew enough not to bother."

I exhale my sigh of relief. "So, why me?"

"Because you're different," he says slowly. "And somehow I knew you'd like it."

I cosy into the side of him and rest my head on his shoulder, looking out at the view and loving the way his arm instantly comes down over my shoulder and drags me even closer. "Well, you were right," I say quietly. "I'm glad I'm the first."

His hand tightens and then he releases me. "Let's go and grab our seats. The performance is starting in ten minutes."

"What are we watching?" I ask as we join the people heading towards the steps.

"*The Tempest*. Is that okay? Do you like Shakespeare?"

"I do. I did him for A-Level and we had a school trip to see one in the West End. I loved it that much I dragged Shaun to a few more." I laugh. "I'm not sure it was his cup of tea, to be honest. He used the theatre as a viable alternative to bed and just went to sleep. But I loved it."

He pulls me towards the steps. They're stone and quite steep, and although he takes them easily it's more of a stretch for me with shorter legs, but he waits patiently, a smile of happiness on his face that's hard to resist.

We reach the aisle he indicates and slip in at the end. We're halfway up, with a perfect view of the stage. There's an excited chatter around us as people settle onto the seats. Silas reaches into his bag and pulls out a large thermos flask and two paper cups. "I've got some rosé wine in here."

I smirk and hold the empty cups he hands to me so he can pour the wine. "Won't we be caught?"

He laughs. "No. Everyone does it." I look around and grin when I see an extraordinary amount of thermos flasks being handed around.

He pulls out a brown paper bag that's giving out a heavenly smell. "Are those Maggie's vegetable pasties?" I ask reverently.

He grins. "Two each. They're my favourites. And after that I've got two slices of Mrs Granger's apple cake."

I'm so charmed by this. I'm sure most men and women would expect the Earl of Ashworth to wine and dine them in splendour at expensive restaurants and nightclubs. However, this picnic with wine in paper cups and cake is perfect to me.

I take a sip of my wine, relishing the tart cold taste, and look down at the sea breaking onto the rocks and fountaining into the air. Seagulls dip low over us as if they're tiny ticket dodgers waiting for the performance.

"It's so beautiful," I say. "I don't think I've ever been anywhere so stunning and unusual. It has a nice feel to it."

He nods, happiness in his eyes. "Last time I was here there were basking sharks in the bay. I spent more time watching them than I did the play."

"Do you come here often?"

He nods. "A lot. I like going to the theatre, but I find London theatres so stuffy and stolid. I like the wildness and eccentricity of this. I've sat here through hot sunshine and pouring rain and loved it every time."

He bends down and reaching into his bag again he pulls out two cushions.

"It's like Mary Poppins's carpet bag," I marvel. "Why have we got these?"

"For your arse," he whispers. "These seats aren't the most comfortable."

They're stone seats with grass for a cushion and they seem okay to me, but he's been here before and there's a wealth of experience in his eyes. I take the cushion.

"Okay," I whisper back. "I know you've got a vested interest in my arse tonight. Can't have it going to sleep."

He stills and looks at me and our eyes meet and catch. His darken and I watch him draw in a slow, measured breath. "No," he mutters. "I need it wide awake tonight."

And just like that, we acknowledge that he's going to have me later on. The knowledge forms a subtle undercurrent to the rest of the evening as we watch the play. And even as Shakespeare's beautiful words float out onto the air, I'm aware with a deep, visceral tug in my groin of the heat and strength of the body next to mine.

The sky darkens slowly from the soft lilac of twilight to the plush navy velvet of night and the sea provides its own soundtrack as it crashes onto the rocks. I shiver and lean closer because I need him rather more than I need breath.

"That was amazing," I say quietly when the last bow has been taken.

"You really liked it?"

"It was wonderful." I look around as people start to leave, climbing the stairs slowly until we're among the last ones.

He sits back. "It's got an amazing history. It was the brainchild idea of Rowena Cade. She pushed it every step of the way. She even heaved some of the rock down from her house up there. Apparently, they had to light the first performance using people's car headlights." He points to the side. "Over there are stone seats with the titles of the different plays that have been performed since the beginning."

I peer over. "There are even little balconies," I exclaim.

He rubs his neck. "Did you mind sitting where we were? I don't like it up there. It feels like everyone's eyes are on you."

I stand up and pull him up after me, hugging him affectionately. "I loved where we were," I say softly. "Thank you for a wonderful date." I pause. "I mean, we weren't hiding in a stranger's drawing room and I wasn't blowing you, but not everything can live up to that first date."

"I don't know," he says hoarsely. "The night's young yet."

And just like that, the heat roars back in and my breath catches in my throat. His eyes darken and he grabs my hand. "Let's go home," he mutters, and I follow.

The drive back is quiet and filled with an intense heat that you can almost see shimmer between us. Every move he makes, every time he brakes and the muscles in his thigh work, every time his hand curves around the gear stick, I feel heat run through me and under my skin like I'm connected to him with invisible wires.

He drives with a fierce concentration, but I know he's just as aware as me from his sidelong glances and the way his breathing is deep and heavy.

When we get home, everywhere is dark and still. I climb out and inhale the scent of roses from the bush growing nearby. He comes around the side of the car and pushes me gently into it. He leans over me, not touching anywhere but staring into my eyes. "Are you sure?" he says in a low voice. "Once we do this we can't go back. It's your choice."

I reach up and push his hair back from his forehead, relishing the feel of the silky locks on my fingers. "I'm sure," I say quietly. "I want you, Silas. So much."

He closes his eyes, and when he opens them I inhale at the lust and determination on his face. "Okay, come with me," he says, grabbing my hand. "I want you in my bed."

"This is just like a Catherine Cookson book," I say happily. "Hopefully you'll use me and toss me aside and then I'll go away and make myself into a very rich man and have my revenge."

He shakes his head. "Those books are not good for mental health."

"They're probably better than the shit you've got in your library," I retort.

He snorts. "The library provides the Earl of Ashworth with all of his reading materials," he says in a snooty guide voice and I laugh, feeling it rush through me like a bottle of pop that's been shaken and is waiting to explode if the cap's removed.

I follow him up the staircase and onto the long gallery. I copy his movements as he sneaks across the pine floorboards because he's obviously avoiding the creaky ones.

"I detect a misspent childhood," I whisper as he creeps to the side. "Alternatively, this could be like dating The Pink Panther."

"Merci beaucoup," he says in the most terrible French accent I've ever heard, and I snort, trying not to laugh.

He pulls me after him, past the family portraits that glare down at us, and to the door at the end of the gallery. I know it houses the earl's apartments but I've never been in.

We walk into a lounge that's long with a low beamed ceiling. A large fireplace sits at one end, but the only other furniture is a battered leather sofa and chairs sitting on a beautiful old oriental carpet and one of the biggest TVs I've ever seen. My lip quirks and he looks slightly embarrassed.

"It's not much, I'm afraid. Apart from my bedroom, there are two others that are empty. An old kitchen that needs demolishing, dining room, and a bathroom. When I moved in I got rid of most of my father's furniture, painted the walls white, and that was about it. I'm not here much."

"This isn't the room I'm bothered about," I murmur, and he grins.

"Follow me."

He opens the door at the far end of the lounge and I walk beside him down a flagstoned corridor and through another door, only to stop in disbelief. "This is beautiful," I breathe. It's a huge room with one wall made up of floor-to-ceiling stone mullioned windows. They're open and letting in the roar of the sea and a salt-tinged breeze that rustles the sky-blue embroidered curtains of the huge oak four-poster bed. It's set back against the far wall, the bedlinens a stark white in the moonlight that floods the room, and whoever sleeps in it would have an uninterrupted view through the windows.

I step towards the windows and peer out. Below me the ground slopes steeply down towards the sea which glitters and moves languidly in the moonlight as if in a spell.

I turn back and find him watching me. He's standing still, but every muscle of his body seems taut with expectation. I flick my eyes around and dimly notice a blue velvet settee and armchair positioned in front of a huge stone fireplace. Then my eyes come back to him.

"I've not been down to the beach," I say, and I can hear a high nervousness in my voice that's never been there before. I have slept with more men than I should count, but I haven't felt this nervous since my first time and I wonder why.

He must hear it as well because he looks at me intently before moving slowly to stand next to me. I cast him a wry look to which he responds with a gentle smile.

"The path's down there," he says, and the Cornish burr in his voice sounds a little stronger. I've noticed it appears when he's most at home with someone and not having to behave like an earl. "It's hidden, but it's there." He pauses. "Are you having second thoughts, Oz, because—"

We both twirl round as the door to his room slams shut loudly.

"What the fuck?" I breathe. "There isn't enough breeze in the room to do that." I look at the floor. "Is the floor on a slant?"

He sighs and then grins helplessly. "It's Lionel," he says and shakes his head.

"Lionel, who?"

"Lionel, my ancestor from the Stuart time."

"The *dead* Lionel?" I say, and my voice has definitely gone high.

"I would certainly hope so. Either that or he'd need shares in Oil of Olay." I look at him in stupefaction. "Don't laugh," he says, then laughs himself. "You said yourself he looked friendly. Well, he is. Too friendly. He loves it around this area of the house and he's always locking me in fucking rooms."

"You've got a three-hundred-and thirty-year-old drunken ghost as a pimp." I start to laugh. "Not sure where you'd put that on your Grindr profile."

He snorts and then stares at me. "You're so fucking beautiful when you laugh," he says, and the fervent note in his voice makes me still and stare at him. Moving slowly, he reaches up and cups my cheekbone, staring at my face. "Look at you," he says in a wondering voice. "You're lit up like you're made of a moonbeam and your hair looks so black against your skin."

I reach up and cup my hand over his, and I know he can feel the tremors running through my body because he stills. "I need you," I say hoarsely, feeling it run through my body like a stream of fire. "I want you now."

"Yes," he says and then he's on me.

He kisses me furiously, eating into my mouth with a choked groan and I catch fire from him, want rushing through me like hot chocolate. My back bumps into something and I realise that he's backed me into the window. The glass feels cold on my hot skin as his tongue rubs and twines with mine. He releases my lips and I suck in air and groan as his mouth slides down my neck suckling on the skin, almost, but not quite leaving a mark. And I want him to. I hate that sort of thing normally, but now I want a bruise on me that I can look at and know his mouth left it there like a signature on my skin.

I moan pleadingly, and he looks up deep into my eyes and his lip quirks in a half smile as if something has passed unsaid between us. Then I give a high, reedy cry as he pushes my shirt collar to one side and fastens his mouth onto the skin he's just revealed. He sucks powerfully and I arch up, shoving my hips against his demandingly and rubbing my dick against him. He grunts and moves onto another area, the delicacy of the way he moves my shirt a stark contrast to the heat and pressure of his mouth.

His fingers lower as he sucks, and I feel them against the waistband of my jeans. There's a jingle as the belt loosens, and then my jeans sag open.

"Christ," I whisper, and then moan as he comes back at my mouth as if declaring war. He shoves his hands down the back of my jeans and grabs my arse cheeks, squeezing them and using them to pull me against him. Encouraging me to rut against him. And all the while he kisses me, his breaths harsh on my cheek.

I feel almost like I've been caught up in a whirlwind. He's so gentle outside the bedroom, but after the blow job I'm starting to suspect that he's very different during sex. This is desperate and animalistic and he's turning me on so much I can feel my balls lift and tighten, and I pull away, sucking in air and staring at him. He looks debauched, his cheeks flushed and his eyes lowered to half-mast. His mouth is red and swollen, and his chest rises and falls with his panting breaths.

"Take your clothes off," he says in a guttural whisper, and I shiver. Gone is the polite, cool tone of voice, and here in this room it's lowered to a rough, demanding drawl. I kick off my shoes quickly and peel off my jeans, shirt, and underwear, watching him avidly as he tears off his own clothes.

I reach out and touch his chest when his shirt vanishes, running my fingers through the thick hair. "Yes," I whisper. "I love this."

His mouth twists with hunger as he shudders under my touch, kicking his jeans and underwear off until he's as naked as I am. Then he grabs me and pulls me into him and I feel that hairy torso against mine, abrading my sensitive nipples so that hot lightning runs through them like they're attached to my cock.

I writhe against him and he groans, reaching down and grabbing my arse in the palms of his hands. Obeying his unspoken command, I jump and he lifts me easily, winding my legs around him and taking two strides to the chair where he sits down.

For a second, I'm taken by surprise. I expected him to go for that huge bed, but I shudder as I realise that he's at the end of his tether. I straddle him, sinking into the cradle of his hips and then sitting back slightly on his thighs so I can feel his cock against mine.

He lifts my hand and spits into my palm. "Wank us together," he orders me and reaches for a small bag on the table by the chair. I obey him instantly, fumbling to align his cock with mine. I'm narrow and long, but he dwarfs me with the thickness of his. Veins marble the surface and the head is slick and angry looking.

I twist my wrist and thrust my cock alongside his, and his hand clutches into a claw on the bag as he throws his head back and shouts out. "Yes," he hisses and starts to move his own hips. Within seconds, we're moving together as if synchronised. As if we did this for an Olympic sport.

I moan and close my eyes, the visual of our two cocks rubbing together too insanely hot. If I look too long, I'll come. Instead, I focus on the silky feel of his flesh against mine, the heat and hardness of his cock, and the tart scent of his pre-come and sweat.

I hear the rustle of the bag and the pop of a cap and jump when I feel cool fingers at my hole. "Lift up," he says gutturally. Abandoning our cocks, I open my eyes and stare into his. They're almost black, the pupil expanding to cover the pretty colour. For a second we just hang there panting and looking, and then letting our cocks go, I lift my hands to his wide shoulders and use them to move upwards so he can get at my arse.

"Yes," he says hoarsely. "Just like that. You're so fucking good."

I feel the praise heat me inside and cry out as he taps against my hole, massaging it with a slick finger before pushing it gently and steadily into me. It burns for a second but I relax into it, loving that first feeling of being breached and knowing what's to come and that somehow, it's going to be better with him than anyone else.

"God yes, Silas," I groan. "More. Give me another."

He pushes another finger into me, moving steadily, and when he taps my gland I cry out and my hips move involuntarily.

"Look at you," he mutters. "Riding my hand. Fuck, you're so sexy." He opens me steadily and pushes another finger in, the digits rubbing continuously over my prostate heating me up. I feel sweat run down my body and moan as he licks it up, his tongue warm and abrasive. He gives a satisfied grunt. "I want to see you ride my cock like this."

I open my eyes to look down at him blearily. Sweat runs down my brow and my dick is throbbing like a toothache. I give a great shudder. "Yes."

He nods, looking just as wrecked as me. "Stand up, sweetheart," he grunts. "Let me get the condom on."

I rise up slightly and watch as he opens the packet, his fingers looking huge on the shiny golden square. I shiver as he reaches behind me and I hear the snap as he rolls it on and settles it. Then one hand is on my hip.

"Slowly," he says, and I lower myself down onto his cock that he has steadied for me with his other hand. I feel his cock tap my hole and wait as he readies me. Once he grunts an assent I lower myself, taking the tip inside me. I pause for a second and then breathe out as I continue to lower myself slowly. As soon as he can, he releases his cock and switches his grasp to my hips.

"Take it easy," he says, and while his voice is even, he's given away by the quick rise and fall of his chest and the way his hands flex on my hips as if he's forcibly stopping himself from forcing me down on his dick. His eyes are dark and riveted between my legs and my stiff cock bobbing.

"It's intense," I slur. "You feel so big." I give a wild cry as he bottoms out, and I grab his shoulders, digging my nails in. I can feel the burn in my thighs as I crouch over him, as well as the shaking of my legs.

"Are you alright, darling?"

I nod frantically, squeezing my eyes shut. "You feel fucking amazing, but give me a second. This position is deep."

His hips stay still, letting me sit in his lap, but his hands move, caressing my chest and tweaking my nipples, before tugging gently in my hair and pulling my head towards him for a deep kiss. Our lips rub and suck and still his hand moves, flirting over my shoulders. Light brushes of touch that feel almost burning hot on my sweat-slick skin. They move down my back and we both groan as he runs his fingers under my arse and touches my hole.

"You're stuffed full of my cock," he mutters, and the deep, satisfied rasp in his voice makes me shudder. I can feel his cock throbbing inside me, rubbing slightly with the rhythm of our breaths and the faint thrust of our hips that seems to have happened almost without us knowing. It makes heat bloom in me.

Lust suddenly fills me like a grenade going off and I grab his head and kiss him roughly, feeling his lips catch and the faint taste of copper on my tongue. I pull away. "You need to fuck me," I groan. "I won't last long."

He throws his head back and I watch as the muscles on his stomach tense and bunch as he lowers his hips so he almost comes out, and then without any warning, he thrusts up and tunnels back in abruptly. Heat bursts inside me like little fireworks going off and I shout out, my head falling back.

Then, as if timed, we both lose it. He pushes up inside me, grunting heavily every time he bottoms out, while I crouch, feeling my legs shake with the strain as I paw at his body, rubbing his chest and nipples and feeling his hairy thighs against my arse.

As if sensing my legs are going to give way, he grabs my hips and lowers me down onto him so I sit stuffed with his cock. Kissing me furiously and licking into my mouth, he pulls at my knees until I set them into the chair on either side of his hips. I groan. Now, he's really deep. I couldn't have done this earlier, but I'm loose enough now to take him and I feel my hips start to move, almost out of my control.

I move up and down, kissing him frantically and feeling his hands come down to my bum. He grabs both of my arse cheeks, squeezing them hard, lifting me and thrusting into me from underneath. I can feel the muscles in his arms shifting and bunching and I pull back enough to watch his torso move.

Sweat drips from me to him and he takes my mouth again, his hands on my arse tightening almost painfully. His cock shuttles in and out of my hole, catching on the rim, and he begins a series of short, battering thrusts that graze my prostate and make sparks dance in front of my eyes.

My cock bobs between us, rock hard with pre-come sliding steadily down it, and I lower my hand.

"Yes," he grunts. "I'm nearly there. Do it. I want your come all over me. Squeeze that hole for me."

I grunt and rub down in tight circles and he shouts out. His hands squeeze tight as he forces himself upwards, losing his rhythm as he gets close, and the knowledge sears through me as I jerk myself furiously, feeling myself getting close.

"Silas," I shout, and he gives a deep guttural groan, his hips stuttering as he goes deep once, twice, and three times. The knowledge that he's coming acts like a match and I rut down furiously. He bats my hand away from my cock, flicking it as he does, and the slight pain sets me off.

I lean back, bracing my hands on his thighs, pistoning on his dick as he jacks me. His eyes are riveted between my legs and the glaze in them makes the heat burst. I cry out and watch through slitted eyes as he angles my cock so that my spunk pumps all over his stomach and chest, droplets glistening in the hair.

Then I collapse back on him and we both sit, slumped and covered with come and sweat. After a few minutes he levers me up, holding onto the edge of the condom, and I clutch at him, muttering an obscenity. He laughs.

"I'm just going to get a towel, Pika," he says, his voice sex-deep and hoarse. "Let me take care of you."

He ties the condom off and chucks it into a rubbish basket and then I gasp as he lifts me up and walks me over to the bed. I cling for a second as he lowers me, and he chuckles as he drops me with a bounce. I watch as he moves towards a door which I presume is a bathroom. The moonlight limns his body, highlighting the wide shoulders and long legs and his full, tight arse.

I shudder and look around the room, trying to concentrate on that and not how my body is thrumming with a bone-deep satisfaction that I can feel to my toes. I've never felt like this before. Wrung out and utterly replete.

He returns, padding across the floorboards, and I lay back into the mattress, moving my body languidly as he directs me. He cleans me with a single-minded focus and gentle hands. When he's finished, he tosses the towel towards the bathroom and slides into bed.

"I should go," I say slowly, suddenly aware that I'm lounging in his bed like I own the fucking thing. Any minute now he's going to roll over and direct me to the spare room the way James did, claiming that I was too fidgety to sleep with.

I open my eyes as a sudden breeze blows around the room,

ruffling the bed curtains. I sniff. "Can you smell something sweet? It's like pipe tobacco and leather."

He pulls me towards him. "That's Lionel."

I jerk. "Really?" I pause. "Oh my God, I smelt that in my room when I was–" I come to a stop and he immediately looks interested.

"Oh, do go on. This sounds interesting."

I prod him. "I was using my dildo, okay?"

He looks like he's had a revelation. "Was that the night I heard you shout my name?"

"Shut up."

He laughs. "No, really. Give me the full details. I love a good bedtime story." He pauses. "Only be really, *really* meticulous with the details."

I shake my head, looking around the room warily, half expecting a drunken peeping tom ghost to step out. "Has that dirty old git been here all the time?"

He snorts. "Probably. And now he wants you to sleep in here with me."

"Oh, he does, does he?" I say wryly. "Does Lionel also want me to cook breakfast in the morning and wash your clothes because his needs seem to coincide with yours?"

He laughs. "We're kin, Oz. It's inevitable." He sighs heavily and manoeuvres me onto my side. He throws his arm over me and snuggles up to me. "For the record, Lionel wants bacon and eggs in the morning with orange juice."

"You and Lionel will get a cold shoulder and a sharp tongue," I say, using my mum's old saying and hearing the Irish brogue in my voice.

"I'll take anything you want to give," he says sleepily, his voice deep and warm in the dim room.

Within minutes he's asleep, and I lie for a few minutes, feeling the scratchiness of his chest hair rubbing down my back. His leg is pushed between my own and I send my toes exploratively down his shin, then I wriggle, feeling his cock and balls damp and soft against my bum.

"I'll never fall asleep like this," I whisper. "I can't sleep with anyone. I'll go in a minute." I smell the tobacco and leather on the air again, mingling with the brine of the sea, and with the suddenness of a child I slip into the peaceful darkness of sleep as if someone has pressed a button.

CHAPTER 12

I'LL WARM YOU UP

Silas

I stand at the window looking down at my land. It's still dark and the sky is that clear deep blue that presages a hot day. There's a hint of lemon light showing across the horizon and a cooling breeze is blowing off the sea, lessening the sticky heat. Usually I can stand here for ages because I love my home with a passion and fervour that I've never felt for a human being. But today there's a major distraction, and I turn away from the view and pad silently back to the bed and Oz.

It's draped in shadows but the lessening in the darkness reveals him. He's lying on his side, his head cradled in the pillow and his body a graceful italic in the bed. I smile because he's patently unused to sharing a bed. No matter where I lay on the bed, and it's big, his sleeping body would find me. We'd ended up in a half sprawl with the sheets tucked around us, his head on my chest and his legs entangled with mine. It had been surprisingly comfortable.

The sheets have come away from him and I pause for a second. I feel like a bit of a creeper, but I can't help staring. This is Oz in my bed. Beautiful, complicated, tart-tongued Oz with the badly hidden soft centre. His fierceness and energy are shuttered in sleep and I can see the soft fullness of his lips and the shadows that his long sooty lashes leave on his cheeks.

The long line of his body is on show and his pale skin glows in the dim light. He's a true Celt, my Oz. No matter how much sun he walks about in, it doesn't touch the white skin. Unlike me his chest is hairless, the only hair on his body the thin happy trail under his belly button leading to the black bush of his pubes. His cock is lying soft on his thigh and his hand lies outstretched across the mattress as if reaching for me.

I dismiss the silly notion of putting my hand in his and instead climb onto the bed behind him and cuddle up to his warm body. He nestles back against me, pushing his arse into the cradle of my groin and murmuring sleepily. I curl closer and inhale his cologne which smells of ginger. Now, it's mixed with the smell of sex and musk. It smells warm and safe and happy and I'm so tempted to stay here, but I'm on a timetable so I move back and push my face into his neck. Inhaling the scent of his shampoo, I murmur, "Wake up."

He moves his head on the pillow and his nose wrinkles like a hamster, although I'd never dare tell him that. I nestle my face into his shoulder and kiss him there gently, and he mutters indignantly and reaches up a hand to smack me away. Unfortunately, he misses and smacks himself in the face, and I try hard to repress my smile as he bolts upright, looking around crossly as if someone has dared to sneak up on him and kiss him.

"What the hell?" he mutters, and then I see memory and recognition creep back into his eyes, replacing the soft sleepiness of before. I can more or less see the exact moment that Daytime Oz appears. His expression becomes intent as if he's mentally running through the list of offenders he's going to deal with, mountains he's going to scale, and fires he's going to put out. It's peculiarly fascinating and gives the already intimate feeling of waking up in the same bed a deeper and more privileged feel. It's like I'm watching a small mythical creature donning its armour.

He tilts his head and looks down at me where I'm lying. His eyes flick down my body and seem to linger on my chest. I hope he likes hairy men because I'll never be a twink, and there isn't much refined about me despite the efforts my mother made. I feel a flicker of worry, but it vanishes when I see heat fill those pretty gin-bottle eyes.

"Hmm. This is definitely a better way to wake up," he says, and the Irish lilt is heavy in his early morning hoarseness. It makes my dick stir and he grins evilly and reaches for me, but I suddenly remember my plan and scoot back.

"Hands off," I say smartly. "Get dressed quickly, Oz." He looks befuddled and I gesture with my hands. "We don't have much time and I want to show you something."

With other lovers I'd have had to go into lengthy explanations and with a few of them I'd have had to wait another hour while they got ready. Not Oz. That ready-for-anything wicked smile appears and he throws the covers back. With a quick pitstop in the bathroom, he's dressed and ready by the door in a few minutes.

"Come on then," he laughs. "Hurry up."

I shake my head and, grabbing the bag I packed with one hand and his hand with my other, I pull him after me. I open the door and come to a stop. Chewwy is lying across the doorway. When the door opens he looks up almost accusingly. "You do know the dogs live in the kitchen, don't you?" I say wryly.

"It isn't my fault," he says indignantly. "Your dog's stalking me." The way he reaches down and coos and pets my dog slightly belies his words and I grin.

"I think he's switched his allegiance."

He immediately looks worried. "Are you bothered?"

I smile. "Of course not. I can't blame him. I'd follow you everywhere if I could too."

I watch with interest the flush on his cheeks, and when he captures my gaze, he grimaces and elbows me.

"Weren't you showing me something?"

I nod and whistle for Chewwy to follow us. We creep down the gallery in the dark hush. I've done this so many times that it's almost muscle memory to avoid the creaky plank outside my mother's old room and to know that the first stair is uneven, but somehow with him it's brand-new and everything seems more colourful and real.

I can smell the scent of beeswax in the air and feel the breeze from an open window wash over us as we walk by. I can feel the rough calluses on his palm against mine and the blue of his eyes looks almost neon in the dim light.

I pull him down the stairs and through the kitchen and out of the back door, clicking my tongue for Boris who rises from his bed near the Aga and frolics around Chewwy as if he hasn't seen him in years. We walk over the grass and we're silent as if by mutual consent.

The early morning is cool and fragrant while the dampness of the dew wets our trainers. Boris and Chewy race around tracking scents excitedly and raising their legs against handy trees and bushes. I've always loved this time of the morning when everything is fresh and new, like when you open the first exercise book of the school year. No blots or ink stains. Just a fresh start.

The sound of the sea gets louder, and I tug him after me towards the entrance to the cove which is partially concealed these days by a rhododendron bush that's bigger than me. I push the blowsy flowers to one side and reveal the steep steps.

"This is the entrance to the cove?" he says. "Milo told me you could get down there, but I couldn't find it." He looks at me. "Going to murder me and chuck my body in the sea?"

I blink. "Well, I wasn't intending to. It's a bit warm to be murdering people. If you don't mind, I thought we'd just watch the sunrise."

He grins, but there's a softness to his smile and a warmth in his eyes that I want always to be there when he looks at me. I don't know what's happening here, but I've never had such an intense reaction to a man or woman. There's just something about him that seems to call to something in me. Something that echoes and matches him. That makes us kindred spirits in some strange way.

I become aware that he's staring at me, and I shake my head at my silly thoughts and smile. "Come on. We need to be on the beach before the sun rises."

The dogs bound ahead of us as we make our way down the steep steps and I'm gratified that he doesn't become self-conscious about his shorter stature. Instead he seems comfortable, his eyes darting here, there, and everywhere, taking in one of my favourite places on earth.

It's part of my land and it's typically Cornish, being rocky and practically inaccessible. Trees line one side and the rest is high rock and stone and a small sandy beach. But the water is a clear turquoise in the sun and a soft navy in this light, and I love this small spot with a passion.

My parents would never come down here because of the steepness of the steps. Our nannies always hated it too and invariably would sit at the top while Henry and I ran wild on the sand. I'm not sure what they'd have done if we'd had an accident, but we never cared, loving the solitude and the wildness.

As I grew older my love for it deepened. Here I could hide Henry away when my father was on a rampage. Here was where I came to be alone with my thoughts and to walk the dogs.

We step down onto the cold damp sand and he pushes his messy hair back from his forehead, those piercing eyes everywhere. He turns to me and I tense slightly but relax as he smiles.

"It's amazing, Silas. Like a magic cove."

I grin at him and for a second, he looks almost befuddled, but he snaps to and helps me with the blanket I pull out from my bag. I sit down and pat the space in front of me between my legs. He looks at me, almost confused, and I smile.

"Come and sit down. The sun's about to rise and you don't want to miss it."

He lowers himself gracefully in front of me and I'm not imagining the contented grunt he gives when I draw up my knees and wrap my arms around him. He rests against me and I tighten my grip on the warm strength of his body, breathing in the scent of shampoo that clings to the messy waves of his hair. It gleams in the light like the wing of a blackbird.

I let go of him with one hand and pull my bag towards me. I open the zip and he shoots me a grin over his shoulder.

"What have you got in that Mary Poppins' bag now?"

"The best thing," I say reverently. "Tea." I extract a thermos and a couple of bright blue enamelled mugs.

His eyes light up. "Tea," he says happily. "I can't start my morning without it."

"Not coffee? Everyone seems to drink that lately," I ask, pouring him a cup of the milky tea he likes best. I prefer it a bit stronger, but this morning is about him.

He shakes his head. "We're Irish. My mum can't start the day right without it and I got into the habit of it too." He looks down into his mug. "It was one of our things when I lived at home. No matter what time she or I got in, we'd always have tea at the table and talk over the happenings of the day."

"You're very close, aren't you?"

He smiles tenderly. "She's my everything. I don't know my dad and she could have given me up, but she never did. She's the strongest woman I know, and I'd do anything for her."

I realise with a shock that I passionately want to have him look like that about me. To have him recognise me as a member of his tribe. To have that warm, soft regard turned on me. I swallow hard. *What the fuck is this?*

He takes a sip of his tea and groans, and my cock stirs at the deep sound. "God, I'll love you forever if you make me this every morning."

There's a sudden shocked silence and he looks poleaxed as if he's taken a blow to the head. I watch as a red flush travels down his cheeks and he looks suddenly embarrassed. "I obviously didn't mean that," he stutters. "I mean, that's just a turn of phrase."

I stare at him for a long minute, feeling shock rush through me. Then I clear my throat and pull him back against me. "I know," I whisper. "Just watch the sun and be easy."

He relaxes immediately back against me, and we watch the sun slowly rise above the shimmering line of the sea until it lays a red carpet in front of us like it's a magic path to a faraway land. Seemingly by mutual accord we don't speak, and the silence is easy and almost familiar as if we're so used to one another we don't need to fill every second with speech.

I'm relieved that we don't speak because while I try to pay attention to the moment, every atom of my body is clanging and bouncing around in shock because I know what this is now. This feeling I have for him, this tenderness and desire to be with him. It's love. I'm in love with him. I look down at his dark head nestled into my shoulder and let the realisation echo around me.

I've never been in love before. The only formative relationship I saw was that of my parents and that was nowhere near love. I love Henry and I've felt fondness for lovers that I've thought might develop into love, but now I know with emphatic certainty that it never was. This is the real thing.

I always thought that love comes softly and gradually along with a knowledge of the other person, but that was from books. Because now I know that for me it's come suddenly and powerfully out of the blue with an almost instinctive reaching towards Oz as if my heart knows it will be safe with him and find refuge. It's incredibly sudden but I know instinctively that this is it for me.

I still slightly. I've finally met the person for me. He's nothing like I imagined but somehow everything I should have known enough to wish for. Clever and kind and sharp, he fills me with joy. However, I also know that he isn't ready for any of this.

For a person who believes that he meets everything head-on, he doesn't do it with his own softer feelings. He seems to look on love and relationships as something alien and almost hostile, and instinctively shies away from any examination of his own feelings. He's fine when other people need him and is there instinctively, but any chance of *him* needing something and he curls up like a hedgehog.

I smile slightly. My Oz is like a hedgehog. Bright eyes, prickly and fierce on the outside with a soft underbelly that he'll roll into a ball to hide. I sigh as another thought occurs. We only have a few months left of his contract. When the house opens he'll go back to London.

My arms tighten at the thought of not seeing him every day, not hearing his Irish lilt echoing through the house as he lays down the law and solves problems like a small Irish superhero.

He squirms at my suddenly tight grip and looks questioningly at me.

"Got a bit chilly in the sea breeze," I say hoarsely, and he instantly rolls up and throws his arms around me.

"I'll warm you up," he says, laughing and giving me a lascivious look, and I let him fuss over me and kiss me but inside I'm planning.

He's not going to go under gladly or willingly but he's right, even though he was joking. He does warm me all the way through into the dark, cold corners that have always been there. I need to be patient and love him silently because if he guesses he'll be off quicker than a greyhound.

CHAPTER 13

I JUST DIDN'T WANT TO GET HIS HOPES UP

ONE MONTH LATER

Oz

I come awake to soft kisses on the nape of my neck and warm arms around me. "Mmm," I say meditatively and snuggle back.

He chuckles, and I feel the vibrations run through me. "Time to get up, Pika."

I open one eye blearily. "When are you going to stop calling me that?"

He laughs and throws back the sheets and smacks my arse.

"Never. You're my Pika and that's how you're going to stay. Now get that cute backside out of bed and walk the dogs with me."

I roll over and look at him indignantly, which is hard because he's naked and warm and rumpled. "I think I'm going to have trouble walking this morning, let alone going on one of your route marches through the Cornish countryside."

"One time we went further than a mile, Oz. *One time*. You act like I'm inducting you into the SAS."

"I'm sure the SAS didn't have you pounding their arse all night."

He grins and rubs my bum. "Aw, are you sore?"

I nestle back into the bed and grab the sheets. "Yes. I think that the NHS Direct prescribes bed rest in these circumstances."

His eyebrow arches. "They've obviously got very worldly since I last rang them." He strokes my hair back. "You work so hard, Pika. Lie in today," he says, and it almost sounds like tenderness in his voice. I'm not sure because I've never had that directed at me by a man before.

I eye him, and he flushes slightly and gets up. "I'll walk the dogs."

He pads over to the window and looks out while stretching. I settle back into the sheets and watch him. This is my favourite part of every morning. Silas is one of the busiest people I know. He rushes here, there, and everywhere and consequently has no time for the gym. However, his work is so physical that he has an amazing body. He isn't gym-honed and doesn't have a perfect six-pack, but he's muscled and fit and very masculine.

I think this early morning tradition of standing at the window and stretching is his own version of yoga, when he stretches his body to be ready to meet the day and runs things through in that busy mind of his. I love it because his eyes are tranquil and content before the stresses of the day hit him.

I think back over the last month and relax into the mattress even more. It's been a strange and amazing time. If I'd been worried that the relationship would impact my work, I needn't have bothered. I'm not the type to take advantage. If anything, I work harder, and Silas has been so busy that the decisions have been left to me anyway.

However, the nights have been ours, and it's an old-fashioned word to use but I feel almost courted by him. We've criss-crossed across South Cornwall as he's shown me places that the tourists can't find. One night we loaded the dogs into the car and drove to a deserted cove. We'd walked them across the sands in the moonlight and talked and laughed. Another night he took me to a small pub on the cliffs where we ate mussels and drank a dry white wine while we watched a beautiful sunset lay stripes across the sea.

On the nights that he's worked, I've waited for him and cooked. One night I packed a picnic and we took it down to his cove where I lit candles that guttered in the breeze as we ate and talked. He laughed when he found the lube and condoms in the picnic basket, declaring his mother would have been horrified, but he stopped laughing when I stripped naked and rode him in the moonlight.

I swallow hard because the sex just keeps getting better and it was pretty fucking epic to start with. I have no experience of relationships, but I can definitely see the pros for them if this is what happens. That lack of experience, however, leaves me floundering slightly. We've made no ties or commitments, and my contract ends in a few weeks, but surely there shouldn't be this tenderness and care in something that should by definition be casual.

I'll catch him looking at me sometimes with a focused look in his eyes. I know that look has never been directed at me before. It combines intense interest and a lively affection, as if in that moment I'm everything he can see.

I run my tongue over my lips nervously because it isn't just him. He fascinates me. I've never met anyone who I can talk to like Silas. He's clever and dry and has a snarky, sarcastic tongue on him. However, he's also kind and decent and generous and sometimes I want to wrap him up in bubble wrap and save him from being hurt because his heart is so fucking wide open. My brow wrinkles because I don't want to be the one who hurts him, and I sense I could.

He turns from the window, and he looks so unconcerned by anything that I clear my expression because my mind is wandering this morning. I'm getting fanciful in my old age. He grabs a pair of old black shorts and a grey sweatshirt that says Hogwarts on it and rather geekily proclaims him to be a house captain at Quidditch. It's a favourite of his and it's so ancient that it's stretched out and the print is faded and barely legible. His eyes are sleepy and his face has a pillow mark down one cheek but he makes me warm inside.

I clear my throat. "No underwear, Silas. You're quite the hussy these days."

He laughs and makes a slow production of tucking his cock in and zipping up. I swallow hard as I feel my cock stir despite the fact that I started the morning off with two orgasms before I fell asleep again.

He stamps his feet into an old pair of checked Vans and I smile. He may have a title and a heritage that goes back centuries, but half the time he looks like a bit of a tramp. His clothes are good labels but they're old and comfortable and seem to mould to his body. In my clubbing days I'd have been horrified by his appearance, but here he fits. His hair is wild looking after a night of me pulling it and his beard needs trimming, but all I can see are those pretty eyes clear and green in the early morning light and the smile that tugs his pouty lips.

He cocks his head to one side. "Isn't today when your friend is coming?"

I grin and sit up, running my hands through my hair and enjoying the leisurely way he runs his eyes down my body. "It is."

"You look happy."

"I am. I've missed him."

He comes to stand by the bed, running his finger down the bedpost and tracing the delicate carving. "I suppose you miss London," he says, and his voice is too casual.

I narrow my eyes. For a split second I think about lying and saying I do. It will make the inevitable separation much easier if we get used to it. For a few wild moments over the last month my mind has toyed with the idea of a long-distance relationship, but I run into the same stumbling blocks every time. He's too busy to ever undertake that sort of relationship, and I'm not what he must be looking for.

With his title and history, he'll be looking to settle down with someone from the same class. Someone who won't embarrass him at social functions when I get the cutlery mixed up or my accent gets heavier. Someone without eyeliner and nail varnish and too-tight jeans. I picture the invisible man or woman and I sigh because they'll probably wear a lot of tweed and cord and have an accent you could cut glass with. My stomach churns.

"Oz?" he says, and I jerk.

"Sorry." I look into his eyes and I can't do it. I can't lie to him. "I don't miss London," I say in a low voice, my usually agile tongue tripping and stuttering. "I don't miss it at all."

His eyes flare for a second but then he shutters his expression and gives a calm smile. My eyes narrow. I went on a call once and watched him with a sick horse. If he uses that even voice with me, I'll punch him.

Luckily, he just swings away and grabs his watch from the side table. "I hope you're not working today," he says distractedly and therefore misses the guilty expression that I just know my face is wearing.

"Not at all," I say brightly. "I'm going to take him out for lunch and show him around."

"I'll be back fairly early tonight," he says and there's a definite wistful tone in his voice. "Do you think I'll have a chance to meet him?"

I still. I've been so concerned that Silas not be here for this meeting that I think I've given him the impression that I'm hiding him. My stomach twists in a way I've learnt to associate with disappointing him. I hate the idea that I've inadvertently hurt him. I come up on my knees. "Silas," I say urgently.

He turns back to me and stills when he sees me naked and kneeling in the sheets. I reach for him, and when he comes close I grab his face gently and cup his high cheekbones. "I would love you to meet Shaun," I say clearly. "I want him to meet you. You're both important to me."

His face lights up. "I am?" He stops and clears his throat. "I mean, that's lovely. I'll try and get back a bit earlier. Perhaps we could take him to that pub we ate at last week?"

"The one with the homemade fish cakes?" I ask, distracted at once, and he grins when my stomach rumbles.

"That's the one." He hesitates. "What do you think?"

"It's perfect," I declare, and he relaxes instantly.

"Okay, I'll book a table."

"Erm, ask for a bigger table," I say, thinking hard. "I know there are three of us, but you and Shaun are big men."

He looks puzzled but nods obligingly. "Okay, Pika."

"Don't call me that," I protest, but it dies to a moan as he pulls me to the edge of the bed and kneels and takes my cock down his throat in one swift, assured move.

I moan and tangle my hands in his thick, soft hair. I hate not telling him the full truth about today, but I don't want to get his hopes up. That's my last thought apart from *harder* and *oh my fucking god* before I fall back into the sheets in a tangled, sweaty mess.

∾

A couple of hours later I hear the sound of a car on the gravel at the front of the house and race to open the door. I fling it open and dart down the steps in time to see Shaun getting out and stretching as if it was a clown car rather than a very swanky BMW.

I whistle. "Nice car."

"Obviously not mine," he says wryly, laughing as I fling myself at him and hug him tight.

"It's so good to see you," I whisper, and he chuckles.

"I've missed you too, Ozzy."

He grabs me in a tight hug and I inhale the scent of Shaun which is one part weed to two parts Calvin Klein aftershave. It smells like home, or at least what home used to smell like.

I step back and he grins. "Bloody hell, Oz, you look good."

I look down at myself. "Really?"

He nods. "Those bags have gone under your eyes and you look—" He hesitates. "You look rested."

"That makes me sound like an OAP."

He shrugs. "I can't put my finger on it."

"Well, don't. You'll catch something."

He bursts out laughing and I smile at him affectionately. The next second he jerks. "What the hell is that?"

I look behind me and find Chewwy staring rather gloomily at Shaun. "It's Chewwy."

"Is it a yeti?"

"Yes, of course he is. Man has searched for the mythical creature for years when they could have just caught the train to Cornwall."

I hear the sound of a door opening and I turn to see the other occupant of the car easing out of the driving seat. "Fuck, that was a shitty drive," he says. "We got stuck behind a whole row of fucking caravans. Who the hell would ever want one of those?"

I look at his outfit of perfectly ironed beige shorts and a white shirt and his sleek appearance and grin. "I'm trying to imagine you in one, Jasper, but it's just not coming."

"Not usually a problem of yours," he says, and I shake my head, looking at one of my old hook-ups. I met Jasper at uni. He's from a very well-to-do family and I'd been fascinated by him for a long time. He's funny, good looking, and effortlessly confident. We shared a house for a year and I willingly shared my arse, but we never moved beyond casual hook-up status despite my hidden wish. I'd taken him home once and the almost horrified fascination on his face had woken me up quicker than a bucket of water in the face. I'd ended things when we got back to uni, and after a slightly rocky reaction to that we'd moved into friendship.

He comes around the car and I look at him for a long second. I can't help comparing him to Silas. Jasper is sleek and rich, like a Siamese cat who will always find the sunny side of any street. Silas is more battle weary. He wears his years on his face but it's a face that fascinates me. I become aware that I'm staring and jump when he pulls me into a hug.

He pushes his nose into my neck and inhales deeply. "You still smell the same," he murmurs. "Mmm, I like it."

I wriggle back instantly. "Oi, watch the hands, Mr Grabby."

He laughs but jumps back when Chewwy gives a low growl. "What the *fuck*?"

Shaun laughs. "Oz's yeti doesn't like you, Jasper. Better watch your step. He looks like he might rip your throat out," he adds with gloomy relish.

"Of course he wouldn't," I scold. "He's very gentle." I look at Chewwy, who's watching Jasper intently. "He'd be more likely to gloom you to death," I coo, bending down to pet him. "Wouldn't you, my furry baby?"

I look up and find Shaun and Jasper studying me as if I'm an exhibit in a museum. I flush. "Are you here to examine me or the house?" I ask, and as if synchronised they turn to look at the building.

"Oh my God, Oz," Shaun breathes. "It's so beautiful."

The house is looking its best today, the mellow honey gold of the stones standing out against a periwinkle-blue sky. I feel a sense of pride and instantly want to fucking kick myself. This isn't my house. I don't have a house, and what home I have is in London with Shaun and my mum.

I shake my head. "What do you think?" I say to Jasper.

He's less moved, probably because his family are very wealthy, but he's still staring contemplatively at the house and chewing on the end of his sunglasses. "It looks good," he finally says, and I nudge him.

"Okay, Captain Cryptic. Do you want to look around outside?"

He nods, and as we walk Shaun flings his arm around my shoulder. "What's it like living here?" he whispers as Jasper paces ahead of us, stopping now and then to take a shot with the expensive camera on his shoulder.

I shrug. "It's a house, Shaun. Just bigger than most. It took me a while to get used to it, but it's not home or anything."

"I never said anything about it being home," he says in a bewildered voice, and we both look up as Jasper stops.

"How far do his lands stretch?"

"Erm, I'm not sure, but as far as the eye can see."

"Does it include the headland over there?"

I nod. "Oh yes. That's all Silas's."

"Silas?" Jasper enquires.

"The Earl of Ashworth."

He shoots me a strange look. "You call him Silas? Hmm."

"Well, I do work for him and he's really relaxed around the staff."

I smile at the thought of him up that ladder dusting cobwebs, then flush when I realise Shaun is staring at me. He opens his mouth to say something, but Jasper interrupts him.

"Can we look inside?"

I gesture him inside and we blink as our eyes adjust to the Great Hall. Jasper looks around at the huge mullioned windows, the carved wooden panels, and the massive stone fireplace. "Shit," he says and then whistles.

I laugh. "I know. I said the same thing."

"Are they the original curtains? What a bag of shit. They look like they're about to disintegrate."

I shoot him a killing glare. "That's not the only thing that will disintegrate if you don't keep your shitty remarks to yourself."

He turns to me, his mouth slightly open. "Really?"

I nod. "I won't have it. This is a lovely house, Jasper, and the people here are lovely too. Don't be crappy. Money might be short but fucking decency isn't."

He stares at me for a long second and then nods slowly as if he's realised something. "Okay," he says quietly. "Show me the rest."

I nod sternly and, aware of Shaun looking at me open-mouthed, I show him over the house, letting him poke into cupboards and open doors. When he's finally finished looking and taken what must be the one billionth photograph, I lead them down to the kitchen and put the kettle to boil on the Aga.

Bustling around the kitchen, I make coffee and huge doorstep sandwiches using the fresh bread that Maggie baked this morning and ham from the village butcher. They fall on the food with gusto and for a while we eat and chat about friends and family.

Finally, when they've finished, I push my chair back and look at Jasper. "Going to tell me what you're looking for?"

He grins. "Do you remember *The Pendarke Saga?*"

I nod. "The steampunk series you were addicted to at uni?" He nods and I sit up straight. "Get out. *Really?* They're filming that?"

He nods again. "I've been sent here to scope out properties to film in. Cornwall will be fantastic for the world of the series, and the producers want a really special house for the family." He smiles. "Your call came at just the right moment."

I can feel my heart beating fast. I hold my breath. "And?"

He lets the silence last for far longer than anyone should and then grins. "I think it's fucking perfect. I looked at the Branton estate up the road." I can't help my grimace, but he doesn't notice as he's reaching for his diary and looking at his notes. "It was just too perfect. I know I was a bit sneery about the slightly tumbledown appearance of this but it's actually just what the producers want."

I punch my fist in the air. "Yes!" Then I straighten up. "How much will they pay?"

Shaun laughs and Jasper grins. "You're like a fucking pimp with money, Oz. Nothing ever changes."

"I watch my money. No one else will," they intone together, and I stick my finger up at them.

"How much?"

He grins and gives me an astronomical figure. I make sure my only reaction is a slow blink. "Is that it? Can you make it more?"

He stares at me. "This means a lot to you, doesn't it?" I nod, and he shakes his head, leaning forward. "Okay. That's the bottom line they're prepared to pay, but confidentially I can tell you to add another zero when you bargain." He looks at the old kitchen. "They're going to want this."

I nod. "And will you need us to do anything?" I pause. "You won't damage the house, will you?"

He shakes his head immediately. "Of course not. We're extremely careful. We'll put our own stuff up anyway, but we take every care to leave everything as we find it." He shudders slightly, and I smile. He carries on. "It's good for the local area, anyway. The crew will use the local hotels and bed and breakfasts for accommodation and once the series hits the TV, the tourists will come. Shaun says the earl's thinking of opening to the public?" I nod and he shrugs. "Well then, more for the pot." He pauses. "I'll have to talk to him anyway before we go back."

There's a short silence as I bite my lip and Shaun nudges me. "Confess, Ozzy. It'll make you happier." I grin. It's a well-used phrase that he got from my mum.

"I might not have told him yet."

"*What?*" Jasper explodes, and I hold my hands up.

"Don't worry, he'll be absolutely fine with it. I just didn't want to get his hopes up."

He nods. "I'm just nipping outside to make a phone call." He looks around the house. "Fucking Cornish phone reception."

Silence falls until Shaun stirs. "You didn't want to get his *hopes* up?"

I flush. "Shut up."

Shaun shakes his head. "I'm not sure how the aristocracy works, but I'm pretty certain that their staff don't keep things from them because they don't want them to be upset."

I jump up and gather their plates together and throw the scraps into the bin. "He's different. You'll see."

"Oh, what have you done, Oz?" Shaun intones. That's a well-used phrase too, by the way.

"I haven't done anything." I avoid his eyes by stacking the plates in the dishwasher.

"How old is this earl?"

"Erm, about thirty-seven, I think," I say, my voice awkward as I bend over the sink.

"Well, that's a relief."

I spin round. "What?"

He grins, his face dear and familiar. "I thought he was in his eighties and you'd embarked on a hobby of necrophilia."

"You're disgusting," I breathe, and he laughs harder.

"Whatever. You're obviously fucking him." He shakes his head. "You know what, Oz. I reckon you've got a boss fetish."

"Oh, fuck off," I mutter as he laughs harder, holding his sides.

"You'd be fucking murder on *The Apprentice*."

I come back to the table and slump in my chair. "I'm an idiot."

He shakes his head. "That remains to be seen."

"How?"

"I need to meet him and ask him what his intentions are." He puffs up his chest. "I must make sure that my beloved Ozzy is not being used and thrown away by a member of the nobility and left destitute and shamed in the dirt."

"Christ, you've been reading Catherine Cookson too," comes an amused posh voice from the kitchen door.

We both jump. "Silas," I breathe.

At that moment Jasper comes into the kitchen. "I've cleared it with production. They'll need to talk to your boss." Not seeing Silas, he ambles over to the table and bends over me. "Want to celebrate, Oz? As I recall, you give the best celebrations."

Silas's face clouds over. "What's going on?" he asks in a very hostile voice.

CHAPTER 14

I'M QUITE SURE THIS NEVER HAPPENS IN CROWN GREEN BOWLING

Oz

I shoot up from my chair and race over to Silas, grabbing his arm and dragging him to face Shaun.

"Shaun, this is Silas," I say and grin at Silas. "This is my best friend."

His expression clears slightly and he smiles at Shaun. "I'm so pleased to meet you. Oz has told me a lot about you."

Shaun hesitates because Silas's voice when he's feeling awkward is very cut glass, but he looks closely at the man. He must see the gentle eyes and kind smile that I see because he relaxes and puts out his hand to shake. "I hope not too much."

Silas smiles. "You know Oz. The line between those two is very thin."

Shaun throws his head back and laughs loudly and I see Jasper's eyes narrow on Silas, speculation on his face.

I turn quickly to Silas. "Can I talk to you?" I ask urgently.

He stares at me, his brow furrowing. "Of course," he finally says. "Study?"

I nod and with a quick "I'll be back" to the men I race after him, trying to catch up with his long strides. He walks into the study and I follow him, turning to face him as he shuts the door.

"You'll never guess–" I start to say.

"Who's that man?" he asks, interrupting me with a very focused look on his face.

"Oh. Oh shit. I forgot to introduce you. That's Jasper and he's from–"

"Is he an old boyfriend from London?"

I stare at him. "Sentences usually end with a full stop and a pause. You're usually better at conversation than this."

He doesn't smile. "Well?"

I fidget. "Well, I wouldn't say he was an old boyfriend."

"He's a *current* one?" His voice rises. "I thought you were single."

I gape at him. "I am single," I say slowly. He flinches slightly and my eyes narrow. "What the fuck?" Then I realise what I just said. "I mean I'm not sleeping with anyone else." His shoulders relax slightly but his eyes are still turbulent. "I knew him at uni, and yes we have slept together, but that's old news."

"It looked to me like he wanted the old news to wrap his hot chips in."

I stare at him. "That is singlehandedly the oddest euphemism I've ever heard." I jerk. "You're *jealous*."

He shrugs awkwardly. "No, I'm not."

"Yes, you are. You're totally jealous."

"And if I am?"

Without even thinking about it I step into him and hug him, resting my head on his chest and feeling his arms automatically come down to hold me. "Then it's adorable," I say softly.

His body stiffens, and he puts me back enough to look at me. "You don't mind?"

I shake my head. "Why on earth would I mind?"

"Well, it's not very attractive. You're not a piece of meat and I don't own you."

"Who said it wasn't attractive? Oh, Silas, cut yourself some bloody slack. You aren't beating him up or shouting and swinging from the beams. A bit of jealousy shows you care."

"I do care," he says slowly. "Oz, I–"

"I can't wait anymore. I have something amazing to tell you," I exclaim and shove him into his chair. I then immediately climb into his lap and straddle him. "That's better," I say happily. "All our meetings should be like this."

He swallows hard and it seems like he's going to say something, but he hesitates and then smiles. "I'm not sure an employment tribunal would approve."

"Pshaw. We don't abide by silly things like that."

He grabs my arse and lifts me into him. "You'd be amazing in Brexit negotiations." He looks at me. "Okay, tell me, now that you have me captive."

"Come closer." He leans in and I whisper into his ear. When I come to the figure his eyes widen. I lean back. "Well? What do you think?"

He looks at me and I can't read his expression fully. There's excitement there and happiness but something else.

"You did this for me?"

I stare at him, something in the atmosphere killing any joke I'd make. "Yes," I say simply. "I didn't want to say anything because I didn't want to get your hopes up."

"And you're not interested in Jasper?"

"Are you not happy?" I ask uncertainly but he looks at me stubbornly, so I shake my head. "No," I say firmly. "Not at all. That ship set sail a long time ago. It's probably docked and sold for spare parts by now."

A smile spreads across his face wider than anything I've seen. "Okay, now I'm excited. Jesus Christ, Oz. This will cut a huge wedge out of the debts. I could probably clear one of them."

"And Jasper says once one production company comes calling they all sniff around, and think of the tourists." I pause. "Oh my God, we should totally stock the books and any other memorabilia they have in our shop."

He shoots me a curious look, but I ignore him. I try to wriggle off him and his arms tighten. "Where are you going?"

"To get my diary. This is amazing."

"No. When I blow you it's going to be amazing. Notes in your diary are just meh."

I grin at him and trace one finger over his eyebrow. "You're going to blow me? Why, Lord Ashworth. When you have guests here too. What a cad you are." I laugh as he dumps me off his lap. "What are you doing?"

"Locking the door," he says. "But maybe don't do your impression of someone from *A Woman of Substance* until we're finished. It's a bit off-putting."

It's hard to laugh when someone has your cock in their mouth, but for a full few seconds I manage it.

∼

Later that evening we sit over dessert and coffee. Silas and Jasper are talking intently about provisions for livestock and restrictions around the estate, so Shaun and I are footloose and fancy-free.

Shaun's looking at Silas contemplatively and I can't stand it anymore.

I nudge him. "So, what do you think?"

He turns to look at me. "I really like him."

I sag a bit in relief. They'd talked and laughed over dinner, but you never know with Shaun because he keeps a lot close to his chest. "Oh, that's good." He shoots me a knowing look and I flush. "Because obviously he's my boss and I like that you think he's okay."

"Yeah," he says, elongating the word, so I poke him. He snorts with laughter and Silas and Jasper look up. Silas gives Shaun a wide smile, but he and Jasper instantly return to their conversation.

I sip my coffee. "So, does that mean you're not going to lecture me?"

"When do I ever lecture you, Ozzy?"

I shake my head. "You lecture that much you should work at a university."

He laughs but then falls silent, staring across the table at Silas who has his head bent over some plans that Jasper has. "I don't think I'm going to lecture you this time."

"Why?" I hesitate. "Not that it means anything. I mean, I'm only here for another few weeks and then I'll be back home with you."

He turns to me and there's something almost sad about his face. "Sure, you will, Ozzy. Sure, you will."

I open my mouth to argue but the waitress comes with the bill. As we stand up he seizes my arm. "Did you say you were coming up to London soon?"

"Yes. I need a dinner suit for the party and Silas needs to look at some deeds at his solicitor's office. Why?"

"Why don't you show him around, take him to some of your old haunts."

I stare at him. "You want me to take the Earl of Ashworth to the Pig and Fiddle in Tottenham and then maybe to Mungos for Bear Night?"

"Why not?" There's something challenging in his eyes that I can't work out. "After all, you call him Silas and that's who you're involved with. So why not show *Silas* your old life?"

"It isn't my old life. It's my *actual* life. I'll be back in a few weeks."

"Then it won't hurt, will it? It might show you something that you're happily ignoring at the moment."

"What am I ignoring?" I'm totally bewildered and it shows in my voice.

He shrugs and hugs me. "What's staring you in the face. The difference this time around."

"You're so cryptic today I think it's time for you to read *The Da Vinci Code*."

He laughs and nothing more is said.

~

Later on, I wander out of the house and into the gardens with Chewwy at my heels. The heatwave is slowly cooling as we head into September and the night has a delicate bite to it now, a harbinger of autumn. I look around at the gardens which are a riot of last-minute blowsy colour and sigh. I won't be here when the trees turn colour and the winds roar around the house. I'll be in London, working in another office.

I wonder fancifully if a part of me will stay here and roam the halls with Lionel. Maybe we'll become drinking buddies and look critically at Silas's next choice of bedmate. My stomach twists and I rub it absentmindedly. I'm not thinking of that now. I have a few weeks left with him and I'm going to make the most of it.

At the thought of him, I wonder where he is. Then on the breeze I hear a faint thud and a clinking coming from the far end of the gardens. This is a much wilder, isolated area where the apple orchard can be found along with an overgrown grassy area where, according to Silas, the Home Guard used to do their drills during the war. The sheep are often in the fields nearest to it, so their bleating and complaining drifts in.

The old bowling green is also there, and I smile when I step onto the grass and see that my guess was right. Silas is just standing up from straightening the rows of skittles that are now as orderly as a military parade. He's drinking from a bottle of Jack Daniels and dressed in a pair of denim cutoffs, their ends white with age, and a faded red Edinburgh University t-shirt. He looks like a student and completely at home.

He smiles widely when he sees me and holds one arm out in invitation. I wander into his embrace immediately and feel his arm close around me. Chewwy slumps down under a blackberry bush and gives a gusty sigh of contentment.

Silas grins and kisses the top of my head before handing me the bottle. I take a sip, the alcohol heating my throat, and sigh happily.

"Have they gone?" he asks.

"Yes. They've gone back to the hotel tonight and back to London tomorrow."

"They could have stayed here and been welcome."

I smile. "I know. Thank you. Shaun would have been happy to, but I think it's probably best that Jasper doesn't experience firsthand the idiosyncrasies of our house before we rent it out."

Something about that statement makes him smile but he covers it quickly. "Like the cupboard in the kitchen when the handle comes off in your hand?"

I nod. "And the toilet where you have to put your hand into the cistern to be able to flush it."

He laughs. "It never happens in Lord Branton's house."

I stand for a minute, enjoying the warmth of the sun and inhaling the scent of cut grass and Silas's aftershave. Finally, I stir with Shaun's words on my mind. They'd seemed like a challenge and an invitation to see something about Silas that I'm not noticing. "So, when are you thinking of going to London?"

He kisses my hair. "Next week. I'll only be a couple of hours with the solicitor. Then we can get your suit and afterwards whatever you fancy. What about a play?"

I shake my head. "Nope. It'll seem too confining in a theatre after Minack." He looks extraordinarily pleased and I carry on hurriedly. "Where are we staying?"

"In a hotel? There's a nice one in Knightsbridge."

I take a glug of Jack Daniels and my thoughts whirl. *Am I really going to do this?* I think of James and his disdain for my upbringing, Jasper who barely concealed his astonishment and some of the others, and my mind is made up. It's a test and I know he'll fail. It's awful of me but it might be the jumpstart I need to get my life going when I get back to London. I've done nothing so far, as if in my head I'm staying with him eternally.

"Why don't we stay with my mum?"

I thought he'd be horrified and polite, but instead he grins. "Really? She won't mind?"

I shrug awkwardly. "She'll be fine. Anyway, she'd go barmy if I didn't go home when I was in London, and you don't want to risk the wrath of an Irish woman."

He laughs. "Okay then. Give her a ring and arrange it. Shall we say Tuesday?"

I nod, incapable of coherent speech. I settle for looking at the old game. "Is this like bowling?"

He steps back and grins. "Sort of. It's Kayling. It's been played in Cornwall for at least five hundred years."

"Oh, that explains why I've heard this called the Kayling Lawn?"

He nods. "The skittles are called by their Cornish name, kayles. The ball is called a cheese." He points at the two groupings of baluster-shaped skittles. "This is a really old set."

I laugh. "I'm trying to imagine a game of cosmic bowling like they do at home. We could paint them neon and play trance music."

A shadow chases across his face when I mention home, but he smiles. "I will even provide you with clown shoes that give you a foot fungus to make the experience truly worthwhile." I laugh and he shrugs. "Bowling used to be restricted by law to the rich, but the locals always used to come here and have a game when I was little."

"Your father let the peasants that near the house?"

"He locked the windows and had a constable on duty," he says in a snooty voice and I throw my head back and laugh, feeling my worries melt away. "Fancy a game?" he asks and there's a glint in his eye.

"Why am I getting nervous?"

He shrugs. "I don't know. Maybe you're shit and you don't want me to know."

I laugh. "Trash talking. Really, Silas?"

He nods. "It's the only way to do it."

He looks up at the sky, which is a deep blue shot through with red, and taps his finger against his lips in a thinking pose which is belied by the twinkle in his eyes. "Why don't we make this interesting?"

"How?"

"Strip Kayling."

"What the *fuck*?" I laugh loudly. "Oh my God, have you no shame? This is a part of your *heritage*."

He shrugs. "So is interbreeding and alcoholism. Well?"

I straighten. My competitive nature is raising its head. "Okay, what are the rules?"

"The one who knocks over the least amount of kayles with one throw of the ball has to lose one item of clothing. The winner gets to ask a question of their choice and the loser has to answer honestly."

I stare at him. "That's extraordinarily detailed for an off-the-cuff game. You'll be telling me next that you've got membership cards printed out."

"Only little ones, but they are laminated very nicely. And you'll get the hang of the words to the club song when you've sung it once."

I laugh. "I'm quite sure this never happens in crown green bowling."

He grins. "You on?"

I curl my fingers at him. "Bring it on."

He hands me the large ball. It's heavy and cold. "Okay, short stuff. Give it your best shot."

I snort. "Fuck me. That's terrible heckling." I pass him the ball and stand back. "I insist you go first. Age before beauty."

He shakes his head wryly and rolls his ball hard at the row of skittles. Unfortunately, it hits a lump of grass and it sends it off course ending up with ... "No kayles knocked over," I say gleefully.

He laughs. "I'm starting to detect a very competitive streak in you, Ozzy."

I smile evilly. "I'm a very sore loser."

His gaze drops to my lower half. "You will be," he promises.

I feel my cock stir and shake my head. "Do not distract me with your sexual wiles, you jezebel."

I take the ball from him and bowl it smartly down my run and then jump and cheer when it knocks over four kayles.

I turn to find him grinning at me. I tap a finger against my teeth, affecting deep thought. "Okay, get rid of some clothes, loser."

He throws his head back and laughs. "Very well." He reaches down and unties the laces on his faded navy Converse and kicks them off.

"Spoilsport."

"Yep." He grins. "Okay, ask me your question."

"What is the naughtiest thing you did as a teenager?" I love hearing funny stories of him and his brother.

He thinks hard. "Jesus, that's difficult. We did so much. Okay, once we put laxatives in my father's tea."

I laugh. "Did he deserve it?"

"Oh, totally. The old bastard. I don't think he quite deserved the *quantity* we put in though. He sat on the toilet for so long that the loo seat had an imprint of his buttocks."

I throw my head back and laugh. He starts to put the skittles back into order and I help him. He grins at me. "Prepare to go down. I know the lay of the course now."

I nudge him. "Pride goes before a fall."

A minute later I watch as he does some sort of strange victory dance that makes him look rather like a dying chicken. He stops and grins at me. "Aren't you supposed to be losing something?"

I smile slowly at him before reaching down and pulling my t-shirt off. His eyes darken and I grin at him. "Only wusses remove shoes first."

He shakes his head. "Okay, my question for you is, what is the stupidest thing you did as a child?"

I grin. "I ran away from home once and decided to hitchhike back to Ireland."

"Why?"

"Isn't that another question?" He shoves me and I relent. "I didn't like London when we arrived. I hated it because I'd run very free in Ireland. Anyway, matters came to a head when my mum refused to let me watch the Brit Awards so I packed up all my worldly belongings and headed out."

"How far did you get?"

I laugh. "The bus stop. It was raining and dark and I knew my mum was making a fish pie, so I headed back and we watched *Coronation Street* instead." I laugh. "I know you're thinking what a rebel I am."

He grins and hands me the ball. "I might be too intimidated by your bad boy reputation now to play at my best."

A few minutes later I grin. "I don't think there's any 'might' about it. Lose something interesting this time."

He smirks and takes a very long time to remove his top. I stare at his wide, hairy chest and the way his shorts hang from his narrow hips, showing the skin that I know is as soft as silk and drives him mad when it's kissed. I look up to find his lips quirked queryingly and jerk. "Oh yes, my question. Let me see. I know. How old were you when you lost your virginity?"

He whistles in appreciation. "Good one. Which gender?"

I swallow. "Both."

"Okay. Fifteen to a girl and sixteen to a boy." I look at him and he smiles. "There was very little in the way of entertainment at boarding school," he says wryly. "What about you?"

I grin. "I thought I won the question."

"This is for the hill of grass on my side of the run."

"That's not a hill. It's a pouch." I smile. "I was fifteen."

"Was it good?"

I shake my head. "No, but I thought I was in love, so it didn't matter." I laugh. "I should have known better. He told everyone at school about it and I got beaten up and my head stuck down a toilet."

His face darkens. "What a little fucker." He pauses. "What did you do?"

I stare at him for a second, struck that he already knows me well enough to guess I did something.

"I told everyone he had a four-inch penis, suffered from premature ejaculation, and called me mummy when he came." He laughs loudly and I smile. "Shaun helped spread the rumour." I pause. "Actually, I think Shaun is still spreading the rumour."

I hand him the ball. "Try and challenge me this time, please," I say in a bored voice.

Half an hour later I'm dressed in my briefs and one sock while he's wearing just a smile and listing slightly from the bottle of Jack Daniels we've finished.

I look at him and laugh, but my mouth waters at the sight of all that tanned skin and hair and the long cock that's plumping up nicely. "Don't you think I've won?" I ask. "You have nothing left to lose."

"Only my virtue," he says primly. "I play to the death, Oz. Now bowl." I go to throw the ball and he steps beside me. "Afterwards I'm going to fuck you against that tree."

"You wouldn't dare," I say, trying to sound modest, but I know I'm failing.

He would dare. One of the things that I've found out about Silas is that he's shameless. In bed he's amazing. He's earthy with a bawdy sense of humour and lacks any inhibitions. He does whatever feels good and he's not afraid to laugh. Sex has never felt like it does with him. Immediate and raw and fun.

I'd thought he would just top but he's happy to bottom too. It's not my preferred position, but the other night he'd asked to be fucked, and pushing down on him and into him brought me a pleasure I've never felt so strongly. I'd crouched over him, watching my cock shiny with lube disappear into his arse as he groaned and panted beneath me.

"Oh look," he says happily. "Someone likes the idea."

I look down at my hard-on which is barely contained by my electric blue briefs, the head poking out impudently, and then shake my head. "I will not fall for your diversionary tactics," I say loftily and throw the ball.

I don't get the chance to look where it lands because at that moment he grabs me and turns me, taking my mouth with a deep groan. His callused hands slide my briefs down, throwing them impatiently over his shoulder.

"Fuck! I can't believe we're doing this," I say. "Are you sure we can't be seen?"

From a pocket in his shorts he produces a condom and a small sachet of lube. "No. But I don't care anyway. If someone wants to spy on us, then they must accept the eye bleach they'll need afterwards."

"I like your attitude," I laugh, but it turns into a groan as he backs me up to the tree and kisses me hard. He fucks me against it ruthlessly, waiting until I've come twice before he finds his own release. When we finish we're covered in sweat, and we half collapse, half lower ourselves to the ground.

"I like Kayling," I say slowly, hearing the slur in my voice. "I think I'm quite good at it. I could take it up professionally."

He chuckles from his position lying crossways with his head pillowed on my stomach so I can stroke his hair. "I don't think professionally you'll be required to strip."

"Oh," I say in a disappointed voice. "I won't bother then." I glance towards the kayles and poke him. "Hey," I say indignantly. "I fucking won that last round. You totally cheated."

He laughs and snuggles closer, patting my hand demandingly to resume the stroking of hair. "You can have your question then."

My question must be borne from my soft feelings of satiation and contentment because I'd never fucking ask it normally. "What do you most want in a boyfriend?"

Other men might have answered with looks or money or just lied, but Silas's answer is simple and honest to his bones. "I want someone to love me for just me. Someone who will watch out for me and someone who will feel like home."

"That's lovely," I say hoarsely. He doesn't reply which is good because I want to shout, *I can do that. I want to be your home.*

I don't. Instead I lie naked with him hidden in the shadow of the tree, stroking his hair on a drowsy summer's evening and wishing I had more time.

CHAPTER 15

WHY DON'T YOU EVER PERFORM ACCORDING TO EXPECTATIONS?

Oz

The drive to London is relatively pain free. Silas has an appointment with his solicitors and I need to get a dinner suit, so we separate with a kiss and a promise to meet at a pub nearby in a few hours.

I walk off, my lips still feeling sensitive. I look back, but he's gone, and for a second everything feels strange, like I've been set adrift on an unfamiliar sea.

I love London. It's been my home since I was twelve and came over from Ireland with my mum. I love the history, the bustle of the dirty streets, and the sudden quiet when you come into some backwater. However, today I feel like my twelve-year-old self again. Everything feels wrong, as if I've tried to put on someone else's clothes.

There are just so many people. They shove past me, rude in their rush to get somewhere, and everyone seems to be en route to something important. And the noise. Buses and car engines. Horns blaring and the asthmatic wheeze as a bus drops another load of people off to join the throng.

At first, I can't place the problem, but then I realise. I've lost my edge. Before Cornwall I was one of this throng. I was fast and impatient. I'd move quickly, coffee in hand, eyes on somewhere further along the road, elbows out and with that hip-swivelling strut of someone who knows that this is my home.

Now, I'm used to a slower pace in everything. I'm used to a wide-open space where the noise comes from the sea or the sheep in the field. The smells around me now are beeswax and lavender and salt, not car exhaust and someone's perfume that's choking in close proximity.

It's lunchtime, and I remember my lunch the other day which was spent in the knot garden with Silas, who'd stolen some time in between calls. We ate thick doorstep sandwiches of cheese and ham and drank fresh coffee while the sun beat down on us from a clear blue sky and bees buzzed busily and importantly. We talked and laughed and it seemed like there was just us in the world. Well, us and Sid, who was snoring behind an Elderberry bush.

For the first time I feel a shard of worry. What happens when I come back here? I'd thought that eventually Cornwall would just be a faraway place in my memory, but what if that doesn't happen and instead London is the stranger and I'll be trying to move through it without a map?

I shake my head at the silly thoughts and plough through the crowds, brightening as I see Shaun waiting outside John Lewis. He grins as soon as he spots me and wades through the shoppers to grab me in a big hug.

"How are you?" he mutters. "It seems almost strange to see you here."

I jerk. "God, I was just thinking that. It feels weird being here."

"Bound to," he says comfortingly. "You're used to something different now."

"Well, that's just silly. It took me ages to get used to London. I've only been in Cornwall for five fucking minutes."

He looks at me thoughtfully. "Perhaps that's because Cornwall feels more like home." I open my mouth, but he carries on talking. "I remember when you first came here; you were a country boy through and through. Maybe that never left you. Maybe you're more at home in the peace and quiet." He shrugs. "Or maybe it's the company you're keeping nowadays."

His words stick with me through the long, sweaty process of buying a dinner suit and they stay as I bitch and moan my way through the cramped underground journey. I look around at the compartment stuffed as full of people as a tin of sardines. Then I breathe in deeply and choke slightly at the odour that fills the area. It's like fish left out in the sun.

Shaun shakes his head. "Rookie mistake." I shoot him a finger and he laughs.

We push ourselves off the train, then fight our way up the stairs and through the ticket machines, but even when we're out I feel itchy and grumpy. I tug at my shirt irritably and look up at the pub we've arranged to meet Silas in. It's one of our old haunts, principally because the beer is cheap and Mick, the owner, turns a blind eye to everything going on. It's hard to care too much when you're asleep at the end of your own bar.

Now, I look up at the dirty windows, the peeling paint, and the sign swinging in the slight breeze that would proclaim the pub's name if anyone had a few buckets of soapy water.

"Why did I agree to meet him here?" I say faintly.

"Because it's near home and you needed alcohol before you introduced him to your mum," Shaun says placidly. "If you have too much to drink, you're hoping that you won't have to do it and we can just carry you home unconscious."

"That sounds horrible," I groan. "I love my mum. I'm not ashamed of her."

"Of course you're not," he says simply. "You're just a bit scarred by introducing her to some of the pricks that came before."

"I don't want him to look at me like they did," I whisper.

He turns on me fiercely. "Stop it," he says crossly. "That's not going to happen and there are two very good reasons for that." He holds up a finger. "One, he isn't that type of bloke. He's real class and I don't mean titles and posh houses. I mean he's decent and honest and he cares about people. I felt at home with him instantly even in that big fucking house. He's got the ability to put people at ease because he cares about them. That's class and there aren't too many people like that."

I feel a surge of warmth and smile at him as I wait. And wait. "Hang on, that's only one reason."

"What?" he says, turning to open the door and letting out a tide of air that combines stale beer and cigarette smoke because Mick persists in ignoring EU regulations. He acts like he's fucking Robin Hood, but in reality he can't pack up himself and he's usually too lazy or pissed to go outside.

I persist. "That's one reason. You said there were two reasons for why it wouldn't happen with him."

"Did I? What a forgetful little thing I am. I'll probably remember later."

I look around and groan. *This place looks worse every second. What was I thinking?*

A great roar of laughter and cheers comes from the bar. "Well, would you look at that?" Shaun says.

"Is Mick's wife stripping again?" I ask idly, looking round for Silas and not seeing him. *Did he take one look and run back to Sloane Street checking his Rolex on the way?*

"No, but she looks like she's thinking about it," Shaun says cheerfully. "No. Look at that."

He steps back and my mouth falls open. Silas is standing at the bar, apparently buying a round for a group of men he appears to be playing … darts with. I watch as they clap him on the back and he steps towards the dartboard, darts in one hand and a pint in the other. I look at the men and blink.

"When did Vic get out of prison?"

"Last week. Reckon he's making the most of his time off before he goes back in."

"He's not an oil rig worker," I snipe. "What the fuck is going on here?"

Silas throws his darts to more loud cheering. He turns around and Shaun whistles. Looking up, he sees us, and a huge grin crosses his face. "Hey," he shouts. "Come here."

I shake my head and rush over. He hugs me and gives me a quick kiss to many catcalls but luckily no abuse. Mick's son is gay and it's a sure way to see his baseball bat come out from behind the bar if you say anything homophobic.

"Alright, Ozzy?" Vic says, grabbing the darts from Silas. "How you doing?"

"Fine, mate. How about you?"

"Not so bad. Enjoying the freedom before I have to start again. You've got a fucking good bloke here." He leans forward and whispers, "I can't understand a word he says though. Is he German?"

He wheels off, bouncing off the side of the jukebox as he goes. I watch his progress. "You do know he doesn't work on the cruise liners, don't you?" I mutter and Silas laughs.

"I figured that out after a bit. I thought at first he was in the army."

I laugh and he grins at me before giving Shaun a smile of thanks as he hands him a pint and gives me mine.

"Cheers," Shaun says, clinking glasses with Silas. "I'll be glad to hand Ozzy over to you, to be honest."

"Why?" Silas looks startled.

"Because he's turning into a whiny little bitch."

I shove him. "Oh, fuck off. I'm not."

"Yes, you are." He raises his voice in a terrible parody of mine. "Oh, London is so busy nowadays. How I long for my Cornish manor house and the peace and serenity of the Elizabethan knot garden. Blah blah wooden carvings blah blah."

"Please don't consider a career on the stage," I say sourly as Silas throws his head back and laughs loudly.

He hugs me. "It's a bit weird, isn't it? I feel it every time I come here."

I feel the weight of his arm on my shoulder and inhale the clean scent of him, and for the first time all day I feel centred and calm. I smile. "Don't let Shaun bang on too much. He'll be telling you about the day the local perv flashed him. Shaun hadn't got his glasses on and ran after the man, trying to tell him that his belt had fallen on the ground and his coat was open."

"Oh, fuck off," Shaun mouths as Silas bursts into peals of laughter before persuading us into a few raucous rounds of darts.

It's almost five o'clock when we emerge from the pub. Shaun reels off up the street towards home after promising to meet us for breakfast in the morning and after many long hugs with Silas, who he seems to have taken a real liking to.

Silas turns to me. "Alone at last," he says, grinning and slinging his bag over his shoulder.

"Did you get your legal stuff done?" I ask, grabbing my own backpack and gesturing for him to follow me.

"I did."

He falls into step beside me but when we come to a florist, he stops. "Wait here. I just need to get something I ordered earlier."

I wait outside patiently and blink when he emerges with a gigantic bunch of lilies.

"You did say that these were your mum's favourite flowers, didn't you?" he asks, sounding worried.

"I did," I say faintly. "About a month ago in an aside. How the fuck did you remember that?"

He shrugs, looking a little bashful. "Because you told me," he says simply. "That makes it important."

I stare at his warm face and clear greeny-gold eyes and he looks back calmly. I sigh. "What do you want from me?" They aren't the words I was planning to say but they are the words I want to say.

He smiles calmly and steps closer, the scent of the lilies rich around us. "I can't tell you yet. You're not quite there."

"Where?"

He ignores me and starts to amble along. I catch up and walk next to him, guiding him down the side street leading to my mum's home.

"What is it with you and Shaun today?" I grumble. "Full of all these cryptic comments, and don't think I didn't see you whispering and looking at me."

He shrugs. "Just discussing your personality defects."

I shake my head. "No, you weren't. I haven't got any." I smile. "Okay, keep your secrets, Silas. I'll get it out of you somehow."

"I know you will," he says placidly. "And I look forward very much to experiencing you trying."

I come to a stop. "Here we are."

He looks up at the building towering over us. It looks grim in this light. It's grey and utilitarian and nothing like his home. But still, when I look up I see the lit windows gleaming cheerily and I remember that feeling of home. This is where my mum is, and I remember all the years of Shaun and I playing around here in the streets and practically living in each other's flats. It was a culture shock when we came from Ireland, but my mum always impressed on me that we carry our home with us because it's with the people we love.

But it hasn't stopped other men's reactions. This is normally when the comments start. I obviously have a terrible taste for posh boys. The wince and sneer barely suppressed, the slight panic that they're actually in this place. I don't really expect that from Silas because he's classier than anyone I've ever met, but this place shines a light on the differences between us that I grow more conscious of every day.

I wait for something that he'll cover up with his good manners. Instead he looks around with a lively curiosity. "Which floor is yours?"

I blink. "Seventeenth floor." I nudge him. "A nice bracing climb for a good view of London."

He laughs, and I direct him into the lobby. He moves towards the lifts, but I put a hand out to stop him. "I wouldn't. They're working at the moment, but that only usually lasts for a few hours. If you get stuck in there at this time you'll wait all night and cry and have to pee in a bottle." He looks at me and I grin. "But that's a long story. Let's not discuss that ever again."

I direct him to the stairs. "Okay, this isn't pleasant because apparently some people who live here are under the fucking impression that this is actually a fucking toilet. So, maybe hold your breath in until the need for air becomes impossible to ignore. If you have a heart attack from the climb, I'll try to cushion your fall with my dinner jacket."

"I think what I find most attractive about you, Oz, is your sunny and optimistic nature." I laugh and go to walk ahead of him up the steps, but he grabs my arm on the first stair. "Wait," he says. I look enquiringly at him and he gives me a little smile. "I'm a bit nervous."

I'm instantly concerned. "Oh, don't worry about anything. You're with me and no one is going to fucking mug you." I sigh. "I could hardly get James out of the car when he came, and he spent most of the first visit looking out of the window in case someone stole his tyre rims."

He shakes his head impatiently. "I'm not worried about *that*."

"Well, what's the matter then?"

He shrugs. "I'm just worried that she won't like me. This is really important to me."

"Why?" I say sharply. "You probably won't meet her again." For a second he looks as if I've punched him and remorse runs through me. "I'm sorry," I say quickly, grabbing his waist to stop his instinctive movement away from me. I can't allow that. "That was a shitty thing to say. I'm just nervous too."

"Why?"

I sigh and rest my head against his chest, inhaling his fresh sea scent. "Because I want her to like you too," I whisper. "I don't know why, but this is really important to me too." I inhale deeply. "I think in some way I thought you'd take one look at this place and hightail it out of here and I just wanted to get it over with." I shake my head and dig my forehead into his chest. "Why don't you ever perform according to expectations?"

I relax as he chuckles and hugs me the best he can with a bouquet of flowers in his hands. As it is, the cellophane goes up my nose. "My performances are beyond expectations every time," he says grandly.

"As is your big head," I say wryly, loving the sound of his rich, warm laughter in this dank stairwell. I stop him as he goes to move. "She'll love you," I say quietly.

He stills. "How do you know?"

I scratch my nose awkwardly. "I just know," I finally say, and he holds my gaze for a long second before a slow smile spreads across his face.

"Okay," he says softly.

The smile's long gone by the time we reach the seventeenth floor. "You okay?" I gasp.

"I don't know," he croaks. "I think I coughed up my spleen on the twelfth floor."

"You're very unfit."

"Whatever," he says indignantly. "Wasn't it you begging me to carry you on floor thirteen?"

"That was just for your fitness. I'm fine," I say primly.

He laughs and groans. "Well, I can cross Everest off my bucket list. It would just be a massive disappointment now." I laugh loudly and he shakes his head. "If I didn't want your mum to like me so much I'd have used the bouquet as a crutch."

I shove him gently. "Come on. We need to get in quickly before either of her neighbours spot us."

"Why?"

"Well, one of them might try to sell you weed while the other might try to fuck you."

He blinks. "I think living here would really improve my social life."

"You'll never know." I ring the doorbell and brush his hair back off his forehead. "You ready?"

He breathes in. "Yes."

"It's my mother, Silas. Not the firing squad." I pause. "Unless you're coming in late without ringing her. Then the firing squad looks attractive."

I hear quick footsteps and I'm smiling before the door opens. I see him look at me but instead I grin widely. "Ma," I exclaim, and she grabs me, hugging and kissing.

"A ghrá geal. How are you?" She pushes me back. "You look so well," she says happily. "Your hair's longer and you've lost those awful bags under your eyes from keeping bad company every single bloody night."

There's a smothered snort from my right and I turn. "Ma, I want you to meet someone." I reach out and snag his hand and pull him forward. "This is Silas."

She looks at him for a long second, her gaze catching and holding on our clasped hands, and worry crosses her open face.

Silas smiles at her. "I'm very pleased to meet you," he says. The cut-glass accent is far posher than anything James could manage and it makes my mum's eyes widen. It sounds wrong on this dingy landing. "Oz has told me so much about you."

For a long second, she stands still and my heart sinks. Silas must sense this because he steps back, looking at me in concern. He squeezes my hand, and when I look at him he smiles reassuringly at me, which immediately makes me relax a bit. He winks and I shake my head.

When I look back at my mum she's still staring at him as though I've brought a Tory MP to her door, but all of a sudden her expression changes and she smiles widely.

"Come in, lad," she urges. "Oz has told me a lot about you too."

He offers her the flowers, smiling almost shyly. "These are for you."

She looks down at the fragrant blooms and her face goes soft. "For *me*? Oh, they're so beautiful. Thank you."

I feel a lump in my throat and act quickly. "Are we having dinner on the doorstep because that's definitely too al fresco for around here?"

She grimaces at me before grabbing Silas by his arm and hauling him over the threshold. I watch as she escorts him down the corridor, talking energetically about cruises and holding onto him like a very tiny Irish prison warder.

I almost expect him to look around the lounge with disdain. My mum's a bit of a one for colour but has zero chance of ever matching two so it's a bit like walking into a packet of Skittles. One old hook-up had taken the piss once. That's why he became an old hook-up.

I tense as Silas looks around the bright blue and orange living room, but he grins widely and picks up one of the photos of me at primary school. They line the glass cabinet three and five deep in some areas.

"Tell me there are more of these?"

"Of course there are," I say sourly. "I'm surprised I didn't need a guide dog, the damage this woman did to my retinas."

My mum smacks my arm. "I don't know why I bothered. Jesus, he was an ugly baby."

"Ma!" I say, scandalized.

"It's the truth. The Lord says not to be afraid of that. Why, when Father McConnell picked you up the first time it was only the fear of dropping you that stopped him crossing himself."

I glare at her, but Silas breaks into roars of laughter. "It's the nose. He has such a distinguished nose."

"No child needs a distinguished nose like that. He looked like Bernard Bresslaw."

I shake my head, but Silas has tears of laughter in his eyes. My mum grins at him and just like that I see the click as she falls for him.

The love fest continues as she cooks for him.

"You've done steamed mussels with cider and bacon," I exclaim. "We only eat this on birthdays. Ow!"

She retracts the wooden spoon she's just whacked my hand with. "This is for Silas, not you, and as such you'll take a smaller portion."

Silas smiles smugly and I kick his ankle. "Shut up."

His smile widens and stays there all through dinner as we sit around the kitchen table and she regales us with tales of her cruise.

"Ma, please," I say finally. "Did you not think adult entertainers meant porn stars?"

"I did not," she says crossly. "I just thought they wouldn't be singing Disney tunes."

"What was your first clue?" Silas asks.

My mum taps her finger on the table. "I think it was the trick with the watermelon. Auntie Vera's eyes nearly popped out of her head."

"Oh God, please help me," I sigh.

Silas laughs and, reaching over, he grabs my head, kissing me on the forehead before excusing himself to go to the loo.

We watch him go and the pinch she gives me surprises me. "What the hell?" I hiss. "What have I done now?"

"Not what you've done, but what you might do. Don't ruin this, Oz."

I stare at her. Her face is as serious as I've ever seen it. "What do you mean?"

She shakes her head. "That man is amazing."

I can't help my smile. It takes over my face and she relaxes slightly but still looks at me with caution. The smile falls from my face and I sigh. "Ma, he's an earl. An *earl,* for fuck's sake, is having dinner here."

She shakes her head chidingly. "No. A man is having dinner here. *Your* man, finally, and he's lovely."

"He's not my man."

She gives me her clearsighted glance that since I was little has always seen right through me. "Is he not then? Oh, I must have been mistaken." I shoot her a look and she smiles. "I said when you finally brought a man home who looked at you the way you should be looked at, I'd be happy." She kisses me and stands up to arrange her flowers. "Well, Oz, I'm happy."

I pat her shoulder and go into the lounge. Silas is just coming down the hall and he grins at me.

"Alright?" I ask. "Were your eyes blinded by the bathroom?"

He grins. "I've never seen that shade of pink before. It's very powerful."

I shake my head. "She's got the colour picking ability of Timmy Mallet." He laughs and I sigh. "Well, you've seen it all. What do you think?"

To my surprise he glares at me. "There's still almost a challenge about you at the moment. It's like you're waiting impatiently for me to look down on you and your mum for living here."

"Can you blame me?" I say sharply. "The others–"

"Weren't me," he says sharply, the anger in his eyes startling. "Please do me the courtesy of not treating me as if I'm the ghost of your old boyfriends."

When Silas is angry his voice gets impossibly posh. I open my mouth and what comes out is instinctive. "It's very different from where you grew up."

He nods. "It is. But that's not your or your mum's fault. I admire you both."

"Why?"

"Because you've both had a lot thrown at you and you've risen from that as this tightknit loving family. When we're here, I don't see what you see. I see a warm home and the two of you. You're this special club of two who love and protect each other above everything, and all I want is to join that club and have you care for me like that."

He looks so vulnerable that I can't fucking stand it. It hurts my stomach and my heart. I cup his cheek in my hand, feeling the softness of his skin and the warmth as if he's brought the Cornish sun with him. "I *do*," I say fiercely, for once not considering my words and the consequences and just speaking bluntly and from the depths of me. "I do, Silas."

His smile is glorious.

CHAPTER 16

FROM NOW ON I'M GOING TO BE KNOWN AS
HERBERT HUMPADICK

Oz

The next few days pass in a rush as everybody gets into gear for the party. It's held twice a year. The winter one is held inside the house but the summer one takes place in a marquee on the west lawn that looks out to sea.

Events like this are a bit like a juggernaut gathering speed. You think you're ready, but then everything happens at once and the fact that the word Oz seems to be on every single fucker's lips doesn't make it any easier.

"Oz, when shall I tell the marquee people to come?" "Oz, when are the tables coming?" "Oz, the caterers need to know when to set up tomorrow." "Oz, can you sign this?" "Oz, where is the seating plan?"

"Oz, do you–"

"Oh my *God*, I'm changing my fucking name," I snap without turning around. "From now on I'm going to be known as Herbert Humpadick and I won't be answering to that poor fucker Oz's name any more. Please pass all your questions onto someone that can actually find a fuck to give."

There's a soft snort, and when Chewwy barks I turn to see Silas standing in the entrance of the marquee. Beside him are two men. One is a very beautiful man with shoulder-length wavy blond hair who is staring at me with a smile quirking his lips, and the other ... oh shit! This one is a redhead, but even though he looks very little like Silas apart from the nose and pretty eyes I know instantly that this is Henry, his brother.

"Good afternoon," he says, coming forward, his voice so similar to Silas's that it's uncanny. "Herbert Humpadick, I presume?"

"Oh shit!" I sigh. "Just ignore me, for Christ's sake."

Silas laughs and Henry's lip quirks. "I think that might prove to be difficult."

He looks me up and down and it's so quick that I almost miss it. I wonder what he's thinking. I'd hoped to meet them on the steps of the house with Silas. I'd have been dressed in something elegant. Okay, strike that. I'd have been dressed in something clean and ironed. I don't own anything elegant. Instead I'm dressed in shorts that used to be black but are now a greyish sort of colour, a black vest, and Converse hi tops that have so many holes they're actually airy. I'm also a sweaty mess and highly fucking sick of this event.

"This is Henry, my brother," Silas says, coming around to sling his arm over my shoulder. He's a brave fucker as I'm very sweaty after moving a load of tables. "And this is his boyfriend and our former stepbrother, Ivo."

I blink.

"*Why* do we always lead with that?" Henry sighs and Ivo smirks.

"Because it saves a lot of awkward questions later," Silas says patiently. "You do remember at Christmas when Mrs Patrick seemed to think that you were starring in your own personal gay version of *The Borgias*?"

"Weren't they on *EastEnders*?" I ask and Ivo bursts into laughter.

Henry shakes his head and smiles at me. "I'd say welcome to the family, Oz, but I think you'll fit in easily."

I blink and Silas clears his throat awkwardly. "Oh, erm, thank you," I finally say. I'm hardly family but it seems rude to correct whatever delusion he's suffering from. Henry looks confused and I rush into speech.

"I'll just grab the seating plan and we can leave this fucking marquee." Behind me I hear a dull thud and a stifled "ouch," but when I turn back they're all standing innocently watching me. I smile. "I don't want to know," I say airily. I wave the plan at Silas. "You need to look at this."

"Why?" he asks, taking it from me and scanning the tables and names.

"Because I don't work for the fucking United Nations. Although after trying to sort out the factions around here I'm actually considering a career change."

Henry breaks into laughter. "Oh my God, it's terrible. I remember when our mother used to do it."

"Yes, but she adopted the Boadicea approach," Ivo says, and I can hear a French accent in his drawl.

Silas nods. "You're right. She did do exactly as she wanted."

"I actually meant more that she'd crush you under the wheels of her BMW if you crossed her. Olivia is not the most compassionate woman."

Silas winces. "Let's not mention her name," he says in a hushed voice. "It's like *Beetlejuice*. If we say it, she'll appear." Shudders run through all three men as if they're taking part in a silent Mexican wave of nerves.

I shake my head. "I'll leave it with you," I say cheerily. "I'm off for a shower."

"Me too," Silas says enthusiastically, and Henry and Ivo's heads turn to him. He flushes slightly and I want to laugh. "Not with each other," he says over-heartily. "I mean separately, obviously."

I shake my head and take pity on him. "We're into water conservation around here," I say blithely. "There's a national heatwave on, you know."

Ivo laughs. "That's so civil-minded of you."

I wink. "That's me. Civil."

Silas smirks. "I really don't think so. Your mouth gets you into more trouble than anyone I've ever met." Affection passes over his face as he runs his hand down my back.

To my embarrassment I arch slightly like a cat being petted, and Henry looks at us assessingly. When he looks up and catches my eye he looks unrepentant. Instead he winks.

"We'll all go in. Are we in the Blue Room, Oz?"

"Oh, erm, yes." I shoot Silas a look. I don't know why Henry's asking me rather than his brother who the house belongs to. "That's your room, isn't it?"

Henry smiles. "And please tell me that you've put my mother on the other side of the house?"

"I have. She's in the bedroom with the wisteria wallpaper." I look at my diary. "Actually, I've still got to check her room. Niall was sleeping in there while they repaired the window in his room."

"Thank God she'll be far away," Ivo mutters. "It'd be like sleeping next to the Queen of the Undead otherwise." He shudders. "I'd have had to get out the crosses and the garlic, and I'm pretty sure we had to leave that bag behind because it wouldn't fit in the car with all of Henry's luggage."

Henry glares. Silas laughs. And I check the marquee again. It looks beautiful, all cream fabric and the late afternoon sun sliding lazily across the wooden flooring.

"You done?" Silas asks and I nod.

"Flowers are coming tomorrow morning and the bar and caterers are setting up at nine. The band's arriving at ten."

"Make sure they play a jaunty tune to mark my mother's arrival," he mutters.

Henry laughs. "Something like *The Funeral March*."

I look around at them with a question hovering on my lips. Henry looks at me and his smile is wide and kind, and I relax all of a sudden because that's Silas's smile. "Yes, she is horrible," he says. "We're really not making it up. Stay out of her way and don't meet her eyes."

"Weren't they the instructions for dealing with Medusa?"

Silas laughs loudly. "She'd have been nagging Medusa about being too kind and friendly to visitors."

Ivo snorts and, grabbing Henry's hand, he tugs him out of the marquee. I stare after them. "They really are a beautiful-looking couple."

Silas twists to face me. "Are you okay?" he asks, pushing my hair back off my hot forehead. "You look a bit stressed. I'm so sorry I haven't been around."

"I'm fine." I grab his hand and drop a kiss on it. "And how could you help? You've been so busy since we got back from London and Theo went ill." He hasn't been home each night until after two, and he's back out again at nine the next morning. "When this is done I want you to take a few days off," I say sternly. "You'll be making yourself ill the way you're going on."

"I can't take time off," he immediately and predictably argues. "I'm needed."

"Not half as much as you think," I say patiently. "You have an overexaggerated sense of importance." He laughs and I carry on. "The world will get on fine if you spend a few days in bed."

"Will you be in it? Because you could really do with some time off too," he whispers, dropping a light kiss on my lips and then coming back for a deeper one.

"Of course." I lean into him, chasing his mouth until a cough makes us move apart.

"Sorry," Henry says, looking slightly flustered. He shoots me a look which seems to combine approval and happiness. Then he blinks and the freaked-out look reappears. "Did you say that Mother was coming tomorrow and she'd only maybe be staying if she felt like it and we couldn't shove her into the boot of a car in time?"

Silas slings an arm over my shoulder and tugs me into his side. "I did. Why?"

"Because she's outside ordering the distribution of her luggage."

"You're fucking joking," Silas explodes.

"It's not a joking matter," Henry says primly. "Mr Peters, the taxi driver, does not look happy to have become an Ashworth servant. I don't think it was in his job description."

"Shit!" Silas breathes, and I feel nerves take root and explode in my stomach like ugly butterflies. He turns to me. "Come on. Meet her and get it over with. It probably won't hurt too much."

"It probably will," Henry says glumly.

When we get outside it's to find a taxi parked slightly askew on the drive. An extremely disgruntled man is staggering towards the main entrance carrying a load of bags and being directed by a very beautiful woman.

I stare at her from my vantage position slightly behind the brothers. I now see where Silas's looks come from. She has black hair, greying slightly, cut in a very elegant bob. Dressed in a pale blue dress, she's a picture of cool English beauty.

Silas moves towards her and after being shoved by Ivo, Henry follows, directing a glare at his unrepentant boyfriend as he goes. I look at Ivo.

"Aren't you family? Shouldn't you be joining the welcoming committee?"

"I'm luckily from the side of the family they like to pretend didn't exist." He grins at me. "My mother and Olivia never got on. Fucking hated each other, in fact, because of a difference in opinion."

"What was that?" I ask curiously.

"Their mother felt all the family money belonged to her. So did mine."

I laugh involuntarily. The sound carries on the air, and I'm horrified to see it interrupt the hushed and slightly irritated family discussion going on. Olivia's head swings our way and she raises her hand in a very regal gesture.

"Shit," Ivo sighs. "We've been summoned." He turns to me. "Whatever you do, don't take any notice of her. She's a shitty person and she was a shitty mother. Her words carry no weight."

I stare at him. "Well, that was honest."

He grins, the smile lighting up his face and making him startlingly beautiful. "Okay, let's do it."

I fall into step next to him as we approach the car. The three people turn to watch us. Henry immediately holds out his hand to Ivo, who takes it and goes to stand next to him. Olivia sighs heavily, a frown on her face. "Ivo," she says coolly. "Still around?"

Ivo smiles. "Yes, still here, Olivia. How lovely to see you. Two years has been too long. Let's not leave it that long next time."

"Of course," she says distantly, turning to face me and missing Ivo's aside of, "Let's leave it a lot longer."

I look into eyes that are so pale a blue they're nearly grey. "And who is this?" she asks.

"Oz Gallagher," I say and then hesitate. *Does she have a title? How am I supposed to address her?* The silence stretches and her mouth tilts in a cruel fashion.

Before she can say anything, Silas is next to me. "This is Oz," he says coolly. "Oz, this is my mother." He pauses. "You can call her Olivia." She opens her mouth and shuts it quickly when he levels her with a look. "Now, Mother, how is it that you're here early? Where's Martin?"

"At home," she says expressionlessly. "He's got a golf match tomorrow, so I came early. Perfect timing for me to see my two sons."

"See or petrify?" Ivo mutters and Henry laughs.

Olivia levels them with a glare. She turns back to me. "So, you are

Silas's house manager then," she says. "And what qualifications do you possess to do this job?"

"Erm, well I've got a degree in Fine Art and the History of Art."

"He's already had an interview," Silas says brusquely. "Let's not perform another one."

"Well, Silas, how rude. I was just making conversation. Please don't talk to me in that manner in front of the staff."

"Oz isn't just staff," he says, and her eyes narrow as she sees his hand take mine and squeeze.

"I see," she says in a glacial voice. "How quaint. It's uncanny how you grow more like your father as you get older. Wasn't the fourth wife a maid here?" She sighs. "I can just see him chasing her round the servants' quarters. So common."

"I'm trying to unsee that," Henry says wryly. "Thank you for the image. I'll try and bleach it away later."

"That's enough, Mother," Silas says and it's loud and carrying. His mother and Ivo look startled and Henry looks gleeful.

"What do you mean?"

"Stop it with your horrible comments."

She shakes her head. "Doesn't the Bible mention the serpent's tongue of a child answering back?"

"Don't pretend you read anything but Jilly Cooper, Mother. I don't think she covers the finer points of theology," Henry says glibly.

"Enough," Silas says. "Let's get you settled in. Have you eaten?"

"I never eat after seven," she murmurs and sweeps up the steps, the rest of us following her like courtiers.

As soon as we're inside I excuse myself and race up the servants' stairs to the first floor and her room. I rush in and sag with relief. Her luggage has been delivered and the room is clean and smells of the perfume from a vase of roses I'd cut from the gardens and set on the polished mahogany of her dressing table. I do a quick check around the room, straightening the fresh towels and checking the drawers. It's lucky I do because Niall has left a very old copy of *Men*, the gay porn magazine, in the bedside table.

"What in the ever-living *fuck*, Niall?" I mutter and grab it out of the drawer. "I'm going to fucking kill you, you moron." I pause, looking at the cover which might be the last edition they printed before they went out of business. "After I find out where you got this from." I slam the drawer and whirl around as I hear voices coming down the corridor.

"So, you're telling me that he's actually doing this job and you don't know his parents? I don't think that's ever happened before."

"I have met his mother, but nowadays we don't make meeting the parents a part of the interview process. Not unless we're employing five-year-olds," Silas says, and I can hear the patience in his voice and underneath the strain.

I wince sympathetically and then look frantically at the porn mag. Where the fuck am I going to put it? I look at the open window and for one wild moment I consider throwing it out but then they enter the room and it's too late. I hold it behind my back in one hand.

She comes to a stop. "Oh, Oz, what are you doing in here?"

I stifle a grimace. She makes it sound like they've caught me rifling through her knicker drawer. "I was just checking you've got everything you need," I say cheerily, edging towards the door with my hand still behind my back.

She eyes me suspiciously and then smiles maliciously. "Why, whatever have you got behind your back? Is it a gift for me?" The wicked old witch obviously thinks she's caught me red-handed with some of her belongings.

"Oh, erm," I stutter. My mind is a blank. Silas looks at me incredulously and I try to think while she waits, tapping her foot gently on the carpet. "I was just looking to see whether you needed any reading material," I say feebly and want to punch myself. Some part of me is shouting abort abort, but the rest of me isn't listening. "But you have," I say hurriedly. "So, I'll be off and hope you have a good night's sleep."

"Hold on," she says commandingly. "I'm sure I can always have more to read. I usually like magazines like *Vogue* and *Harper's Bazaar*. What have you brought me?"

"Not *Vogue* or *Harper's Bazaar*," I say faintly. I back up to the door slightly and she shifts position like an animal tracking me for lunch.

She holds out her hand. "It's a very sweet gesture. It's probably not what I'm used to, but I'd love to see what you've got." Silence stretches like toffee as she keeps her hand held out. The woman's obviously up on her Pilates as there's no sign of shaking muscles. "Oz?" she says and I just give in.

I set the magazine neatly into her raised palm and silence falls on the room apart from Silas's choked intake of breath. She stares at the magazine in her hand like I've just put a big poo in her palm and it's abruptly too much.

"It's a collector's edition," I say and leg it out of her room as fast as I can.

Half an hour later I hear Silas's bedroom door open. "Go away," I say, not taking my hand from across my eyes.

"Oh Oz, you do know what a very special person you are, don't you?" I can hear the barely suppressed mirth in his voice.

"Fuck off," I mutter.

"No, really. Mother's face will live in my memory until the day I die. It was utterly ... stupendous."

"What did she say when I left?" I ask, removing my hand. He's standing at the bottom of the bed with the biggest grin I've ever seen on his face.

"It's actually the first time I've ever seen her speechless. It lasted for a full two minutes."

I groan. "Oh my *God*, that's the most awful thing that's ever happened to me."

"Oh, don't say that. You haven't had a proper conversation with her yet. There's plenty of time for things to get a lot worse."

"I just gave your mother a gay porn magazine."

"It was a collector's edition," he says helpfully. His eyes run down my body clad in just a towel. "Have I missed your shower?"

"Yes, but you caught the ritual humiliation instead," I say sourly.

He throws himself down on the bed next to me and raises his arm for me to snuggle in. "Don't even bother getting worried."

"This is your mother." I come up on one elbow. "She's never going to like me now."

"She was never going to like you anyway."

I draw back, stunned at the sharp sting. "Because of my background?"

"No. Because she doesn't like anyone," he says simply. "She's not a nice person and I'd like you to spend as little time as you can with her. Stay out of her way."

"I can look after myself."

"I know you can, but you've never encountered anyone like her. She's utterly poisonous."

I rest my chin on his warm chest and he strokes my hair back. "What was she like when you were growing up?"

"Exactly the same," he says steadily and sighs. He stares into space for a second and then looks at me. "She was cold and haughty. She wasn't loving like your mum. But she's still my mother and …" He hesitates.

"And you love her," I say softly.

He shakes his head. "I'm a twat."

"No, you're a son and you're a good man. It doesn't make it easy when you have parents like that, but I know you. You're loyal and you don't stop loving people just because their behaviour means you should."

He leans sideways and catches my mouth in a soft kiss. "It's very tiring," he sighs. "I'm glad when she goes and then I feel guilty."

We lie silently for a few minutes, my fingers brushing his chest in a hypnotic motion. Finally, I stir.

"Where's the magazine?"

He snorts. "Over there."

I sigh and fall on my back in a dramatic fashion. "*Why* have you brought it in here? Are you taunting me?"

I laugh as he twists over and straddles me. He pins my shoulders down, the strain falling away from his face and his eyes sparkling. "There are some very interesting articles. I've even seen two positions that we haven't tried yet."

"You're actually subjugating me with the tool of my humiliation."

He shakes his head. "I somehow feel that I'm a lot more interesting in your head."

I shrug. "You can't help it," I say cheekily and then shout out laughing as he falls on me. The laughter turns to moans and panting, hurried breaths, but it stays underneath, running like a sparkling river through my blood.

CHAPTER 17

BE MY OZ AGAIN, BECAUSE THAT OZ IS
UTTERLY PERFECT TO ME THE WAY HE IS

Silas

The sea pounds onto the sand of the cove and I exhale in satisfaction, lying back and resting my head on my jumper. "I love this place."

"Me too," Henry murmurs.

I crack one eye open. He's staring out to sea, his expression contemplative.

"What's up?" I ask, coming up onto my elbows.

He shoots me a grin. "I love you," he says affectionately.

I smile at him, feeling warmth run through me for this brother of mine. Quirky and funny and kind. "I love you too. What brought that on?"

He shrugs and stares back out to sea again. "Memories, I suppose. Brought on by being here."

I sigh. "It wasn't the place's fault, Henry. We just had shitty people for parents."

"I know that," he protests. "I also know how much you love it here."

"I do," I say simply. "It's home."

"I know, and I'm so cross with you."

"*What?*" I sit up. "Why, for fuck's sake?"

"Because you're tied here. How on earth are you going to have a life with all of Dad's shit piling up around you? I'm so fucking angry that you didn't tell me."

"How did you know?" I hesitate. "Did Oz tell you?"

He huffs. "No, of course he didn't. As if he'd let anything slip that's private to you. Mother took a lot of pleasure telling me over breakfast this morning."

"Shit!"

"Oh, you can say that again and do better. How could you not tell me about the mess he left us in?"

"Me," I correct gently.

He sighs heavily and crossly. "No. It's *us*, Silas. I might not want anything to do with this place particularly. My home's with Ivo. But I do want something to do with *you* and I'd really rather you didn't work and worry yourself into a fucking early grave like he did. I love you and I want you around." He glares at me. "I'm giving you back the money you gave me after father's death."

I jerk. "You are fucking not. That's yours."

"He didn't leave it to me."

"Well, that's because he was a wanker. It's yours and that's an end to it."

"Oh, Silas, I love how you think your word is law." He shakes his head. "It isn't." He holds up a hand to stem the flow. "No. It's nonnegotiable. I've never used it. It's just been sitting in my bank account gathering dust."

"Why?"

"Because it's tainted. It should go to help here. It'll make me very happy to know it's paid a bill. Then I can stick two fingers up at the old tosser because he hasn't fucked us over."

"He won't," I say urgently. "We've got it under control."

"Who's we?"

"Me and Oz, of course."

A smile ticks his mouth. "Oh, of course. You and Oz."

I can't figure out his mood. "Don't you like him?" I ask, and I'm absolutely astonished when he starts to laugh. "*Henry*," I warn.

He stops laughing and slings his arm around my shoulder, kissing my forehead. "I adore him," he says quietly. "Absolutely and utterly. He's perfect."

"Well, I wouldn't say perfect," I mutter.

"Perfect for you," he whispers. He drops his arm and we stare out to sea. If someone had left a camera filming this beach during our childhood and adolescence, at some point every day our figures would have appeared and done exactly this. Stared out to sea, laughed and talked.

"I was worried about you," he mutters, and I jerk.

"Why?"

"Because you never had anyone of your own."

"I've had lots of anyones."

"But now you've got a someone," he says solemnly. "And it's right."

I sigh. "You do know he's going back in a few weeks? His job is nearly done. He'll go back to London because that's where he belongs."

"He belongs here with you," he says fiercely. "I always worried because we know from firsthand experience that Ashworth partners don't seem to adapt well to living here."

"That's an understatement," I mutter.

"But I'm not worried now. He belongs here as if he was made for this place and it was waiting for him. He's just at home."

"I know," I say low. "But I can't make him stay and he always said this was just for the summer. I think he's close to admitting that he feels something for me, but he's gun shy to say the least and I can't push." I shrug. "It's hard because I want to grab him and force him to see how right we are together, but that would send him scurrying back to London quicker than Dick fucking Whittington. I don't think your welcome to the family comment last night went down too well either."

"Shit!" He sighs. "I didn't mean that. It just came out."

"Well, zip it back up again and don't say things like that. Save the honesty about feelings for your boyfriend."

He snorts but then sobers. "Do you love him?"

"Of course," I say, and I can hear the astonishment in my voice.

"Then it will all be okay," he says peacefully.

I stare at the side of his face which is reddening slightly with a blush. "Henry, tell me it isn't true. Have you become a *romantic?*" I enquire in an astonished voice.

"Oh, fuck off," he says sourly. He shrugs. "I just believe in love more now that I'm in it."

I shake my head. "Come what, come may."

He shoves me. "Okay there, Shakespeare. I'll take your very fatalistic words to heart." He shakes his head. "Just be careful. Shakespeare didn't know Mother. If he had, his plays would have been a mega fuckton darker. Keep her away from Oz because I think she could hurt your chances."

Oz

Richard Ashcroft's *A Song for the Lovers* is playing on my iPod, the moody song seeming to twine itself around the shadows of twilight in the room. I stare at myself in the huge old mirror on Silas's bedroom wall and wrinkle my nose. I twist around and check the back. Then I face forwards and sigh again before shrugging.

I look down at Chewwy, who's watching me with a fairly jaundiced air. "It'll have to do," I say to him, and he sighs heavily before jumping onto the sofa and settling down as if he's been walking for hours rather than sitting in the visitor's centre with a bone.

The door opens with a click and Silas appears. "You alright?" he asks.

"I am now," I sigh. "Look at you."

Silas is built for a dinner suit. His wide shoulders stretch the black material perfectly and the trousers show off the long length of his legs. His hair glows dark in the low light. His face is tanned and his eyes a clear sparkling green.

He strikes a model pose, sucking in his cheeks and looking sulky, and I laugh. "No. Just no. You look pissed."

He grins and reverts back to normal until a strange look comes over his face.

"What's the matter?" I ask alarmed as he comes towards me and grabs my shoulders gently to hold me at arm's length. He sends an intense look down my body and I squirm. "What is it? Do I look wrong? It's the first time I've worn a dinner suit."

He flicks me a searing look. "You look amazing but you're missing something."

"Oh my God, have I got to wear a sash or something?"

He smiles but it fades quickly. "Where's your nail varnish and eyeliner?"

I shrug. "It's not appropriate for this. I'll embarrass you."

"What the *fuck*?" he breathes. "Where has that come from?"

"Well, your mother said—"

He breathes in deeply and flashes his teeth in a very dark smile. "What did she say?"

"Oh, she didn't say anything horrible," I interject quickly. I don't need him roaring off and falling out with her. "She just spoke about all the important people coming tonight."

I'm telling the truth. She's never said a horrible word to me, but all day I've felt her eyes on me. Judging and weighing me up and finding me wanting in everything I did. The staff weren't being managed properly and poor dear Silas needed his peace of mind. Was I really considering using candles in the gift shop from a woman on a council estate when there was a very posh candlemaker down the road she'd been at school with?

On and on. Little jibes and digs that have left me feeling ... unsure. Yes. I admit it. For the first time in my life I don't know if I'm doing right. I've always been so sure, so focused on myself. But now I have Silas and he means more than ... I stop that chain of thought immediately.

I sigh. "I just don't want to humiliate you and make you a laughing stock."

For a long second there's silence in the room and then he moves over to the table and rummages through the drawer. "Okay, come here," he says sharply.

"What?"

He gestures. "Come here, darling."

"I don't know why you're calling me–"

"I want you to come and sit down here," he interrupts, and I huff slightly before drifting over and settling on the chair he indicates.

"What are you going to do?" I ask and then grin as he lowers himself to his knees in front of me. "Oh, okay, I am fully on board with that," I murmur and start to unzip my fly.

I stop when he puts his hand over mine. "Lovely as that idea is, I have something else in mind." He opens his hand to show me the small bottle in his large palm.

I swallow hard and look up. "What are you doing?"

"I am going to paint your nails," he says in a voice that has outrage and fierceness running through it. "Because I will not have you fucking *ever* muting even a millimetre of your personality to suit anyone." He glares at me. "Then you are going to outline those pretty eyes and you are going to put your fucking combat boots on with this dinner suit and be my Oz again, because that Oz is utterly perfect to me the way he is." He takes a breath. "Now hold out your hand. I can't claim to be an expert at this and you'll probably look a tit, but at least you'll look yourself again."

He bends over my hands, the sweet scent of his shampoo wafting around me. His hair shines and his eyes are intent and focused as his large fingers paint black sparkly polish very badly onto my nails.

The polish is smudged and my cuticles are painted nearly as much as the nails but I swallow hard, feeling tears in the back of my throat. I'd thought the moment when I fell in love would be dramatic and full of noise and energy. Instead, it's in a quiet bedroom where a soft song plays and the light dances on the man's hair and the planes of his face as he makes me back into me. The only man who's ever valued that person.

I hold that knowledge tight to me, examining it and waiting for the fear to hit me. It doesn't take long. This will never work. I've always known that. At the moment he likes the way I am, but how long will it be before the enchantment fades on his side and I disappoint or embarrass him? It seems almost inevitable lately, and I don't know how I'll bear to see the letdown in his eyes. All I can see ahead of us is a prolonged goodbye. Then I'll crawl back to London, and at some point I'll pick up a newspaper and see a picture of him with another man. One who will look like he belongs next to him.

I flinch and inhale slowly and he looks up. "Alright?" he asks quietly.

"I'm fine," I say. And I try to hold onto that feeling of love rather than the fear. It feels as fragile as a spiderweb in my hands.

∼

I manage it for as long as it takes us to leave that quiet bedroom and right up until he insists I join the welcoming line. Henry and Ivo are waiting along with Olivia and a portly red-faced man who I presume is her husband, Martin. Ivo looks slightly resigned and Henry just looks cross as his mother talks to him.

As we walk up, she catches sight of Silas first. "Where have you been?" she scolds. "The first guests will be here soon and–" Her voice dies away as she sees me behind Silas and the way he's holding onto my hand.

"Problem, Mother?" Silas says in a slightly challenging voice.

"You know very well there is a problem. What is *he* doing here?"

I go to move back but he stays me. "No," he says firmly. "Oz is joining us because he's with me. I want him standing by my side."

She turns to her husband. "Martin, talk to him. He's making a mockery of the family."

"Yes, Martin," Silas drawls. "Please do try and talk to me about something that is quite patently none of your business." Martin huffs and puffs but obviously decides that discretion is better than a stand-up row which I now see that Silas is spoiling for. He and his mother glare at each other.

"This is epic," Henry whispers happily and Ivo smiles at him.

Milo darts up. "First guests are on their way."

Silas moves into position at the top of the line and pulls me after him.

"Oh no, I am putting my foot down," Olivia says querulously. "He is *not* standing in front of me."

"Oh really?" Silas says silkily, but I've abruptly had enough.

"I'm actually going to help Milo," I say firmly and tug my hand away. I feel unsettled and cross like I'm a toy that's being tugged between the two of them. I know Silas is standing up for me, but I'm getting fucked off with her constant asides and the speaking about me as if I'm below her notice.

Ignoring the hurt look on his face which makes me feel like shit and even crosser at the same time, I pace over to the back of the marquee and duck in next to Milo.

"What are you doing here?" he hisses. "Aren't you supposed to be in the receiving line?"

"And why the fuck would I want to be there?" I snap, and he shakes his head.

"Don't let her get under your skin."

"She's already there and I must say I'd rather have a fucking tapeworm than that witch."

He rubs my arm, but at that point one of the groundsmen comes up with a problem in the carpark and he dashes off to sort it.

I edge to the side of the room and watch unnoticed as the family greet their guests. The late afternoon sun falls on them, gilding them as if they're on stage. I examine them. Silas and Henry and Ivo's suits are obviously hand tailored as they cling to their lean figures, while Olivia looks expensive in a long silver-coloured dress and pearls. They look expensive and refined, greeting their guests and within seconds putting them at their ease. Even Ivo, who has maintained a conspicuous distance until now, looks practised at this and part of them.

I look down at my off-the-rack suit and my fingers, and for a second I want to hold my hands out of sight. I look wrong here. Out of place and tacky, like neon tinsel on a designer's Christmas tree. I look up and Olivia is watching me. Her thin lips are tight with disapproval but as she looks at me, a smile twists them that I'm sure doesn't bode well. I raise my chin, but she shakes her head and dismisses me as she turns to the next guest.

The next hour passes quickly and I'm ashamed to say that I'm undertaking avoidance manoeuvres. Every time Silas gets close to me I dart off to check something else. I think it's fair to say that I'm getting on the caterer's nerves and pretty soon a member of staff is going to lynch me.

I watch as the last hors d'oeuvre tray comes back past my hiding spot behind a large plant. All around is the sound of happy and lively conversation accompanied by the smooth sound of the jazz band playing.

Milo pops up next to me, muttering into a walkie talkie.

I eye him. "Haven't we got anything more modern? You look like you're auditioning for a role on *The Professionals*."

He shakes his head, all business. "Shall we start getting everyone seated?"

I look around and gauge the mood. "Yes. Get Silas to make the announcement."

He gapes at me. "Have you lost the power of your own mouth?" I glare at him and he shakes his head. "Men would pay for this moment of silence," he mutters and stalks off.

I watch him edge to Silas's side who is currently charming a group of people, one of the women hanging on his arm. Silas bends to listen as Milo talks and then his head shoots up and he looks straight over at me. I sigh. *Bloody interfering Milo.*

I straighten as Silas walks over to me. "Is there a particular reason why you are hiding behind this lemon tree?"

"I like the scent of the leaves," I say feebly, and he shakes his head.

"What is going on right now? I thought you were going to be by my side for the evening and it appears that I'm dating The Invisible Man."

"Perhaps you'd be better off with him," I mutter.

"*What?*" he says sharply. He tries to take my hand, then steps back with a hurt look all over his face as I wriggle out of his grip and step back. "What is going on?" he asks hoarsely.

"Nothing," I say, panicked. "I just don't think we should be seen holding hands. That's all. It's silly to be all over each other anyway." I nod to make my statement more emphatic.

He stares at me for a long moment with turbulent eyes and then without another word he turns and walks away.

"Shit!" I say. "Oh fuck, Silas." I've just hurt him. With a sinking heart I remember him talking about how he's never had anyone to stand up for him and be with him. He wants that. He's given me everything and I just behaved like a stupid fucking kid and hurt him by throwing it back at him and telling him he's silly.

I go to walk after him but there's a rustle of silk behind me and I turn, knowing who I'm going to find.

"Oz," Olivia says smoothly. "Surely you can see that this infatuation of my son's is absolutely ridiculous. He's a very important figure around here. People look up to him to set the tone. It's bad enough that he has a male lover. It's an absolute joke that he's picked you. He could have had other men. I know that. Men much better than you." She shakes her head, the poison falling smoothly from her lips. "The whole county will be laughing at him. He'll be the subject of whispers and jokes. *My son*. The Earl of Ashworth. A man who can trace his lineage back hundreds of years sleeping with a man who can't trace his back more than two minutes because he doesn't even know his own father."

I stare at her. "How do you know that?"

She shakes her head and sips her champagne. I notice her hand is absolutely still, unlike mine. I'm shaking slightly with an outraged tremble. "Darling, I know everything that happens around here. When I found out my son was jaunting all over South Cornwall in the company of someone very undesirable and upsetting neighbours of ours who've been friends for years, I knew I had to have someone look into you."

"You had me investigated?"

"I did." She smiles. "And I found a young man who really doesn't have much going for him. A good brain, but it's rotting because he's drinking too much and sleeping with his bosses and getting fired." She looks me up and down. "Hardly what a peer of the realm needs as his companion. Silas needs someone from a good family. Someone able to entertain in this sort of setting. Someone who will never embarrass him by dressing in cheap clothes and talking with that awful common accent. Ashworth House needs someone better."

"But does *Chi an Mor*?" She looks at me in confusion. "You've spoken a lot about what you think Silas needs. Have you actually asked him?" I say hoarsely.

All my words that would normally come flowing out when confronted with someone like this have gone because she's voicing my inner fears. I don't think I'm good enough to be here at his side and I really am scared stiff of disappointing him. This is what happens when people make themselves so nice that you fall in love with them and bend yourself backwards to avoid hurting them.

She looks at me steadily, her eyes full of a cold disdain. "I don't need to ask Silas. He was a silly boy and he's grown into a foolish man who obeys his heart in everything. I speak because I know the world you've fallen into. It will reject you, Oz, as surely as the sun will rise."

I look back at her, dumb for once in my life, and Martin calls her name. She smiles at me and without another word brushes past me and goes towards her husband.

I look up and Niall is coming towards me. He looks after her departing figure and concern flares in his eyes. I hold up my hand to stop him. "I'm going to see how the caterers are getting on," I say hoarsely and hightail it out of the tent.

CHAPTER 18

I WENT LOOKING FOR MY COURAGE AND COMMON SENSE

Oz

I march quickly up the steps towards the house and then in through the main door. I just need to get my breath back and think because my mind is fucking whirling, but at that point I hear Niall call my name.

"Absolutely not at the moment," I mutter, and spotting the door to the coat cupboard in the hall, I whisk in and shut the door. A second later I hear scratching and a deep whine that's familiar.

I huff and open the door a crack. "Get in here," I hiss at Chewwy, who is looking at me in a slightly accusing manner. "How did you get out of the kitchen?" I ask the dog, grabbing his collar and tugging him into the cupboard.

He obviously doesn't answer. Instead, he plonks himself next to me and licks my hand. I look down at him and stroke his ears. He looks anxious, as if he knows I'm unhappy, and I pet him until he relaxes. For a second peace descends and then I jump out of my skin when I hear a thump and a snort of laughter.

"What the fuck?" I breathe, peering into the darkness.

"Oz, is that you?"

"Yes. *Ivo?*"

"In the flesh," comes his wry retort. There's movement near me, then a click, and light floods the cupboard revealing the dishevelled figures of Henry and Ivo. Ivo's shirt is open and his mouth swollen, while Henry's trousers are unbuttoned and his hair is standing straight up like he's stuck his finger in a socket.

"What the fuck?" I mutter. "In the *coat cupboard?* You've got a bedroom upstairs."

They exchange sheepish looks and start buttoning and zipping up. "We've got fond memories of this cupboard," Henry says. "It's sort of a tradition."

I shake my head. "Don't traditions centre around events like Christmas?"

Henry grins. "It's the same thing. I'm just letting Ivo come in my chimney instead of Father Christmas."

"*Henry*," Ivo groans and shakes his head. "That's so lame."

Henry shrugs, looking unrepentant. Then his gaze sharpens. "What are you doing in here with Chewwy?"

I fidget slightly. "I just needed a quiet space for a second." I pause. "And Niall was going to lecture me."

"Why?" He looks searchingly at me. "Is it anything to do with your disappearing act tonight?"

I shrug. "Maybe." I dart a look at him. "I just got things turned around in my head. It's my fault."

"I doubt it," Ivo says. "I saw Olivia talking to you earlier."

"What the fuck?" Henry explodes and we shush him quickly. "I mean what the *fuck?*" he whispers furiously. "What did she say to you?"

"It doesn't matter."

"Yes, it does," he says implacably, and I can tell that he and Silas are brothers at this moment.

"She mentioned how unsuited we are and how much damage I could do to him with the local gentry."

"Like Silas spends any fucking time with the local gentry," he scoffs. "He's too bloody busy and he spent enough time with half of them at school." His gaze softens. "You do know it's total bollocks, don't you? Other people's opinions have never mattered to Silas."

"I know that," I start to say, but then we hear the click of heels and Olivia's cut-glass tones coming up the steps.

"Shush!" I say frantically. "She'll find us."

Ivo reaches up and cuts the light out just as we hear Silas call "Mother" very loudly.

"Ooh, that's Silas's pissed-off voice," Henry says gleefully. "Budge up, Ivo. I can't hear properly."

"Did you mean to put your hand there?" Ivo says calmly, and Henry snorts.

"Sort of. Are you complaining?"

"No. By all means go ahead."

"Shush!" I say again and stroke Chewwy when he shifts about.

"What is it, Silas?" Olivia says. Her voice sounds clear, so she's right by our door and there's no chance of escape. I groan under my breath and slump against the wall.

"I'd like a word with you."

"Must you do it now? They'll be serving supper any minute."

"Yes, it won't wait. What did you say to Oz?"

"Oh, Oz, Oz, Oz. I think I'd like to go an hour without hearing his name being mentioned."

"Try not upsetting him then," Silas says with an edge to his voice.

"Upsetting *him*. What about me, Silas? What about your mother's feelings?"

"Hmm, let me think. No, I still don't care."

"Yes," Henry whispers. "I told you. Epic."

"That's a disgraceful thing to say, Silas. And to your own mother."

"Stop it." His voice is weary and harsh, and I feel my slight smile fade off my face. "I can't find him, and I want to know what you said."

There's a pause before she gives a long-suffering sigh. "Very well. I'm obviously not going to be allowed to have supper before we do this. I simply pointed out to him that he's not good enough for you. A fact which should be blindingly obvious to him and to you."

"You did *what*?" Silas's voice is low and so cold now that I shiver.

She obviously senses it because her laugh sounds nervous. "Darling, be reasonable. He's a boy from a council estate and a single-parent family. Look at all those tattoos on him. And the nail varnish and eye makeup. It makes me shudder."

"I'm appalled at you." His voice is cold and still.

"Oh, don't be so dramatic. Have your fun with him but then pack him back where he came from and select someone respectable. Maybe a woman next time."

"It doesn't work like that, Mother. I wish you'd understand."

"I understand that you're naïve in a lot of ways. That boy is using you. He's seen the money and—"

She stops as he laughs. "*What* bloody money? There is none. Father left so much debt I could suffocate myself with the paperwork. But you knew that and did nothing. The only person who has, is him. He's done everything in his power to help me and he's the only one. You've done nothing."

"You cannot be serious about this man. I forbid it. Think of your position."

I curl my fingers into fists. This is awful. A warm hand squeezes mine and in the faint light coming through the side of the door Henry looks at me. He smiles. "Wait," he whispers.

Silas's voice is solemn. "I've done everything you've ever asked of me. I've always done my duty for you and everyone else. And now I want something of my own. *Someone* of my own. I want to pick my partner, not because of money and status but because I love them with all my heart." I inhale sharply as his voice goes quiet. "I love Oz. I love him so very much. He's clever and kind. He sees me and he loves me, and he will always protect me the way I do him. I won't tolerate anyone speaking to him the way you just did. We're a team and I couldn't be happier with him."

I feel a rush of happiness run through me that's so strong it nearly knocks me to my knees.

"But you could do better." Her voice is sharp and querulous.

I tense but his voice comes clear now. "No, I couldn't." There's a simple truth and honesty in his voice that brings tears to my eyes. "I can *never* do better than him because he's everything I have ever wanted. He's quick and funny and loyal, and this man who could have anyone actually waits up for me at night for the simple reason that he wants to see *me*. He listens when I talk because it's me. Not the Earl of Ashworth. Just me. He makes me think, makes me laugh, makes me want to be a better man because his opinion is the only one that matters."

"But what will people think, Silas?" I tense because this is all my fears in one sentence. "He's so low class and brash."

Unbelievably he laughs. "Who the fuck cares about everyone's opinions? I certainly don't. Not when I have him. I don't care where he comes from, Mother. I only care that in him I've found my home, my safety, and my ease." He pauses. "Do you know how many people want to live out here? You should think hard because you weren't one of them. Oz loves it here the way I do, like it's in his bones, and if I have my way we'll grow old here together and die with the salt on our lips and sand in our hair."

"I don't understand."

He sounds sad. "I'm sorry for that because you've missed out on loving with your heart rather than with a copy of their CV and

Debretts in your hand. Don't you see it doesn't matter to me? Yes, Oz may have a different background to us, but I've been to his home and I've met his mother and I've got to tell you that I was jealous."

"Of what?" The incredulity is loud in her voice.

"Of the love and care they give each other. The fierceness, the devotion. I want that, and I want to give it to him because he's the most amazing person I've ever met in my life. So, if you feel that you can't be civil to him and can't be kind then please don't come here anymore."

"You'd throw your family out for him. Shame on you."

"*He's* my family and I would do a lot more for him."

There's a short silence and her voice when she speaks is cold and my heart aches for him. "As you wish, Silas. You've made your bed. Don't come whining to me when things go wrong."

"Why would I do that, Mother? I've never been able to do it before."

There's a sharp intake of breath and then the sound of her heels clicking away. I hear a low sigh and then a soft curse before Silas's footsteps stride away.

Henry straightens up as if he's going to open the door, but I put my hand out to stop him.

"Don't. I wasn't meant to hear that."

"But you did. Don't you want to acknowledge what he said?"

I shake my head. "He'll tell me anyway," I say serenely with the sudden surety that's come to me.

Ivo looks at me and nods. "It's good that you heard that, Oz."

"Why?"

He smiles. "Because I think you needed to know that he would stick up for you."

"Not at the cost of his mother."

Henry snorts and Ivo makes a moue of distaste. "She's not worth being sorry over and Silas knows it. She can't see how you fit and balance each other and she probably never will."

"Do we fit?"

He nods calmly. "It's like you're on a seesaw. It's been somewhat battered by previous users, but you both balance it perfectly. If one of you got off it would make the other fall. He needed someone who would put him first. He hasn't ever had that in a partner or a parent. And you needed someone who would accept you for who you really are. Accept you and love you." He gives a very Gallic shrug. "Perfect balance."

"Sometimes I forget how clever you are about people," Henry says.

"Would that sometimes be when I'm disagreeing with you?" Ivo asks wryly, and Henry gives him an impish smirk.

"Probably."

"Okay." I straighten my jacket and run a hand through my hair.

"Where are you going?" Henry asks with a thread of nervousness running through his voice.

"To the kitchen to shut Chewwy in again and then out to the marquee. Dinner's being served," I say calmly. "And Silas will be looking for me."

I go to open the door and he stays me with a hand on my arm. "Welcome to the family," he whispers. "I'm so happy you're here."

I squeeze his hand. "Thank you."

The sound of talking in the marquee is like a wall of noise after the quietness of the cupboard. I look around, quickly noting the servers moving with dexterity and the happy faces. Satisfied, I move over to the central table. Olivia is there with a face like thunder sitting next to Martin who is drinking wine as if they're going to outlaw it at any second. Silas is looking around with a worried expression on his face that eases slightly as he sees me. He stands up hurriedly and strides over.

"Are you alright?" he asks in a rushed voice. "I know my mother spoke to you."

I grab his arm and rub it gently, watching his eyes close slightly in relief. "I'm so sorry I ran away. I'm okay now," I whisper. "Don't worry. Everything's fine."

"Where have you been?" he whispers. "I've been looking everywhere for you."

I shrug and smile at him. "I went looking for my courage and common sense."

"Sounds like *The Wizard of Oz*," he says gently. "Did you find them?"

I lower my hand and take his. Then I raise it to my lips and kiss it gently and deliberately. His eyes flare at the simple gesture because he knows what this means.

He takes a deep breath and suddenly his face is illuminated with the widest smile I've ever seen. "Okay," he breathes. "Are we doing this?"

I nod and smile tenderly. "Yes, we are." I pause. "Together."

He grins, and I gasp as he grabs my face and pulls me towards him, dropping a gentle kiss on my lips. He pulls back and walks us over to the table.

"Here he is," he says happily. "Everyone, I'd like you to meet my boyfriend, Oz Gallagher."

∽

Later that night I strip my clothes off and step into the shower with a sigh of relief. It had got hot and sticky later on in the marquee when the dancing had started. I look at the shower and smile. Out of everywhere in the house, this is one of my favourite places. It's a huge cubicle tiled with pale blue subway tiles and with plenty of room for two.

"That's a happy sigh."

I look up and smile at the sight of Silas through the shower door leaning against the sink. He's down to his trousers and shirt but the shirt is open and showing off that wonderful hairy chest.

"It's lovely. It was so hot in the tent."

"I was very proud of you tonight." His quiet voice cuts through the noise of the water and I rub my hand down my wet face, staring at him through the glass.

"Why?"

"I was proud to have you by my side. You're so funny and irreverent. You won so many people over."

"Not everyone."

He shrugs. "Of course not. But we can't please them all. That's not something I'm ever going to try to do. As long as the people I love are happy, nothing else matters."

"Your mother won't come round, will she?"

She'd vanished after the meal, taking a drunk Martin with her and returning back to their home. I can't say I'll miss her, but she is his mother.

He looks at me intently. "I can't bring myself to be bothered. I think a tiny part of me will always care about her because she's my mother, but I don't like her, and her opinion doesn't matter to me." He pauses with a wild-looking expression on his face. "I won't let her come between us."

"She won't," I say loudly, cutting through. "I've learnt my lesson tonight. I know my priorities." I shrug. "It's quite a small list."

"How many items?"

I smile tenderly at him. "Just one, really. It's you, if you're interested."

He smiles and his tension melts away. "That's one of the reasons I'm so proud of you. That fierceness of yours. It's comforting and almost familiar."

"Is the other reason my vanishing act tonight? Are you banking on me becoming a magician?"

He smiles. "That is an idea for sure. If the electricity bill is as big as I think it's going to be, we might have to start sawing people in half and wearing top hats."

I laugh but then sober. "And we'll do that together." He looks at me and gives a glorious smile. I look around the door and beckon him. "Come in here with me," I say in a low voice.

He straightens, looking at me intently, and the atmosphere thickens. I watch as he removes his clothing piece by slow piece and then step back so he can get into the shower enclosure. He brushes past me, my wet skin sliding on his, and I groan as I feel the hairs on his chest rub against my sensitive nipples.

He stands under the spray, letting the water cascade down over him until his hair turns jet black and water beads on his eyelashes like tiny diamonds. He opens his arms and I move instantly into them, lifting my head for the kiss he gives me, opening my mouth and sighing as his tongue rubs against mine.

We kiss for a long while as the water pours down on us, and when he pulls back his lips are swollen and red and his eyes at half-mast.

"I love you," he whispers. "I'm sorry but I can't stop it and I don't want to. I know it's not what you want to hear at the moment, but I can't keep it in anymore."

I put my hand over his mouth and the low impassioned words stop. For a second his eyes register apprehension, which I cannot stand to see there. Not about me.

"I love you too."

The words seem to twine around us like the steam, and for a long second he's silent apart from a gasp.

"Really?" he asks shyly.

I nod firmly. "*Really*. In the interests of being completely honest I have to say that I've never loved anyone before, so I'm absolutely convinced that I'll fuck it up."

He shakes his head. "So what? We'll just mend it again. Oh God, I love you so much."

He bends his head and takes my mouth with a deep groan, and the tenderness is submerged under a flood of intense passion.

The water pours down over us, encasing us in heat and steam, and I drag my mouth away from his to pull in a breath before quickly going back to his lips. I groan in protest as he pulls his lips away but smile when he drops to his knees.

"Okay down there, old timer?" I say, and he grins up at me.

"I'm going to take my teeth out and blow your mind, you young whippersnapper."

I laugh. "Promises, promises."

My laughter dies away to a gasp as he licks a broad stripe up my dick. The rough rasp of his tongue makes my eyes cross and I groan.

"Look at me," he mutters, and when I turn my eyes down he holds my gaze and takes me slowly inside his mouth.

"Oh shit," I groan as he starts to suck. The hot, wet tunnel my dick is enclosed in is like heaven. Silas has many talents, but sucking dick should be right up there at the top. He throws himself into it with all the enthusiasm that he shows in life, and the fact that it turns him on so much is an added bonus. The other week he gave me a blow job and was so turned on that he came hands free, shooting all over the floor.

He sucks hard, the pulling motion seeming to want to tug the come from my balls. I look down at him through the steam of the shower and all my feelings seem to gather into a hot ball inside my chest.

"I love you," I groan, and he looks up, droplets of water spangling on his eyelashes and clumping them together like little starfish.

His eyes soften from their lustful gaze and he releases my cock from its home in his throat and stands up.

"I love you too," he whispers, kissing me and sharing the tang of my pre-come. "Turn around, Pika," he urges, and I steal another kiss before obeying his hands, moving out of the direct flow of the shower and turning to face the tiled wall. I stick my arse out and I feel his hands come down to cup and caress my buttocks.

"Such a gorgeous arse," he says in a low, guttural whisper. He separates my cheeks and stands back to direct the shower stream to cascade over the inside. I shout out as the hot water caresses my opening. "And look at that pretty hole," he murmurs. He moves back behind me. "I'm going to put my cock in there and see it stretch around me. But first I need a taste of it. I haven't had the taste of your arse on my tongue since this morning."

I moan at the sound of his dirty words muttered in that pure, clear accent.

He chuckles and kisses between my shoulder blades. I screw my eyes closed and bend over, resting my head against the cool tiles as his kisses lead slowly down my spine before flaring out to scatter butterfly kisses over my buttocks.

I groan and, reaching back, I use my hands to spread my cheeks. "Silas, please."

"What do you need, darling?" He kneads my backside. "You can have anything you want. I will do anything and be anything you need. Complete honesty."

I twist my head to look down at him. "While that sounds incredibly deviant, all I really want you to do at the moment is stick your tongue in my arse."

He grins impishly up at me, his hair wet and swept back from that elegant face and his eyes shining almost catlike in the steamy light.

"Your wish is my command," he says deeply, and I shudder. "Hold yourself open for me." He looks up. "If your hands let go, I'll stop."

I spread myself wider, feeling my hole stretch, and cry out in pleasured agony when his tongue slips slowly over the surface of my hole, flitting back and forth in delicate catlike licks.

"Oh God," I groan. "So fucking good." He puts his lips over the hole and starts to alternatively suckle it and send his tongue inside my body. The shower fills with the sounds of his slurps and groans over the noise of the running water and I rub my face against the tile and moan pitifully.

I'm still holding my cheeks open and my cock is throbbing almost painfully. All I want to do is send my hand down and touch myself but I don't. I've learnt that he keeps his word and if he says he'll stop, then he will. He's done it before and left me with a hard-on for three hours.

I rut back against his face, feeling the scratch of his beard which is an intense blend of pleasure and almost pain against the sensitive skin of my arse. He rewards me by licking enthusiastically, groaning under his breath, and when I twist my head round and open my eyes I grunt at the sight of him on his knees with his cock in his furiously moving hand.

"Oh God," I whisper. "Mo mhuirnín dílis. I need you inside me. I want you so bad."

He must be nearing the end as well because he stands up quickly, reaching for the lube and starting to open me up. I twist back on his fingers, crying out as they rub me inside, setting up this heated ache in my passage. I reach back and grab his hand when he goes to add a third.

"No," I mutter. "I'm ready. I need you inside me now."

"Are you sure?" he asks hoarsely. "I won't hurt you."

I nod, struggling to find words as all the blood has left my brain and is currently filling my throbbing cock. "Yes. I want to feel this tomorrow. I want to remember it."

He grabs a condom from the shelf and starts to open it. I open my mouth and hesitate, and he stops what he's doing, looking at me intently. "What?"

I shake my head. "I wondered whether seeing as we've admitted that we're together properly now–"

"Wondered what?"

"Whether we'd be seeing anyone else as well?"

His face darkens. "Well, I'm certainly fucking not," he says sharply. He opens his mouth to say more but I put my fingers over his mouth, feeling the soft, swollen lips.

"Neither will I," I promise. "I've no interest in that." I hesitate. "I just wondered whether we needed a condom now?"

He stares at me and his eyes seem to spark a golden green with emotion. "You'd want me bare inside you? You want my come?"

I groan and, twisting sideways, send my fingers through his wet chest hair. "God yes," I mutter. "I want that so bad."

He gives a shudder that seems to move down his body like a powerful wave. "I'm close at just the thought." He looks up. "I'm clear of everything. I was tested last month, and I've only been with you since we started." He swallows and his eyes go soft. "I'll only be with you until the finish."

I nod, incapable of words. He is, after all, the one that does that best. "I'm clear too." I reach down and fist his cock before widening my stance and bending forwards I bring the tip to my hole. "Please," I beg, pushing back so that the head pops in.

"Oh God," he chokes out, and I feel his hands come down on my arse. "It's so fucking hot, Ozzy."

I fold my arms on the tiled shelf and rest my head on them, backing into him. "Now," I cry out and he grunts and suddenly he's sliding inside me fully, the pinch and burn caused by his girth making me cry out.

He stills immediately and wraps his arms around my chest, bringing me back against him. "You okay?" he asks, and I can tell how much effort it's taking for him to keep still as he's practically vibrating.

I breathe out and nod. "Yes. God, yes. I love it. Fuck me."

He inhales a sharp breath and then he starts to move, pulling his hips back before screwing into me, the length of his cock hot and hard as a pipe inside me.

"Fuck," I mutter, and I feel him nod, his face twisting into my back and sending shivers down my spine.

"I won't last long," he says, the words an impassioned mutter. "You're so fucking hot and tight in there. I've never felt anything like it before."

He grabs my hips and I know and love the fact that he's leaving bruises I'll find the next morning, like a handwritten map painting his travels across my body. "We're never using condoms again," he gasps, and I chuckle. He moans as he feels the vibrations through his cock and slaps my bum lightly. "Don't do that," he gasps. "Or this is going to be over embarrassingly fast."

I back up and start to fuck myself on his cock. "It's so fucking good," I whisper. Talk stops and all I can hear in the wet, steamy air are our panting breaths and the slap of flesh against flesh.

He takes control and holding my hair in one hand, he grabs my hip with the other and starts to ram into me, fucking himself in with hard, urgent shoves that make my toes curl.

"Oh shit," I gasp and reach one hand down to grab my cock and start a wet, heated slide. The action sends sparks into my balls and I feel them draw up. "I'm going to come."

"Yes," he gasps, and I feel his hand move and one long finger tracing my pucker. "You're stuffed so full of me," he whispers fiercely. "All red and swollen around me. You're going to come any second, and when you do I'm going to fill you up with my spunk and watch it slip out of you and down your fucking legs."

"Fuck," I scream and the pressure bursts and come shoots out of my cock, painting the tiles with creamy glistening ropes.

"Yes," he shouts out and gives two more battering thrusts before grunting. "So good," he moans. I feel the hot liquid inside me for the first time in my life, and he shudders like he's been tasered.

We ride out the aftershocks, clutching at each other, and I moan complainingly as he pulls slowly out of me. "No. Don't go."

"I have to," he says hoarsely. "I need to see." I turn my head to see him kneeling at my arse. He opens my cheeks and groans. "Fuck, that's so hot. My come's sliding out of you."

"I can feel it," I whisper and then jerk and give a shout as he pushes his face in and I feel him start to lick and suck. "*Silas*," I groan. The feeling is almost overwhelming and just this pleasurable side of painful as he licks the stretched, swollen opening and sends his tongue in to get more. Incredibly I feel my cock stir.

"Silas," I whisper and start to slide my hand down my cock that's still slick with my spunk. I push back against his face demandingly and hear the slick sounds as his hand moves on his own cock. "Don't stop," I beg.

He hums an agreement and his other hand comes up, one finger touching the sore hole before sliding in under his tongue. The dark bite of pain sends electric sparks into my groin, making my balls clench painfully, and before I know it's happening I spurt a second small amount of come into my palm. He pulls back, breathing harshly, and I spin round to watch him arch on the floor and come into his hand.

I grab his hand and lift it to my mouth. Holding his glowing gaze I lick the spunk off it, cleaning it thoroughly. He chuckles and sighs. "No more," he mutters. "I couldn't get it up again if my life depended on it."

"You're the one who ate the come out of my arse." He grins and I pull him to me, hugging him tight and loving the feel of him against me. "You dirty bastard," I say admiringly, and he laughs.

"Your dirty bastard."

"Always."

"What did you call me during sex?" he asks. "It sounded Irish."

I blush. "Mo mhuirnín dílis. It means my own true love."

"I like that," he says softly, pulling me close for a kiss. "I really like being that to you."

I redden even more, and he chuckles. I reach up and kiss him, feeling the smile I can't stop against his lips. He fills his palms with my body wash and starts to wash me, cleaning me up as gently as anything I've ever felt. His smile is soft and warm, and he hums contentedly as I do the same to him.

Eventually when the water starts to cool we stumble out of the shower and dry each other tenderly, dropping kisses onto dry bits and murmuring silly nonsense to each other that I know will make me blush tomorrow.

I move over to the bed, pulling the sheets back and already anticipating sinking into the softness with relish. I pause as I catch sight of him standing against the window, looking out in his customary posture. As I watch, he stretches and gives a satisfied grunt before leaning against the window. My breath catches in my throat at the sight of him. The long, lean length of him touched by moonlight that catches the content, almost dreamy look on his face that's always there when he's in this room with me.

I'm held immobile, almost stunned by the certainty that runs through me, and before I can second-guess myself I walk over to him, sliding under the raised arm and feeling it lower to my shoulders, grounding and warm and everything to me.

"Ask me," I say quietly. I smile tenderly. "I guarantee I'm going to say yes."

He looks down at me, his eyes pellucid in the dim light, but somehow, he catches my meaning like it's written in front of him in neon smoke letters.

"Will you stay with me, Pika? Live with me here in this house always?" he asks softly.

I pull him down to me and wrap my arms around his shoulders as he buries his head in my neck. I feel his breath on my skin and the warmth of his body, and I want it like this forever with a desire that feels like it's taken root in my bones.

I put my mouth to his ear and I whisper one word. "Yes."

EPILOGUE

THIS IS MY KIND OF PERFECT

FIVE YEARS LATER

Oz

I sit back on the sand, feeling the breeze hit me in the face, and listen to the roar of the surf. It's been a sticky, muggy day, but here in our cove it's cool and fresh. I inhale the scent of pine and salt and smile. Chewwy, who's been sitting hovering near me, suddenly jumps to his feet with a whine and I grin.

I know who it is even before I feel his large warm hands come down on my shoulders as he lowers himself behind me, cuddling me back against his bigger frame and burying his face in my neck for a second. The greeting he always gives me is as familiar as my own face in a mirror.

I turn to face him, raising my lips for a kiss. He obliges, and I lift my hand and card my fingers through his still-messy waves that are now touched with a few threads of silver. He's forty-three and grimaces when I mention it, but he's the sexiest forty-three-year-old I know.

"How was your day, dear?" I ask, and he chuckles.

"Long and boring and I spent far too long with my hand up a horse's vajajay."

I snort. "What a daring and scandalous life you lead."

"How's it been here?"

I smile. "I spent the morning in my office trying to go through some figures." I point in front of me at the small figure on the beach watched over by the inquisitive form of Boris. "But I'll give you two guesses how that went."

He laughs and gives a short fluting whistle, and I jerk and poke him in the side. "How many times have I told you not to summon her by whistling? She's not Boris or Chewwy."

"She loves it," he laughs and gets to his feet, waiting for the running figure to reach him. When she does he falls to his knees and grabs her into a tight hug, kissing every millimetre of her tiny face and laughing loudly as she squeals.

Boris barks and jumps around them, and I smile widely at the sight of my husband and daughter laughing. Yes, you heard me. Husband and daughter. I told you before. Time moves quickly in Oz land.

Silas asked me to marry him a few months after I said I'd stay. He'd planned an elaborate proposal, but as things always go in our house it had degenerated into chaos with a fire engine, an ambulance, and a near miss with public indecency. We were sitting in the glow from the lights of the fire engine when he asked me. I think he'd planned to go down on one knee, but events of the evening prevented it, so he'd actually proposed sitting in the ambulance. But that's another story.

I'd always known he harboured a desire to have children. In my eyes he's the perfect person to be a father. Kind and funny, clever and grounded. It had been me who'd worried. I'm not exactly father material. I'm too spiky, too mouthy. I'd gone through my twenties happily avoiding commitments and I couldn't see how that would change.

We'd talked about it, then talked about it some more and then some more before we'd made the decision, but it had still seemed like an impossible dream. Adoption isn't easy, let alone when you're gay, so we'd resigned ourselves to a long wait, which contrarily had meant that I'd immediately decided I was all in and ready for it there and then.

Then one night, Ivo rang us. He'd still got a lot of contacts abroad and one of his interpreters had rung him with a story of a baby girl in Columbia left orphaned with no family. He wanted to know if Ivo knew of anyone in England who would consider taking her because he feared for her if she ended up in an orphanage.

I'd taken a deep breath, looked at Silas and knew from his impassioned, eager face that we were going to do it. Sometimes I don't think I've ever exhaled that breath. We'd spent a frantic and angsty few months jumping through government hoops and signing any paperwork put in front of us, but one afternoon we got the call that she was ours and we packed and went to bring her home.

I'd worried but I needn't have bothered because when Silas put her in my arms, I fell in love. I'd looked at her tiny, scrunched-up face and the sweet bow of her mouth and known that I would happily die for her. Nothing has changed that, and nothing ever will.

We'd come back to *Chi an Mor* a family and that has never altered, only grown stronger.

I look up to see her running towards me. She's gap-toothed and soaking wet. Her dark silky hair is in wild salt-kissed curls, her face is dirty, and she's tanned from the sun like a little baked hazelnut. No matter how often I wash her face and put her in clean clothes she always ends up like this – half wild and full of life.

"Da," she shouts and hurls herself into my arms.

I hug her tight, reaching for the towel and wrapping it round her sturdy little body and rubbing her dry. She nestles into me, resting her little feet on my calf as I brush the sand off her. I don't know why I bother. She'll be mucky within seconds. She's a creature of this place and us, my Cora. Fierce and wild and occasionally sharp like me, but also with Silas's kindness and wide-open heart. To me she's like the sky – vast and sometimes unfathomable.

Silas comes towards us, smiling. "Ready for tea?" he asks. Boris barks and Cora giggles.

"Daddy, can we have cake?"

"If there's anything left," he says, looking at me, and I shrug.

"Not sure. It's been a busy day."

We opened the house three years ago and it's gone from strength to strength. Visitors always comment on the warmth of the welcome, the feel of the house, and how accessible the family are. We have old people from the village who come most mornings and sit in the tea rooms eating homemade teacakes, drinking countless cups of tea, and chatting to Cora who sits happily with everyone biting into her biscuit with sharp white teeth. I introduced a weekly book club for them a few years ago. It's lively and raucous and I was stunned to see the risqué book choices they'd decided on.

However, we're coming up to autumn now. The days are getting cooler and there's an occasional bite to the air. Soon the house will close for the autumn and winter and become ours again. The stairways and paths will fall silent and the house will nestle around us like a benevolent entity sheltering us. Our daughter will run free again and the rooms will smell of wood smoke and pine and echo to the sound of Cora's running footsteps.

Silas had worried that I would hate the cold and desolate months but instead I love the dramatic and wild beauty of the Cornish coast in these months when it feels like it's ours.

Cora unravels herself from the towel like a little butterfly from its chrysalis and dances to Silas, who promptly puts her on his shoulders with a lot of shrieking, and the three of us walk back to the house. My house may be called *Chi an Mor,* but my home is walking next to me. The big man with the gentle spirit and warm eyes who made me fall in love with him despite all my misgivings, and the tiny girl who holds my heart with him.

My family.

Time in Oz's world can now stop as far as I'm concerned, because this is my kind of perfect.

Silas

Cora's snores start halfway through the millionth rendition of *We're Going on a Bear Hunt* and I slow my voice before stopping. I pull the cheerful duvet cover with the embroidered daisies on it over her and look around the room.

When Henry and I were little, we slept in the children's wing, which was as far away from my parent's bedroom as the motorway service station in Plymouth. Our rooms were full of old furniture that nobody wanted and made colourful by posters and an enormous mountain of Blu Tack which drove my father fucking mad.

Cora's room is so different. One wall is painted a warm clear turquoise and the others are sunny yellow, so it looks like she's trapped sunshine in here. Her white painted cast iron bed is so soft it's like sinking into a cloud and her toys and books are everywhere.

She's also near our room rather than being miles away. We live in the family apartments that I'd racketed around in on my own for so long, but they're drastically different now. Oz has completely overhauled the rooms and he has a genius for finding old bits of furniture in the attics, restoring them and putting them in rooms that look fresh and modern. Rather than being dark and dingy, the family rooms are now light and airy, echoing the colours from outside.

Our parenting styles are so different from what I grew up with. I smile as I remember Oz's face when I'd earnestly explained that if Cora had a nightmare she was to come and get in with us rather than toughing it out. His expression had been soft and almost sad, and he'd agreed instantly, rather than pointing out that this is normal behaviour in families not headed by my father.

Sometimes at night I'll wake to hear tiny footsteps padding across the floor in our room and in she'll get, sliding between us like a queen who knows her land. The next morning will always find Oz and me contorted into strange positions and clinging to the sides of the bed while she sleeps horizontally with her feet in our ribs.

Oz seemed to find it easy once she arrived. I think that might come from being brought up by his mum. He's firm but fair and very loving. Fatherhood brings out the softer edge only a few of us ever knew was under there. I struggled a little bit initially. I was so terrified of dropping her or fucking her up. Oz coached me, and I grew into my role the way she grew into hers. I like to roughhouse and play and I'm not always the strictest parent. Sometimes she's just too funny and I have to laugh, even if Oz disapproves. I think a portion of this might be down to me trying so hard not to be my father that I go the other way.

I close the book softly and put it down on the bedside table. My sleeping girl doesn't stir. She runs through the grounds all day the way Henry and I did and then she's out like a light. I stroke her curls back gently and lay a soft kiss on her forehead. I smile. She looks like an angel in sleep, which Niall always says is so ironic, considering she could raise the dead with the volume of her voice during the day. It always leads to him then enquiring whether she could be Oz's biological child after all, to which he usually responds with a lazy raise of his middle finger.

Niall likes to consider himself the matchmaker to end all matchmakers, but I can't begrudge him the title because he changed my life the day he sent Oz to me. I look up and grin as I see Oz leaning against the door and smiling at me.

"Couldn't wait to hear the ending again?" I say.

He shakes his head. "The same book all the time. Surely that's bad for her development, and for the love of *God*, why is she still so astonished that there's a bear?"

I gather him into my arms, loving the way his smaller body fits against mine, his head notching into my neck and his warm smell of ginger weaving around me. "It's tradition," I whisper. "It's good for her, darling."

I feel the smile he gives at the endearment against the skin of my throat, but I also don't miss the slight shiver. He loves that endearment above all others, and one night I'd stretched him out and for every kiss I'd laid on his body I'd whispered "darling" against his skin. I give a swift grin. I'd only got to his upper thigh before he lost patience. My Oz isn't one for delayed gratification.

He pulls away. "Dinner."

I nod and let him take my hand. We wander down the gallery, which is now lit by lamps in case Cora wakes up. I look up at the portraits as we go by, catching their sour expressions which always used to frighten me as a child. I wonder what they'd think of me and Oz. I smile. They're probably still bobbing and rolling over in their graves like miserable Lilos in a pool.

At the end of the row of portraits I look up at my father. He glowers down at me, looking eerily similar to that one summer when Henry and I had decided to slide down the main stairs on tea trays. We'd nearly taken out some members of the Women's Institute and had damaged a very old door when we'd smashed right through it. I can still remember the horrified faces of the women as they scattered like pins and the look of apoplectic doom on my father's face as we'd sailed past him.

I smirk. That would register as nothing compared to his son and heir marrying another man and living in this house with him and being so fucking happy.

"Why are you grinning like a moron?" Oz asks, and I shake my head.

"No reason." But my smile widens as behind my back I raise my middle finger at the old bastard's portrait.

When we get down to the kitchen we ease into our routine which is like a dance between the two of us. No matter what time of night I get home, Oz will be there. He'll heat the dinner up and I will lay the table. I'll uncork the wine and last of all I will open the back door so the sound of the surf fills the room in a muted grumble.

Sometimes he won't eat with me. Sometimes he'll just make a cup of tea. But he always perches next to me, watching me with that face that's as full of life and interest as the day I looked up and saw him sitting on the fence and staring at me. We'll chat about our day and he'll regale me with tales of Cora and the house. We'll laugh and just be together. It's a simple pleasure that beckons me home every night like a lighthouse beacon.

I stand at the door and breathe in the salty air and turn back to watch him as he moves with the ease of familiarity around the old kitchen, nimbly avoiding the loose flagstone and knowing just the right amount of pressure to open the cutlery drawer. Too much and it will explode out of its tracks like a race horse and throw knives and forks around the room with abandon.

The low light picks out the sheen in his dark hair which is longer now and makes his pale skin seem to glow. The tattoos on his arm are like dark shadows over his skin, and he looks as gorgeous as he ever did. I feel warmth hit my chest because I love him so. Nobody has ever got me like Oz.

When I was little I had yearned for someone to protect me from my childhood, someone to stand for me when no one that I trusted would, when I was tired from sticking up for Henry and then later for Ivo. I'd never have guessed that my knight in armour would come to me later in life when I'd almost forgotten that I needed one. He would be small and fierce and his weapon was the sharpest tongue this side of Ireland. But he was all mine and I, in turn, belonged to him.

That feeling of ownership and steady love gives me everything. When I'm with him I feel whole and safe. And free to be me because he loves simply and deeply. He doesn't ask for expensive gifts, which is a relief because the house will still be in hock for years. All he asks is for me the way I am.

He sets the dinner down and for a few minutes we eat hungrily.

"When is your mum coming down?" I ask when my hunger has been assuaged a little.

"In a couple of weeks." He grins at me. "Get ready because she's staying for a few weeks."

I pour us each a glass of wine. "I love your mum. I wish she'd take the house I offered and live here." When Oz moved in permanently I'd offered her one of the cottages on the estate, but she'd said no.

Oz grins. "She's happy living with my auntie now. The two of them are trouble. Actually, speaking of trouble, don't forget that Henry and Ivo are down at the weekend."

"Is it my imagination or do we see a lot more of them since Cora came home with us?"

He smiles. "I told you the other day. Ivo feels some sort of kinship with her since it was he that found her for us, and Henry's just besotted."

"I'm glad," I say softly. "It always bothered me that Henry didn't love the house the way I did. That he had bad memories of this place, because that was down to my father, not the house."

He nods. "It's a welcoming house. I felt it as soon as I came."

"It knew," I say impulsively, grabbing his fingers and kissing them. "It knew it should keep you."

He laughs but his eyes are soft. "You and this house."

I shrug. "I just think that now it's the way it should be, and Henry is responding to that. This place is built for children running here and there and noise and laughter and arguments. It's built for–"

"A family?" he says softly and astutely as ever. "You want more children, don't you?"

"I do." I watch his expression closely. "I want Cora to have a couple of brothers or sisters. Someone to roughhouse and argue with. Someone to think of apart from herself."

"Someone to protect," he says softly, and I smile as he gets up and falls into my lap with the same ease of movement that he navigates our home. Sure and deft like a sleek little cat. Sun warm and peaceful nowadays, but ready to rear up and wreak some hell if needed.

I run my fingers through his hair and hold him close while we sip our wine and talk. "I love you, Pika," I whisper into his ear, and he gives me the wide, curling smile that first captivated me.

"Mo mhuirnín dílis. I love you too."

He kisses me softly, but the tongue promises other things, and before it gets too heated he levers off me and stands up. "I'm going for a shower. I'll see you up there."

I kiss the palm of his hand and watch him go, followed by the ever-present shadow of Chewwy. I clear the pots away and switch the lights off, but at the last minute I deviate and stand against the open door. The moon lies full on my land and the breeze rustles the trees, sending fantastic shapes over the ground. An owl swoops overhead and the sea roars.

I have always loved this place passionately. My ancestors fought to stay on it, some for glory, some for pride, and I will carry the fight on in my own little way. It will probably be lost in the history of the place, but my fight is to keep it safe for Oz and our children, so we can live the rest of our lives together in a ramshackle old house where sand drifts in and lays a fine layer over everything. Where the booming of the surf is loud and the sweet scent of the lavender drifts through every window. Where we can be at peace. There truly is no place like home.

The End

THANK YOU

My husband. He's always supported me, believed in me and made me laugh when I was down. He had a big part to play in this book because he drove me to Cornwall for the research trip that inspired Chi an Mor. We loved sitting in the lavender garden in the real manor house on a hot summer's afternoon, and he's the one who spotted the bees!

My boys. They're my pride and my joy and I'm beyond thrilled that they're growing into clever and funny young men.

Leslie Copeland. For being such an awesome beta reader and friend. I couldn't do this without her. She's organized, focused and the best judge of books around.

Natasha Snow. I cannot imagine my books without her covers. She's an unfailing joy to work with, and has done an amazing job creating the covers for this new series.

Hailey Turner. I love that despite living so far apart we can spend ages messaging back and forwards. She's enthusiastic and kind and a very good friend. She's also the person who advised that I just acknowledge that I'm writing a series this time rather than have to go back and get more covers later!

Courtney Bassett. She always does such a wonderful editing job. She takes my babies and always dresses them in proper clothes. Here's to commas and that well known wine made from roses!

The members of my Facebook reader's group, Lily's Snark Squad. They're enthusiastic and funny and cope with my erratic posting schedule. I love my time spent with them.

To all the bloggers who spend their valuable time reading, reviewing and promoting the books. Also, the readers who liven up my day with their messages and photos and book recommendations. I've love being a part of this community, so thank you.

Lastly thanks to you, for taking a chance on this book. I hope you enjoyed reading it as much as I enjoyed writing it.

Want to know the proposal story that Oz hinted at? It's over on my website.

I never knew until I wrote my first book how important reviews are. So if you have time, please consider leaving a review on Amazon or Goodreads or any other review sites. I can promise you that I read every one, good or bad, and value all of them. When I've been struggling with writing, sometimes going back and reading the reviews makes it better.

ALSO BY LILY MORTON

Beggar's Choice Series
1. Promise Me (m/f)
2. Trust Me (m/f)
3. Keep Me (m/f)

Mixed Messages Series
Rule Breaker (m/m)
Deal Maker (m/m)
Risk Taker (m/m)

Finding Home Series
Oz (m/m)

Other Novels
The Summer of Us (m/m)

Short Stories
Best Love (m/m)

CONNECT WITH LILY

Website: www.lilymortonauthor.com
This has lots of information and some fun features, including some extra short stories. I've written Silas's proposal and you'll find that here.

I'd love to hear from you, so if you want to say hello or have any questions, please contact me and I'll get back to you:
Email: lilymorton1@outlook.com

Printed in Great
Britain
by Amazon